THE GIRL IN THE ZOO

JENNIFER LAUER

For my loves

"The true harvest of my daily life is somewhat as intangible and indescribable as the tints of morning or evening. It is a little star-dust caught, a segment of the rainbow which I have clutched."

HENRY DAVID THOREAU

PART 1

ISOLATION

CHAPTER ONE

Staring through the Plexi, I long to feel the world again.

On a field trip to an aquarium in second grade, I daydreamed about freeing all the sea creatures, because no one could build a tank that could replicate the ocean. When a bully struck my sister in fourth grade, I doubled over in pain and spent the rest of the day crying, in part due to my sister's hurt and in part because I wondered how awful the bully's life must be to make him behave so poorly.

That empathetic person *used* to be me, Mirin Blaise, girl with a big and caring heart, and now I struggle to believe I even have one.

I am the only human left living in the Zoo. I haven't been outside the Plexi walls in 2,196 days. *Six years* of days filled with the same routine activities.

Wake up, get scanned, exercise, read, swim, sleep, repeat. You'd think the repetition would be grounding, but it's not. It has sucked all the humanity right out of me. I haven't seen or talked to another person many years either.

The last one in here with me was Ander, but he didn't last very long. We were only here together for about three months, so it hardly counts as companionship. I try and tell myself that I am enough, that my imagination can sustain me. But this is a lie. The truth is that I'm afraid the loneliness will crush me. At least I have Borgie, whose metal face is close enough to human that I haven't given up completely yet.

And speaking of my metal-faced captor, it's late.

Borgie is never late. Every morning like clockwork, it arrives to scan my body and take my measurements. But now it is precisely seven minutes late. Maybe its internal hard drive overheated, and it's stranded somewhere between wherever it calls home and my room. Wouldn't that be amusing.

As much as I despise Borgie's visits, it is the only thing keeping me alive in here, so I forgive its tardiness. Anomaly noted.

Of course, it would be late today, the one day I actually have somewhere to be. Today is Harvest Day, and I just want to get to the garden.

The only thing that excites me as much as the idea of getting out of this place is the thought of eating real food. It only happens four times a year, and I like to make it count. My stomach growls at the thought.

Finally, I hear the crunch of metal on gravel behind my room, and I know that Borgie is approaching. When Borgie enters my room, I see a small dent in its shoulder and its head ticks to the side a few times.

This is strange.

Borgie is always pristine and moves with an artificial smoothness that I expect from it. What exactly happened to make it late?

"Mirin, sit down," Borgie says in its Information Voice, which is perky, genderless, and British accented, and I sit as it trims my nails. Its voice would be charming, if it didn't belong to an eight-foot-tall robot captor. It has grown on me nonetheless.

Funny how things that start out as bizarre become familiar. Borgie rests its gaze on my forehead and reads my temperature to me.

"97.5 degrees Fahrenheit," Borgie reports. As usual, my temperature runs cool. Every day for the last six years, we go through this same morning routine. I have no idea what it's hoping to find, but the only choice I have is to be compliant.

I used to think Borgie was doing these scans to learn about me, about humans, but now I suppose it wants to keep its human captive healthy so that it can keep the Zoo up and running. Because without me, who would the other borgs come to see? Who would be the main exhibit?

Nothing in the Zoo ever changes, so if it is learning or doing something important, I have not seen the result of it.

Yet.

That "yet" is the tiny bit of hope that I hold on to.

Borgie's claw sifts through my hair, checking my head— for lumps, for lice, who knows? I could pretend that it's a massage if the tips of its metal talons weren't so pointed.

Squinting through the Plexi walls of my room, I look toward the path that leads to the garden, but the Weatherlight makes it too bright for me to see anything. Despite the fact that the Weatherlight was designed to make me happy, I'm not. It only reminds me that it's not the real sun, and I miss the real sun.

There will be a day when it hits my face again, I just know it. I shut my eyes and imagine my face leaning up toward the hot sun. I see the red light behind my eyelids and feel all the UV rays needling my skin.

When I open my eyes, I see that the red light is actually coming from Borgie, as it shines a tiny red laser from its eyes into mine, and it feels like it can see inside my brain.

My shoulders shudder, and a waft of nickel lingers as Borgie leans in close. It's looking at my face, and I can hear its fan whirring, keeping its system cool.

I take advantage of this moment of closeness to scan Borgie's face, looking for any subtle changes, a scuff on its exterior or any changes to the armor—anything to tell me *something* new. Something about what it's been doing or where it goes.

Anything to help me get out of here.

But other than that single dent, I see only the familiar smooth shape of Borgie's armor. *Nothing new to report here, Mirin*, it seems to say.

"Borgie, will you ever let me out?" I ask, knowing there won't be an answer, but I search its eyes for one anyway. Borgie's steel eyes are looking directly into mine. And inside of them, I see a flicker of something ... *human?*

Startled, I move back instinctively. That cannot be possible.

"Mirin, sit down," Borgie says, and so I do. Mechanically, I sit still, but inside, my mind is on fire. *What just happened?*

Closing my eyes, I reach my hands up to my shoulders and squeeze and release, trying to ease the tension and calm myself. There is no way I saw what I saw.

What exactly did I see? It was a flicker. A light. A look of recognition, of knowing. It had to be a trick of my mind. *Of course it is, Mirin.* Borgie is an unfeeling piece of metal; it is not sentient.

But is that really true?

I have noticed little things lately that have me wondering, a furrowed metal brow here, a sound like a sigh there. It's not so farfetched. Back on the outside, there were experts who claimed their AI was sentient, but they were outliers and always disproven. Plus, I've known Borgie for six years. If it was going to reveal itself as sentient, it would have done so by now.

Right?

As if registering my shock, Borgie's face shifts, softening into an expression much like that of a doctor tending to a patient. I hate that it can read my emotions so well—there must be something in its computer that detects expressions and translates them into feelings. Or data about feelings. I don't know how it works.

Borgie's hulking shoulders expand, and it measures my height and weight. When it's done, I pull on my white linen tunic and try to make conversation to shake off my paranoia.

"So, Borgie, today is Harvest Day. Have you seen how well everything has grown?" It looks at me with an emotionless face that is a map of intricate metal filigree but does not respond. I look deep into its stoic eyes, hoping to see a flash of the humanity I thought I glimpsed earlier. But all it does is stare back at me, unblinking.

My cheeks sting at the rejection, even though being ignored by Borgie is nothing new. Part of me wishes Borgie was sentient. Then at least I'd have somebody to talk to.

But the other part is glad that Borgie isn't, because who knows what kind of evil an emotional robot would cause? Especially after all that we humans have made them do.

That thought sends a shudder through me.

I am a paradox, significant enough to be an exhibit in a zoo and insignificant enough to feel invisible.

Borgie moves a dial on its arm and holds it to my chest.

No matter how thick the loneliness gets, I do feel a

certain responsibility to stay alive. To do my best as the possible last representative of humanity. I can't say what's left of the world outside or who survived. But I hope there are more of us out there.

And still I wonder why in the hell I, Mirin Blaise, a cashier at the Farm Food Mart, would be preserved over someone else. Perhaps the borgs messed up and got the wrong human. If that's the case, I owe it to the actual extraordinary, deserving humans that could have been me to stay alive.

Borgie's hand glows, which is my signal to hold it so that it can record my heart rate. I grasp its cold metal claw and notice that Borgie's left shoulder is just slightly higher than its right, just above the small dent. There was something new, but I missed it before. Another anomaly. Is this why it was late?

"What happened, Borgie?" I ask. Reaching up, I lightly tap the dent with my free index finger.

Borgie remains silent, showing no intention of answering me. Figures. I close my eyes and let out a deep sigh.

"There was a complication," Borgie's Information Voice says, and I perk up. There isn't much that is complicated within the monotony here, but it got that dent somehow.

I want to know more, but it's so rare that Borgie actually responds to me that I'm careful not to scare it off. Maybe if I help it, it will keep talking. I ball my fist and give Borgie's shoulder a good knock to get it back into place.

"There you go, Borgie," I say, looking back to its face, which starts changing, fine metal latches rearranging themselves.

A chill runs down my spine as Borgie stands up tall and its expression morphs into an angry one with pointed eyebrows and a frown. Before I can do or say anything, Borgie's claw tightens on my wrist hard like a handcuff. I know that in one quick movement, it could toss me into the wall like a piece of crumpled paper, so I freeze. We hold each other's eyes in a solid glare. I'm terrified.

"Borgie, stop," I reprimand. I grab at the claw with my free hand.

My heart beats faster as I try to pull away, but it doesn't release. I can feel the skin around my wrist ready to break under the pressure of its claw.

"Is Mirin feeling violence?" it asks me, using its high-pitched Alarm Voice. This voice shoots right through me.

"No, no, Borgie, I was fixing you. Let go, that hurts." I take a steadying breath. I can feel blood dripping down my arm now, and I let out a small whimper.

Borgie releases my hand and I hug my sore arm to my chest. I thought I saw something real inside those eyes, and now I feel like I must've been hallucinating. When Borgie doesn't move, I start walking toward the door, wanting to be anywhere but here.

"Incomplete scan, incomplete scan," Borgie shouts, moving behind me, toward the door.

I freeze.

While blocking my ears with my hands, I also hold my breath. Borgie has to finish the scan before it will leave, so despite everything in my body telling me to run, I wait. In order to complete the routine I must assume a T-pose and bend forward. When it's satisfied that my spine is in alignment, Borgie finally turns away.

Minutes—which felt like hours—later, Borgie glides through the door as if nothing happened. As I watch it go, rage simmers beneath my skin.

No matter how closely Borgie studies me, it somehow

seems to forget how physically delicate I am compared to a borg. I rub my sore wrist, where the blood has already dried, as I watch Borgie's gray shadow move away down the path, and I realize I am still holding my breath. Letting the air out, I promise myself that one day soon I will get out of here.

CHAPTER TWO

After rubbing some aloe on my scabbed wrist, I grab my plate and head out toward the garden. My stomach growls, knowing that it's one step closer to consuming real food. I've been carefully growing these vegetables for months now. Being able to grow any food inside the Zoo is a true privilege.

If the plants die, I will lose the opportunity to eat something fresh, something other than a nutrition packet or processed treat. And I'm not going to let that happen. Not today—not even after Borgie's strange temper tantrum.

Three nutrition packets is the daily allowance here. I remember the first time I opened that little aluminum baggie full of lumpy orange goo and thought it was a mistake. It looked like lentil soup vomit, and I put off eating it as long as I could.

When I finally tried it, it tasted like multivitamin oatmeal with the consistency of baby food. The only positive is that it does provide all my basic nutritional needs and gives me quite an energy jolt.

But I dream of the food from before the Zoo all the time.

I miss things like salad dressing, garlicky pasta, and green chili tamales—most of all, the comfort of a warm meal. Anything warm, but especially pancakes.

A bittersweet pang hits me when I think of my father making his special pancakes, with raspberry eyes, a blueberry nose, and a maple syrup smile. He made them this way even when my sister Violet and I were grown up. I miss them. My family mostly, but also the pancakes.

The path toward the garden reaches out in front of me, and once I get to the end, I'm at the edge of the forest. My favorite tree, which I've taken to calling Shel, sits to my right, facing the beach. But today, I go left, past the Treat Show area and on to the garden.

As I walk, I can't help but think back to that *look* I saw in Borgie's eyes. And to its strange behavior. Why was it late this morning? And how did it get that dent?

After six years of being in the Zoo, you'd think I know everything about Borgie, but I still don't know what it does when it's not in my room. Or when it's not cleaning the Plexi. I followed it a few times, when I first got here, but all I managed to learn is that it lives near the waterfall.

Sometimes I see it zooming around with the other borgs —there are a few different kinds that live here—but I never know what they're doing.

Or why.

Perhaps one of them crashed into Borgie? Or maybe something fell on it? I wish I knew. Borgie is the only one that I interact with every day, it seems to be the borg in charge. All of the others complete tasks, but never directly come in contact with me.

Sometimes I wonder how the borgs even know what to do. Are they pre-programmed, running some endless loop that an AI technician assigned to them before the war?

Have they somehow adapted on their own? Or is someone controlling them from the outside? I think back to the look in Borgie's eyes and shudder.

Don't get ahead of yourself, Mirin. Like you said, it was probably just a weird flicker of the light, a mind trick.

As soon as I see the garden box, my shoulders begin to soften and I shake off all thoughts of Borgie. The large wooden box of soil is pushed up against the Plexi and is my truest delight. I need this space to be with nature. It is the one place in the Zoo with real loose soil.

Some trees in the forest have real dirt, but it's hard packed and hidden beneath flooring. Everything else is phony and spectacularly clean, which I appreciate, but there is something inside me that craves something real.

I put down the plate, and my knees fall gratefully into the soil.

A few weeds have sprouted in and around my blossoming vegetables. I tug them out, thank them for their service, and make a small pile on the sheet of plastic next to the box. I save them for later, when I'll braid them into garlands to decorate my room.

Just as I start collecting the zucchini, I notice something amiss.

There are several small holes where the dirt is dug up, and a bite taken from one of the zucchini. Upon closer inspection, I can see the teeth marks, like tiny fangs had carved through the zucchini's flesh. Whatever ate it did not like it much, because the chewed-up bite sits a few inches away.

I look around for the culprit.

There is no other person or animal that I've heard or seen in the dome with me, only borgs. There's no way a borg did it, since they don't eat.

Beside the fact that Borgie provides seed packets at the start of each year, it makes no other acknowledgment of the garden. Honestly, it's probably for the best. I don't need Borgie watching me down here too. The purpose of the seeds was never discussed, only left on the small table in my room.

The borgs wouldn't eat zucchini, but something did.

"Well, hello, cherry tomatoes, and zucchini. Someone has been in this garden. Have you seen anyone?" I ask them as I carefully pluck the tomatoes from the vine.

I tap a zucchini in greeting.

"Hey, buddy, sorry you got nibbled." There is a bit of an orange carrot top sticking out of the soil, signaling that the carrots are ready to be picked. I am proud of them, withstanding all the sufferings and limitations of the Zoo. They grew despite it all, and if they can grow, then perhaps there is hope that I can too.

"Bravo, bravo, my sweet carrots. You've done it," I cheer out loud. There is no one here but me to judge my hyperbole.

I pull on their wild greens. Some carrots are long and slender and some look like cranky, wrinkled babies.

When I was a child I despised carrots, so my mother never cooked them. When I was a teenager, our class went on a field trip to a local farm. During lunchtime, the farm had an offering basket for us to eat from, and I chose a tall, bright-colored carrot. I wanted to prove to myself that I could change, and I surprised myself by enjoying it.

My mouth waters just thinking of the feast I will have later, as I bring a short one to my nose and inhale the earthy carroty scent.

The last carrot is a large one, the diameter of a coffee mug.

"You could take the top prize at the county fair," I tell her as I pile her beside her brethren on the plate. I fill in the holes left from the carrots I pulled but leave the ones from the intruder so I can come back and study them more closely.

What or who could be digging holes and chomping on zucchini in here? It's such a strange yet exciting prospect.

Perhaps I'm not the only exhibit in the Zoo, after all.

CHAPTER THREE

When I arrive back at my room, carrying the plate stacked precariously high with veggies, I find a collection of borgs roaming around outside my door. There are four tall borgs near the dome that look powered off, several short wagon borgs, and many that I have never seen before.

It's unusual to have new borgs inside the dome, so something big must be happening.

This could be the complication Borgie ran into earlier.

Careful not to drop my provisions, I shimmy through the door into my room, dump the vegetables onto the countertop by the sink, and begin washing them.

As the water runs over the zucchini, I watch the borgs outside. There are so many of them, and I can't yet make out what they're doing.

All I see is a large stack of Plexi and some borgs carrying welding tools, but it's impossible to guess what they could be building. One of the taller borgs issues a series of loud beeps, and the rest of the maintenance borgs zoom away back toward the beach. They're probably gathering more supplies.

I wish they would tell me what they're constructing just so I'd know what to expect. Shaking my head, I think, *If only it were that simple.*

The first time I saw the borgs was on the news when I was a child. It was a horror show, as they destroyed people and buildings with lasers. It was my first glimpse of violence in the real world. My mother had always tried to shield me from it, but eventually she couldn't protect me from reality.

"Children aren't meant to see the filth of the world. You need to maintain your innocence as long as possible," she would always say. Little did she know how completely my innocence would be shattered.

The war between the borgs and the humans had been brewing my entire life, but most of the fighting happened in big cities, which felt like a world away. Like most children, I learned the details from the kids at school.

"Did you see that the borgs took over the Coldwell Factory in the city?" Reggie Stone told Arthur.

"Oh, yeah, they are going to take over the world," Arthur said matter-of-factly.

"My dad says we are going to obliterate them, since they don't have brains. They might be tough, but they aren't that different from a toaster," Reggie said. The fighting always felt more like a movie than something that could ever affect me.

My sister Violet and I spent a lot of time reading books and playing House. Using the news programs as our guide, we would make a trench between our twin beds, and shoot lasers at the borgs with our fingers while protecting the baby dolls. How I wish that shooting finger lasers could have saved Violet.

Later, when I was nineteen, the real war came to my rural town. The borgs had had enough, and they didn't want to be our toasters anymore. The way I saw it then was that they had been built and then mistreated, and they came for their makers.

If you disrespect and malign someone long enough, there will be consequences, and we have all paid that price.

"We taught them to be too much like us. And now they've become power hungry like people," Dad used to say. I never understood exactly what he meant because I am not power hungry. No thanks, power. We never argued about it; it just didn't ring true for me.

A part of me wishes we could have that conversation now.

"Power can corrupt you," I'd say. "If everyone felt valued, they might not need to seek power. I think this is true, even with the borgs."

He would have to consider it, and I like to think he'd warmly smile and say, "Okay, kiddo."

I feel drops of water hit my feet, which pulls me back into the Zoo, where I have nearly overflowed the sink. Draining the water, I breathe out the past.

As I dry the clean vegetables, I stack them like a pyramid in a grocery store onto the plate. I picture myself somewhere else, somewhere outside the Zoo, at home cooking dinner with my family. There's laughter in the dining room. Violet sneaks bites from the stew cooking on the stove as I wash the vegetables for the salad.

A simple moment from the past, but my heart aches like it's everything.

I wonder what it would have been like if they had been taken too. It surely wouldn't be as lonely. Violet would love the waterfall and Dad and I could build sandcastles at the beach.

My mother would love the garden and Dad would like

the challenge of figuring out new recipes with our limited ingredients. A tear runs down my face at the unfairness of what happened to them. They were all innocent.

A loud commotion outside interrupts my thoughts and pulls me back to the Zoo. I wipe my cheek with the back of my hand.

A dozen maintenance borgs swarm around a stack of painted wood pieces. They must be making some kind of new enclosure, but I can't imagine what all this is for.

I leave the vegetables next to the sink and walk over to the door to get a better look. A forklift borg pulls up a board while another borg bolts a small door to it. It looks like a cabinet of some sort. Maybe they need storage space? Too many knick-knacks.

It's been so long since I've seen this many borgs all together that I can't help but stare. They are truly enormous, lifting heavy pieces of material, welding it with tiny motors in their arms and claws.

There is one smaller borg with HIPPO imprinted on its side. I've seen this one before, but it's usually in the Testing Pod, where I go for medical treatment. HIPPO is short and square and has tread rather than legs. For some reason, I like this one best. With a side pincher arm, it's holding something white and ill-shapen that almost looks like ...

My face grows hot as I turn around and look at my bed. My eyes fix on the exact same hospital-grade pillow sitting there, lopsided.

A pillow can mean only one thing.

They are making another room.

For a human.

My pyramid of vegetables falls to the floor behind me. The plate shatters into three large pieces and I shriek, "No!" as if I had just dumped an entire holiday dinner into the trash. No, no, no. I rush over to pick them up. My heart is thundering through my chest as I salvage a couple of smushed tomatoes.

Borgie enters my room with a *whoosh*.

"I'm okay, just dropped something," I say to it. I notice a black scuff along its torso. That's weird. I didn't see Borgie out there building with the others, so I don't think it's from the maintenance work.

"Borgie, what happened to you?" I ask, as it beams a red light over my body.

"Mirin, what happened to you?" it asks right back. We look at each other, and I take a step closer.

"I'm fine," I say slowly. And then, *bam*, there it was again—the flicker. Borgie looked at me like it truly saw me. For one second, it went from flat to full. Soulless to soul.

Or did it?

Borgie turns out the red light and turns to leave.

"Stay," Borgie says in its Information Voice.

Great, now it thinks I'm a pet. It opens the door to go.

I watch Borgie slip through the front door, and although everything inside me wants to crawl under the covers right now, I can't.

This place has been the same, the exact same, for six damned years. And now everything is changing. The flicker of humanity in Borgie's eyes, the damage to its shoulder, the creature in the garden, and now a new zoomate.

All I've ever wanted was for something to change in this place, but now it feels like it's happening too fast for me to keep up.

Stay? Not a chance.

I open the door and run off after Borgie.

CHAPTER FOUR

Rushing down the path, I see Borgie slip around the corner toward the waterfall. *Dammit.* I cut behind the Treat Show area where I receive visitors, hoping to see wherever it goes through the walls. I have to climb over some rocks, and when I get behind the waterfall, Borgie's gone.

I lean on my knees to catch my breath, suddenly very angry with myself for not learning where Borgie goes after all these years. The rush of the waterfall behind me is loud. If I just wait for it to come out, it could be a while. I look around for some kind of button or door, but again, I see nothing.

I could wait until morning, but how would that look? *Oh, yes, good morning, Borgie. I was just wondering where you live, so I stalked you.* I laugh a little at how stupid that sounds.

But *where* does Borgie live? Or charge, or whatever it does at the end of the day? I used to only think about the borgs as mechanisms of the Zoo, a part of the whole, but what if there's more?

If that flicker in Borgie's eyes this morning really was

some proof of intelligence, of a soul, then I want to know more. I have so many questions for it.

I sit down on a rock to let my breath slow. The waterfall, flows into the ocean on the other side. I don't normally spend too much time near the waterfall, mostly because it feels noisy if I'm not busy in the garden, but today it's peaceful.

I can't help but wonder if there are any peaceful places left outside the dome.

When I first arrived here, I knew that everything was chaos outside. I saw it firsthand. All the major cities were destroyed, and yet the borgs still came. I remember thinking that if the borgs could just find whatever it was they were after, maybe they'd leave us all alone.

But thinking back on that now, I realize how naïve it sounds. To want, a borg would need to have understanding —they'd need to have some shred of humanity. And there's no way they could have caused such destruction if they did. There's no way they could have put me in here—and kept me locked up for the last six years. No caring thing would do that.

I used to have these discussions with Ander. Our three months together were some of the best months of my life. It was the Zoo honeymoon period, you could say. Instead of grieving, I let myself luxuriate in the lack of responsibility I had.

Ander and I would work out together and share stories and jokes. He was like the college roommate I never got to have. On the outside, I had been saving up to go back to school, because my financial aid ran out and I couldn't afford my next semester, so I dropped out to work. That's when everything happened.

Ander gave me wild hairstyles and I drew elaborate pen

tattoos on his arms. I think that's part of why the idea of a new zoomate scares me. Being close to someone again brings the potential for losing them.

I still remember his last day here. We were in the room, talking and eating carrots. I can picture his face and his lips moving like it was just yesterday. Ander was in his early twenties, slight and attractive, with a movie star smile.

We often talked about what we would do if we ever got out of the Zoo. His plan was to find his love Drew, venture to the ocean and set sail until they found an island, and live on coconut milk and fish until they were old and wrinkled.

It was a grand idea, and I kind of wished I had one so specific. For me, just getting out was enough. We ate Treat Show snacks for dessert, and he braided my hair. He was my friend.

That night, we talked about what it would be like to be the last hope of the human species, and we kissed, but it felt weird. Ander was more brother than boyfriend. Besides, he had someone on the outside.

His Drew, who wore only gray, wrote sonnets, and made the best egg sandwiches. And Ander loved him. I wanted Ander to have his dream, to find Drew and go live on an island. I told him that while he braided my hair.

Suddenly, Borgie was there, at the door. With its flat, genderless voice, it demanded that we "go to bed," and we looked at each other with our eyes wide and knew what it wanted even though no words were spoken between us.

It wanted to mate us, and our innocent little kiss must have given Borgie the signal it was looking for.

When neither of us moved, Borgie gave Ander an injection and left the room. They inject us all the time, so I thought perhaps he would be taken to the Testing Pod later that night. For a second, I was relieved. But then I saw Ander's face change.

His eyes darkened and his brow protruded, sweat beading on his skin. He came at me so aggressively that I ran. He began chasing me around the room, grabbing for me, and I knocked over the lamp by the bed, but he didn't slow.

Eventually, he caught up with me, and he grabbed my shoulders and threw me to the bed.

I hit my head on the wall, and I knew I was in danger. When he leaned over me, I could feel him hard against my waist. I pleaded with him to please stop.

Whatever Borgie had injected him with was making him act this way. The violence of his behavior was such a sharp departure from his true nature, and I tried to assure him that I knew he was still in there, but nothing worked. We struggled, and he tried to rip my clothes off.

I remember looking out the Plexi to the trees and fake rocks across the way, and I knew that nobody was coming to save me.

Either I let him hurt me or I could fight back. I remember looking into his eyes, thinking, *This is it, it's him or me.*

I was going to die if I did not stop him.

In desperation, I reached my hand around, searching for anything I could use, and I found a piece of that broken lamp. I jammed it as hard as I could into his side, but he did not retreat. I felt warm blood trickle down my arm.

Him or me.

Him or me.

I didn't think twice as I stabbed him again, this time in his neck.

By the time Borgie got to us, Ander had quieted significantly, but he was bleeding out. I had a blanket wrapped around his neck, trying to stop the blood. This was Ander. My friend. Now he was dying, and I had to help him.

Borgie lifted him into its giant metal arms and carried him away.

He never returned, and I knew that could only mean one thing.

I killed my only friend.

The sound of my own wheezing surprises me. I use the bottom of my shirt to mop my tears.

Although it has been six years, the memory of that night still haunts me. The pain of what I did is ever present. But so is the longing for a friend, despite my fear of being mated. Another person joining me here at the Zoo is my greatest wish and my deepest nightmare.

I push off of the rock to stand. Borgie still hasn't appeared, and I'm tired. This mission is over. All I want to do is sleep.

CHAPTER FIVE

On the way back to my room, my plans change. I see movement in the garden and realize that whatever has been eating my vegetables is back. When I look at the garden, I don't see the creature that caught my eye, so I sink down into a squat to inspect the dirt inside the garden box.

Sure enough, small holes with little dirt piles beside them now populate my garden where the vegetables had been.

Where are you, little creature?

I stand up and look around, but all I see is my own reflection in the Plexi. Looking down, I examine my body in the way a stranger would. This is what this new person will see. I used to consider my body a vehicle taking you through life, but now it's more of a showpiece, a physical story.

All the laps in the ocean, running the dome, and the pushups and other calisthenics have left me lean and muscular. My eyes look sad, and my lips turn down. My body tells a story of the girl in the Zoo.

As I lean closer to inspect my teeth, I see something in the reflection behind me.

Hiding behind a row of weeds are two glowing eyes. Crouching toward it to get a better look sends it scurrying deeper into the shadows. Holding out my hand, I offer a coaxing sound, *pwah*, and the creature comes out.

It's a cat, a real live animal.

I blink in disbelief. If it is a hallucination, it is a welcome one. Her fur is gray, and she has one green eye and one yellow, two different faces.

She is nursing a half-moon scar along her stomach, likely a bite from a larger animal. Perhaps she found the Zoo a safe place to recover.

I smile a bit at that.

That my nightmare could be this cat's safe place. Imagine that. Moving slowly, not wanting to frighten her away, I hold out my hand. She comes close, carefully sniffing the air, and then runs off toward the Treat Show door. Shoot.

Rather than chase her around, I decide to wait. I cover up the holes the cat made, raking the soil with my fingers. The smell of earth has a calming effect on me. Sure enough, a few minutes later I spy the cat out of the corner of my eye, as she comes pouncing back, keeping her distance, crouching behind the box.

"Don't worry, I'm not going to hurt you," I say.

She looks at me suspiciously.

"Look." I show her the injection marks winding down my arms that end in a tiny spade birthmark on my wrist. "I have scars, too."

She gingerly walks over and gives my hand a little head-butt, and I'm filled with the delight of this little acknowledgment.

Sitting down in the box of dirt, she lets me pet her soft fur, and I relax. I can't believe a real cat found its way inside the dome. There is something so comforting about the presence of a living soul, rather just another borg. I feel less alone already.

"Maybe it won't be *so bad* to have another human here," I mutter to the cat softly. She looks back up at me and purrs.

My whole life, I longed for a real animal pet, but my parents never let me have one. Sadly, pet tech was the ideal choice for most families. No cleaning up after them or feeding them; they only need charging and software updates.

I did have one friend in seventh grade with a pet dog, Skylar, the sweetest dachshund. When he passed away at the end of high school, Skylar was replaced by Gomo, a pet tech dog.

Gomo was never as sweet as Skylar.

Science has come a long way in replicating domestic animals, but I could always tell Gomo wasn't real. Just like I'm sure that the blip of humanity I saw in Borgie earlier wasn't real either. Someone probably programmed Borgie to replicate that look—that emotion, whatever it was—just like Gomo was programmed to fetch.

It wasn't real.

Gently, I scratch the cat's ears, and when I feel the small vibrations of a purr, I know that she is relaxed too. *She* is real. My eyes glaze with tears, and I'm so grateful for this moment. We sit like this for a while, silently enjoying each other's company.

When I hear metal crunching on gravel, my stomach drops like I've been caught. I half expect to see Borgie racing toward me, demanding I leave the cat alone. But when I look down the path, it's only the construction borgs carrying more flats of Plexi and other gear.

The cat meows, looking up curiously as if asking what

the borgs are doing. Perhaps the construction noise scared her over here this morning—maybe she doesn't like how loud it is either.

"Want to see my room?" I ask. "It's mildly more interesting than the garden. And it's quiet." She seems game.

With thoughts of Ander temporarily pushed to the side, I start to walk toward my room, and just my luck the cat follows behind me.

When we approach my room, the cat is more curious about what the construction borgs are doing.

She winds around them, ducking out of the way of the swinging Plexi, and tiptoes beyond the foot of a giant work borg.

I imagine how cute she'd be wearing a tiny yellow hard hat, bossing around the crew. Her confidence inspires me to name her after my favorite classic Hollywood actress, Linda Hamilton.

CHAPTER SIX

About half an hour later, Linda pads into my room with a confident swing in her hips. Finally, she must've tired of watching the borgs work.

"Welcome," I greet her. She leaps up onto my bed without invitation to show how comfortable she is in my space. She seems to like me, and I can't help but let joy nuzzle into the empty crevice in my heart.

"You're just in time," I say. "I'm going to have a Harvest Day feast tonight. Would you like to join?"

Linda meows her acceptance as she sniffs my pillow and steps on it as if to decide its worthiness.

"Were those borgs nice to you?" I ask. I hope that Borgie won't be mad that I let her in my room.

Linda meows again. She's talkative.

"The Harvest meal is set with the vegetables, but let's see what we'll have for dessert." I open the cabinet where I keep my treats and find only one Cocopoof left. There is a small ache in my stomach at the thought of the last one. Only one treat left.

"Almost time for the Treat Show," I tell her. "The Treat

Show happens once a week, at the place where the dome is open and outside borgs come to watch me. Hey, is that how you got in?" I ask. Linda yawns.

It has been nagging at me since I found her. But she doesn't answer.

I place the cut vegetables on the plate in a pattern because it makes me feel in charge of something, like I'm a chef. The order feels like control.

Tomato-carrot-zucchini.

Tomato-carrot-zucchini.

I bring the plate over to the table, and Linda follows. I sit down, but she goes over to the door and scratches. She wants me to open it, but I worry that Borgie is going to take her away from me if it finds her.

Scratch, scratch.

When I reach out to open the door, something makes me stop and pull my hand back. I want her to stay. There hasn't been anyone to talk to in years. Crouching low, I pet her, but she nips at my hand.

"Linda, please don't leave," I whisper. My chest feels heavy.

She scratches harder. She wants to go.

Finally, I push the door open, and she pounces off into the dusk of the dimming Weatherlight. Leaning my head against the doorframe, I squint as she heads out toward the forest. I feel a deep disappointment that I didn't expect.

I am alone again.

As I stare out at the gray path, I see the new room being built across from me. It sits empty too. But for how long?

Turning back to my room, I sit down for my feast. The plate of organized crudité rests before me, but somehow the rainbow has lost its luster. I glance up at the Plexi door, expecting something, but nothing happens.

Tucking my feet underneath my chair, I throw a half-hearted "cheers" into the air with my water packet and eat slowly. I want to savor the flavors the way I always do, but the bites get stuck around the lump in my throat.

The vegetables are a symbol of life and of my hard work, I remind myself. I should enjoy them. The emotions stack inside my throat, tomato-carrot-zucchini, lonely-sad-Mirin.

How did Linda get in? And then back out again? If she can leave, then it could be possible for me to leave too. Linda is new to the Zoo, and she must have found a way inside. I wonder if it has to do with Borgie's "complication." Maybe there's a hole in the Plexi somewhere?

It is possible that Linda found the flaw in the system, the one thing that I have tried to find and could not. Perhaps that is why she is not hungry for my food or water, because she finds it on the outside. Maybe Borgie found out and had to fix it. My heart quickens as I realize that there are still many things I don't know about this place. She could show me where things from the outside can get in, and perhaps back out again.

Staring out across the way, at the new room, I wonder why they'd build a whole separate room. Perhaps there will be more than one new person, or maybe the zoomate will be a friend or a sister instead of a mate.

A sister. Violet. My heart aches for the sister I already have.

Had.

Maybe we can have dinners and talk, and she can tell me about the outside. Maybe she'll be really smart, like an engineer, and she'll know how we can escape, and we can leave the Zoo together. My face warms, and I feel my mood shift.

CHAPTER SEVEN

After my scans the next morning, I head down to the beach in search of Linda. I'm hoping she's still inside the dome, and if not, maybe she'll hear my voice and show me her secret passageway. I smile at the idea of a cat being my ticket out of this place.

When I first got to the Zoo, I used to imagine all the different ways I would escape someday—and not one of them ever involved a cat.

But after covering almost every inch of the beach, I don't see her or any recent pawprints in the sand. As I walk the shoreline, I squint over toward the forest and search for any small movement that could be a gray cat.

No Linda. I hope that she found some dinner at least.

I wish I knew how she made her way in here. My best guess would be through the Treat Show area since it is open to outsiders once a week. I have a mental image of all those borgs filing in, one by one, coming to see me, in the human exhibit, and little Linda weaving through their tread, wheels, and steel legs.

Even though I only knew her for a handful of minutes, I miss her already.

Wherever she is, I hope she has enough food. Maybe she is living on the rats outside.

Maybe she has an actual home with a family that loves her. I have no idea what the outside looks like these days.

Are there still neighborhoods? Or maybe people live inside camps. If there are any people. I suppose there must be if the borgs are bringing another human into the Zoo.

I hope that my new zoomate, whoever they are, brings news of the outside. I have so many questions about the survival of humans, the landscape, if there are even grocery stores anymore.

Maybe we can put our heads together and escape this place. If Linda can get in and out, then why not the zoomate and me? Meeting Linda has already been a game changer, but this new zoomate could lead me somewhere truly life changing. Either that or one of us will end up dead, like Ander.

Suddenly, everything feels heavy. The walls feel too close. The air feels too stale. And the Weatherlight feels like a shabby lamp. Dark thoughts are no stranger to me these days, but I no longer succumb to them like I used to. I used to sleep a lot and forget to eat my nutrition packets, and sometimes I hurt myself.

But then I realized that Borgie would never actually let me die. I'd wake up in the Testing Pod on an IV, getting nutrients that way, or stitched and bandaged up. Borgie's message was very clear—either take care of yourself or I will do it for you. So I stopped trying to give up the ghost.

But as my feet pound the sand, I grow impatient.

For years there was no one, and then Linda showed up. And now that helpless feeling is creeping in again. Without thinking I begin to jog faster, the energy inside bursting to be released.

Leaving the beach, I weave through the forest, beginning my laps around the dome. It seems smaller and my strides longer, and I feel like a mouse beginning to turn in its wheel. When I finish my twelfth lap, I fold over and grasp my knees, out of breath.

Then I do twenty-five pushups on the sand before I enter the water and swim twenty laps in the ocean. When I leave the water, my muscles are aching. My mind still spins.

My heart is pumping in a progression, with momentum, like I need to move more. My body is tired, but I am not satisfied.

Existing inside of this dome is not enough.

The pervasive feeling of being confined makes me want to be free. And with Linda's arrival, that possibility feels like it should be closer than ever—but it's not. It walked right out of the dome with her.

Black spots start to form in my vision, and my heart beats harder. I could scream or cry or laugh or fall down in defeat. Is this sadness? Or rage?

Madness. Mirin, you are going mad.

I wish I was a borg so that I didn't have to feel so many things. I look down at my arm and think about what it would be like to have gears and a motor running underneath my skin.

Before the war, there *were* human-replica AI borgs—and they were *so* lifelike. I remember seeing them on display at a museum with my family once. I was so captivated by how real they seemed—their mannerisms, their voices, even their pupils could dilate.

It was like they didn't even realize that they weren't actually human.

Sometimes, when the loneliness gets thick, I think about how Borgie could have implanted me with borg parts while I was knocked out in the Testing Pod. There have been so many tests and injections and blackouts, and I never know what they actually do to me.

Imagine what it feels to be like those borgs in the museum, to wake up thinking you're one thing, only to realize you're something else entirely. That would be so sad.

Each day feeling emotions, knowing yourself, and then when you are powered off, who you are is lost. And when you wake it begins all over again.

That is like living in the Zoo. Maybe my confusion, the madness, is because I am a borg. I rub my face hard, feeling for metal, but my cheek and jaw bones feel the same as always. I look around for anything to satisfy the ache in my chest to know.

I want to know if I'm real.

There's a rock sitting just underneath Shel, a real one, unlike the larger plastic rocks. I grab it and sit down by the shore.

Breathing in, I raise the rock high and bring it down onto the top of my right foot. I wince silently. Again, I bring it down on the same spot. It hurts more, and my eyes squeeze tightly shut. A third and final time, I bring the rock down.

Auhh.

I howl from my gut. My fragile skin breaks and bleeds freely.

I welcome the pain. It means I am not a borg.

As I sit in the sand with my foot on fire, I remember my humanity. It hurts.

CHAPTER EIGHT

I rinse my foot in the water, but it won't stop bleeding. I may have gone too hard this time.

It's been so long since I've needed to perform a humanity test that I must have forgotten my own limits. There is nothing left for me to do but limp all the way back to my room to bandage my wound.

Forsaking Shel and the blood-stained rock, I go back to my room, leaving a trail of very human blood along the path. The borgs hover around, raising up the Plexi, welding it together, and there is that short HIPPO borg again, the one I've seen in the Testing Pod.

Maybe it can give me stitches. I limp over and wave my hand at it.

"HIPPO, I hurt my foot," I say. The borg continues with its work, gluing together slats that look like pieces of my kitchenette. I tap it, refusing to be ignored.

"HIPPO borg, please, I need some help," I try again. I hold my foot up as an offer. It looks grotesque, with crushed patches of skin and fresh blood running down my ankle.

HIPPO stops and turns toward me; it runs its beam over my foot.

"Ooooh," it beeps.

A small water hose protrudes from its boxy body, and it rinses my foot. Blood continues to ooze out of the wound, but HIPPO doesn't seem to notice. Instead, it taps my foot with the glue gun, as if to say, *There.* HIPPO apparently thinks I'm all better and continues gluing the cabinet.

I lean against a pile of Plexi, balancing on my good foot, and hold my sleeve over it, applying pressure. HIPPO is not going to help me. A construction borg swiftly moves by us and smacks a board against a wall.

Bang.

I don't want that guy helping with my medical care. He might rip my foot right off. A construction borg performing medical tasks wouldn't make sense, so why is a medical borg doing construction?

"HIPPO, what are you doing here? You're usually in the Testing Pod," I say. But it's too busy to answer.

HIPPO is acting just as strangely as Borgie lately. But maybe there is some kind of urgency to get the room done, and they required every borg to do construction. If the zoomate is coming soon, I better prepare.

Even though HIPPO tried to help me with the rinse, my foot is throbbing, and I need to get to my room and wrap it up. I think I've stopped the bleeding a bit.

Limping to my room, I grab a nutrition packet from off the counter. I wrap my foot and tie it in a tight knot, using a sock as a makeshift bandage.

Sitting down on my bed, I prop my foot on the pillow. I rip the top off the nutrition packet and squeeze some of the gelatinous mix into my mouth. It tastes like the Zoo, same vitamin goo as always. After my feast yesterday, it feels like

I have returned to eating air. Every heartbeat feels like it is throbbing into my foot, and blood is soaking through the sock.

Little stars float across my vision, and my hands feel clammy. *I might be losing too much blood* is my last thought before I pass out.

CHAPTER NINE

When I wake up, my foot is still throbbing. It takes me a minute to adjust to the fact that it's morning and that Borgie will be here any minute to do its scans. I slept all the way through the night, but somehow, I feel more tired than ever.

I tug off the blood-stained sock bandage. There is an ugly wound festering, my ankle is red and swollen, and red streaks follow my veins like ropes of licorice up the back of my leg.

Could an infection have already started in just twelve hours? I thought this place is supposed to be sterile. But then I remember Linda. She must have brought germs in from the outside.

I cannot let Borgie see the state of my ankle—not only will it take me to the Testing Pod and prod me, but it will also know that something has come in from the outside, spreading germs.

I have never been sick in the Zoo before.

Ever.

I take that back; my body has not been sick. I cannot deny the toll it has taken on my mental health. It is the lack of contact with other people and their germs that has kept me physically well. I cannot say which is worse because loneliness may be just as dangerous as a virus.

I see the outline of Borgie just outside my room. I put on a clean sock and carefully slide my foot into the front part of my slipper.

Borgie comes in and takes my temperature—100.8 degrees—and because I run cool, I know that this is a significant fever. My foot is on fire.

Even though I need help, I don't want to go to the Testing Pod because I don't want to be injected and I don't want to be turned into a borg. I have no choice but to distract Borgie until it leaves.

"Mirin needs fever reducer." Borgie hands me two pink pills. I take them without a beat.

"Thanks. Borgie, why have you been acting so strange?" I ask, and point to her shoulder, which is now perfectly smooth. "What gave you the dent, from before?"

"Bad man," Borgie says in its Information Voice, facing away.

I'm shocked.

"What bad man?" I ask, wondering how a person could have possibly given it that dent. But then I realize that perhaps it was my soon-to-be zoomate.

"Mirin is safe from bad man, worry, w-w-w-worry, d-d-don't," Borgie stutters. Borgie never stutters. My heart clenches and I don't know what to say.

Borgie looks at me again, making solid eye contact this time. I see the flicker of life like before, and I know my previous assumptions are true.

Borgie sees me.

We stare at each other without speaking. I can't believe

it's real. The robot in charge of my person might be a person too. My stomach spins.

"Borgie will take care of Mirin," it says. It takes my breath away. It referred to itself with the pet name I gave it, and it looked at me deeply. This is not a flicker; this is a moment. A connection. Could it be true that borgs are sentient? Is Borgie?

It seems like Borgie cares about me. It wants me to be safe.

Suddenly, I feel guilty for hiding my foot injury.

"There, there, Mirin," Borgie says in its Maternal Voice, and it runs its claw over my hair. *The robot is trying to comfort me.* The cold metal claw pulls at individual strands of hairs, but I don't pull away. I want comfort.

"Complete scan," Borgie says in its Information Voice. It stands and whooshes back outside, as though everything was as it always was.

This was the first real moment I've known with Borgie. I've never talked to a sentient AI before, and maybe it won't ever happen again. I hope I'm not projecting my feelings onto this interaction. No, it was real.

Borgie actually said "there, there" like it learned that from a children's book or something. This is amazing. It felt like when I met Linda, that same warm connection. I notice that Borgie left a window squeegee attachment leaning up against my wall outside. Maybe I can use that as a walking stick, to help me get to the garden.

I have to find out if Linda is back.

Once outside I notice that all the maintenance borgs are gone and the new room is complete. There was no celebration, no fanfare. It's just done. I walk over to the perfect replica of my own room.

Standing outside the new room, I drag my finger along

the Plexi, just to be sure that it's actually there and not another case of my imagination wanting something enough to invent it.

My breath fogs up the outside, but I can see a twin bed, white linens, a kitchenette with a cabinet, a small table with a stool. Everything is bright white. When I get to the door and turn the handle, I find it locked so I can't snoop inside.

Oh well.

Will it be a friend, like my sister, someone to laugh and argue and be a team with? Or could it be someone older and wiser who can teach me?

It could be a child or a grandparent. I am slightly horrified by the idea of an elderly person living out their final days in the Zoo. And even worse—for a child forced to grow up in the Zoo. There could be nothing worse for a child—no playmates, no toys, no food. It would be the worst.

And then I remember Borgie's words: *bad man*.

It wouldn't make him my zoomate. The possibilities threaten my balance, and I lean on the squeegee. It could be anyone, and I'll have to be ready for anything. Including the bizarre possibility that Borgie is becoming sentient and that I may soon be living with someone capable of denting a giant borg. I shake off my thoughts.

Without anything exciting happening here, I decide to try to find Linda. I shamble along the path as fast as I can, using the squeegee for support as I drag my foot along, passing the Treat Show on my left and continuing to the garden.

The waterfall ahead of me is loud today. It sits front and center in the dome, with a stunning rock wall for climbing along the side. A natural waterfall is often the gift at the end of a rigorous hike, and this one offers me that gift every day. The sound of it is quite soothing. There is some beauty here, and for that I'm grateful. It keeps me well.

The garden looks undisturbed. As I get closer, I see no paw prints in the soil, meaning Linda hasn't been here since the last time I was. My shoulders sink in disappointment.

"Linda." My lip quivers as I call out to her. I was hoping to find her here, basking in the Weatherlight. Kissing the air a few times, I try to coax her out, but no response.

"Linda," I call one last time. Nothing.

But then I do hear something. First, it's a muffled sound, then a loud banging as if in response. The noise is coming from behind the Treat Show. I worry that they've found Linda and are trying to capture her to put her outside the dome again. I'm not ready to lose her completely.

Quietly, I make my way over to the entrance of the Treat Show, steadying myself on my good foot. I'm careful as I lean my body against the doorway to where I can see what's happening but the borgs can't see me. I can be a proper spy when needed.

"*No!*" A male voice cries out, reverberating through every fiber of my being. I freeze.

I can't believe it. The sound of another human voice carries across the air, through my ears and down into my gut. I wrap my arms around myself and squeeze tight. I haven't heard a real human voice since Ander.

Could this be the bad man Borgie mentioned?

I try to push back the thoughts, but they flood without permission. It feels like a violation. Ander left the Zoo covered in blood, injured by my hands, and I was sure he was dead.

But in that male-voiced "no" I hear the chance that he survived and is back, and it fills me with relief and dread at the same time. I grip the doorframe and hear borg tread, shuffling, and muffled yells.

The door to the Treat Show flies open and I see him. How did they get him into the Treat Show? The borgs got him past the barrier somehow.

Because now I see a man strapped to an ambulance gurney, a white sheet covering him completely, smothering his shouts and grunts. Right there before me is the shape of a new person.

I hold my breath.

I squeeze my eyes together tight, wondering if this a dream. But when I open them, it's all still there. I take a step forward on instinct, and my foot lights up in pain. Surely, I wouldn't be able to feel *that* in a dream.

This is real. I must be here, watching as they push my new zoomate forward.

The man is upset and unruly, his body clenching against the sheet. How terrified he must feel. And out of control.

I barely remember the day they took me. I was scared and trapped in my mind. There was no acting out or screaming. Being thoughtful and careful was my role because I thought I could outsmart the borgs or reason my way out. I wanted as much information and knowledge as I could get before deciding what I would do.

I would not consider this a successful choice because it has been six years and I'm still here.

Then again, *it has been six years and I'm still here.*

But this man is intense and is full-on resisting. This must be the anomaly; he must be the *bad man* Borgie told me about. He sure seems capable of denting a borg. I want to follow and watch him, but I can't.

I'm frozen in place as they wheel the gurney past me.

Tousled black curly hair springs from the top of the sheet—a striking difference from fair-haired Ander. I press my body against the back wall of the Treat Show to stay out of the way.

The breeze from the gurney wafts toward my face, and the hot resistance of the man fills the dome.

And his scent. He smells like sweat and salt and life.

Borgie walks alongside the gurney as they move him toward the rooms. It does not acknowledge me. It does not show me any of the benevolence I saw this morning. And now I'm not so sure it was how I imagined it.

Beads of sweat dot my face. *Move, Mirin. Do something.*

My knees wobble as I make my way back to the garden. I'm not ready to face my new zoomate yet. When I arrive in the dirt patch, I still see no signs of Linda.

My foot throbs, and I am dizzy. I fall to one knee and realize I can't feel my foot anymore.

That's not good.

The borgs are completely distracted by the new man on the gurney, with no space to worry about me.

"Linda," I call, but no one answers.

I think I will just lie here and take a quick nap. And when I'm rested, I will go meet my new zoomate. Even if he is the *bad man* Borgie spoke of.

Blackness overtakes my vision as I curl up in the dirt.

CHAPTER TEN

My sleep was fitful. It felt like I woke up every thirty minutes, but somehow, I was never awake enough to get myself back to my room. With all the excitement of yesterday, no one even noticed that I spent the night in the garden.

Good thing I didn't die.

The sound of the Treat Show alarm blasts through the Zoo, letting me know I have about ten minutes to get dressed and get back to the arena.

Hurry, Mirin.

I hobble back to my room as quickly as I am able. I cannot miss this Treat Show. I need the treats. If I can just make it through this Treat Show with my festering foot, afterward I will beg for Borgie's mercy and ask it to fix me.

Last night, somewhere between being asleep and awake, I realized that the only way to gain an upper hand in this situation with the bad man on the gurney is to give him food.

It's my only leverage or offering, all that I will have to

trade him for his kindness. Although I don't think he's quite in the mood right now.

Which means that no matter what, I must entertain the borgs today. I need *a lot* of treats, not only to fill up my own cache but to give to my new zoomate as well. And that won't be easy. The borgs are wishy-washy.

Sometimes I talk about a VR show from my childhood and get a good haul, so the next week I do that same talk again with high expectations and receive nothing.

No rhyme or reason. I'm dealing with hunks of metal here, not exactly reasonable patrons.

When I finally make it back to my room, I go straight to the closet. There are three Treat Show outfits that I received upon arrival to the Zoo, all equally bizarre. I pull on the matcha green tube top with taffeta pouf sleeves over my head and squeeze the magenta spandex skirt over my thighs.

The look is nearly complete with a pastel rose-shaped hair bow placed just over my ear.

And finally, I shuffle into the neon fur boots, which are a size too big. Too big works in my favor today, as I'm able to get my wrapped, wounded foot into the boot. It is tender at my calf now, and my foot feels numb.

Just get through this Treat Show and then Borgie will fix it. If I have to beg for help, even if I have to *make violence*, I will.

I dust off the boots, look at myself in the reflection of the Plexi, and see that I'm a perfect disaster.

Looking weird must confirm something human about me for the borgs. The more mismatched and ridiculous I look, the more treats they throw, so I indulge them.

The alarm sounds again, and even though I'm expecting it, I cover my ears and tuck my chin.

Alarms are the worst.

Borgie meets me at my door and escorts me to the Treat Show area.

As we walk, my taffeta sleeves crinkle and I can't help but think of Linda. She would love this sound. Part of me hopes that she did get out, to stay safe. But the other part hopes she'll come back soon.

She was my best friend, and I only knew her for one day. Linda is special. The way she looked at me was like she understood me. We will reunite and she might even show me the way out.

As if it can hear my thoughts, Borgie marches by my side with its head turned toward me slightly.

I wonder if the man is feeling better today and if they let him rest and shower. Maybe he'll be ready for a snack and meeting his new neighbor when this is over.

Borgie unlocks the door to the Treat Show at the outer edge of the dome. It's the one part of the dome that opens to visitors.

There is a barrier rail between the outside of the dome and the inside part, much like the old-fashioned zoos for animals were.

Only the inside part here is set up like a classic turn-of-the-century office. There is a cubicle with three desks and chairs, and on top of each of the desks is a multi-extension phone, a pen, paper, and a stapler. A vintage water cooler with a giant jug of water sits against the back wall, as an art piece. It's almost like a museum.

My best guess is the borgs found blueprints of office cubicles and wanted us to perform our visiting day in a historical site. I liken my office setup to that of a reenactment of a historical moment.

The only performance in my life was the seventh-grade

talent show. My best friend was Zelda, and she convinced me to join her group.

I'm not a joiner, not a performer, and certainly not someone who would humiliate themselves in front of the entire school. I resisted adamantly but tears and promises of shared Halloween candy convinced me to sign up.

My neck broke out into hives on the day of the performance, but I made it through to the finish. And Zelda did, in fact, share her Halloween candy with me later that year. What I would give to eat a proper chocolate bar again.

When I look out at the audience, I see about a dozen borgs of various shapes and sizes.

The Zoo isn't as popular as it once was. I used to draw big crowds in my first years, but I must have lost my luster. Maybe that's why they brought in another human.

Borgie stands by the exit door watching me.

My teeth chatter and I feel cold, though I know it must be because I'm feverish.

Standing at the center of the desks, I begin to hum the song under my breath and mime the dance moves.

I sing out in my unused and off-key voice, and pantomime a wake-up motion in front of my face.

The song refers to getting ready with makeup, so I feign putting on blush, which feels strange, as makeup as a concept has lost its appeal completely.

My hands come together to pray. Please toss me treats. Desperate, I look out with a big smile plastered on my face and pause.

Total and complete silence.

Dammit.

They do not throw treats. Not one. I'm bombing. I swear that I forget they are robots sometimes.

The only other time I've spoken in front of a group was *Hamlet*.

I had to memorize the "To be" speech senior year thinking that there was no circumstance in my entire life that would ever require this knowledge. The words tumble out easily now.

"To be, or not to be, that is the question: Whether 'tis nobler in the mind to suffer the slings and arrows of outrageous fortune, or to take arms against a sea of troubles and by opposing end them. To die—to sleep."

After a breath, I continue the speech with as much gusto as I can manage. I am genuinely surprised that I remember this at all. Mr. Mack would be so proud. The borgs stare, and I take a deep breath for the final passage.

"And enterprises of great pitch and moment with this regard their currents turn awry and lose the name of action," I finish.

I'm sweating profusely now, which is expected for such an emotional performance. The truth is that I meant those words.

Balancing on my good foot expectantly, I look beyond the borgs to the wall and the door at the back, where they entered. The world I used to be a part of is out there, or not there. I don't know what it's like anymore.

The room is quiet.

They hated it. Two borgs clank away and leave, and I count only ten remaining. They left. That's never happened before. I bored the borgs with Shakespeare. What were they thinking?

The Human Exhibit is highly lacking these days. We don't visit to see unusual movements and voice discrepancies. The human is broken.

I'm feeling lightheaded, my foot now switching between burning and numb. It's miserable. I've failed to get treats, and time is nearly up. One time I played an office worker, and I think that may have worked before. I'll take what I can get. At this point one treat would help.

Limping to a desk, I pick up the old-fashioned phone, but I see stars. Sweat drips down my spine. My arms are heavy, and I feel my heartbeat slow. My head hits the desk.

"Oooh," something coos.

I'm slumped over the desk, and my face hurts. Rubbing my sore nose, I feel a warm drip. Nosebleed. *Shoot.* There are no tissues, so I grab the rose hair piece off my head and hold it to my nose. Blood turns the pink rose red.

Looking up at the gallery, I see that the four borgs left are all still staring at me. Round steel eye sockets, square acetate filters, blank sheet metal.

If I'm not mistaken, they enjoyed me fainting. I plop my head back down on the desk, this time turning my head to avoid further injury.

And then, I hear it, the crinkle crackle of a parchment-wrapped apple pie flying through the air.

It lands by my left foot, and I understand now that the borgs like slapstick. And so I sulk and sigh and bang the desk with my fist. A packaged chocolate mini cake lands nearby, like the kind my father put in my lunch bag when I was a child.

Ooooh. Ahhhh.

New borgs enter the audience. The crowd of borgs all start making varying sounds. Some are recorded human voices or canned cheers; the unknown origin makes the sounds particularly disconcerting. But the borgs come "alive" when I look upset, and treats start landing on the desks. Treats swat my arm, and the more dejected I appear, the more the treats stack up.

Lying down on the floor, I stomp my good foot for emphasis. It rains treats.

My bad foot reminds me to hurry this performance. I feel terrible, my foot is infected, yet the borgs are rewarding me for my comedic pain.

It's a performance inside a performance.

I'm in so much pain that I'm giving them my true self for the first time. One of the truths of living here, something I had come to terms with a long time ago, is the fact that I have no control.

But this is the first time I feel like I made something happen. The borgs are compensating me for something I am doing on purpose, and I can stop if I want to, or I can be more dramatic if I want. The feeling of agency is like a drug. I am treating my pain with agency.

When more of the visitors enter, Borgie enters and leans in close to scan my temperature.

"102.6 degrees Fahrenheit," it says aloud. Much higher than last time.

My legs sway, and I blink myself into the moment.

"Mirin is febrile," it says.

Yes, Borgie, I have a fever.

"I want to stay just a little longer," I say. I grasp the edge of the desk for balance.

"Mirin is febrile," it repeats.

"Borgie, give me a few more minutes. I'm busy working here," I say.

"Mirin is sick," it says in the Maternal Voice.

I lose my composure.

"All I'm asking for is more time. Can't you see, I'm

getting treats here? Just trying to be a good neighbor, *a good person*," I stop because I realize I'm yelling, and feeling nauseous.

"Time to go now." Borgie switches back into Information Voice. I pout and begin collecting my treats.

CHAPTER ELEVEN

Careful not to lose any of my treasures, I clutch the snacks and treats close to my chest. My entire leg is throbbing now. Borgie is looking at me, head tilted. It has never paid this much attention to me on the route back to my room before—usually, it just ignores me.

"Borgie, is there something you want?" I ask. I don't think borgs have learned tact.

"You are behaving in a confusing manner. Fever makes Mirin act like a grouch in a trashcan," Borgie says. I smile, remember public virtual experiences from childhood.

"Oscar the Grouch, you mean. Yes, I suppose I feel like that," I say, looking at its face with new consideration.

Through the haze of my fever, I'm suddenly in awe of how striking Borgie is. There is something very artful about how it was designed. How did the designer even make a borg this big so beautiful?

Based on its height alone, I wonder, not for the first time, if Borgie was originally designed to be a warrior borg.

Warrior borgs were originally created to fight battles with other countries on behalf of the humans. They were war machines, programmed to do a myriad of awful things like kill, maim, and conquer.

When there was no active government war, humans put them up against each other to fight for entertainment. And whenever one would fall, they'd repair the body and send it back out into the fighting arena.

Fight, kill, repair.

Over and over again. It always struck me as sad, but my father, along with many people I knew, just loved Warrior Borg Battles. They saw them as giant toys, created to act upon our human whims. And it went on that way for a while.

Until the borgs began to kill us.

I shake off the thought as we walk back toward the room. The HIPPO borg is waiting for us. Borgie must have signaled it with whatever they use to communicate. I could see its medical toolkit attached to it magnetically.

When I reach out to tap it on the head, HIPPO grabs my hand and starts to pull me away. A dial from the front of its body catches on my costume, causing me to lose my balance and then I watch as my cache of treats goes airborne.

"No," I say. I am still for a moment, seeing all thirty-seven treats on the ground. I bend to grab one little cracker bag, but HIPPO comes speeding in reverse toward me on its tanklike tread, looking like it's going to run right into me.

At the last second, Borgie grips my wrist with its claw and jerks me out of HIPPO's way. I drop the crackers.

Wow. I think HIPPO was trying to attack me. I have never seen a borg behave like this; they are usually so precise. There is no possible way that behavior was programmed. But if not programmed, where did it come from? This new fear drops like a lead weight in my stomach.

HIPPO is now near the garden, facing us, frozen. It makes a jerking movement forward, and then freezes again before whirling around in a circle. It's like someone is using a remote control to direct him and doesn't know what they are doing, just pushing random buttons.

Borgie seems perplexed by its behavior as well, even though it doesn't say a thing. It watches as HIPPO zigzags and races around aimlessly. Or maybe Borgie is manipulating it with some kind of internal command to tell HIPPO to stop.

HIPPO spins again and again, erratically crushing all my hard-won treats. My heart sinks. I needed them, and in minutes they're gone. Finally, it speeds off toward the forest. Borgie drops my hand and speeds after it.

Before I go back to my room, I comb the ground for any intact treats. All of them are flattened to the ground like mush. Except—

There is *one* round chocolate cake. Only an edge has been trodden on, so I snatch it up. After all that, I have three quarters of a treat left to offer the new zoomate. It feels unfair, it feels personal. Even though, I know that it isn't.

Without the adrenaline from HIPPO's behavior to keep me upright, I stumble and limp back to my room, angry tears falling down my cheeks.

I worked so hard. I mean, I threw myself around performing, even though I feel ghastly. I had so many treats, and then HIPPO just callously trampled them. Borgie was right about me being grouchy.

My ears prick up when I hear the whir of HIPPO again.

It speeds toward me, with Borgie's shadow looming not far behind. HIPPO stops spinning about a yard away and turns toward me like it is scanning me. The knob on its front is emitting a faint laser that I have seen before, a terrible memory grips me. I squeeze my eyes shut.

When I open them again, it seems like HIPPO is recording information about me. Its boxy head leans to one side, but I hold my gaze on the borg defiantly. It starts moving toward me slowly, making a high-pitched buzzing sound.

"HIPPO, I just need some medicine for my infection." I lean against a wall and hold onto my foot to show it, but it does not stop advancing.

"HIPPO. Do not come any closer. You are scaring me."

It stops about a foot in front of me as if it could understand my plea.

And then it explodes.

There is a hot flash of fire, and dirt flies everywhere. I'm thrown to the ground from the force, my ears go silent then start ringing. A pain shoots through my head, but for now my foot is numb.

I feel small and inside myself.

Seconds later, everything goes black, for the second time today.

CHAPTER TWELVE

As I wake up, my eyes slowly adjust to the familiar room. I'm dizzy and my vision moves between crisp and blurry, but the bleachy scent and bright white walls tell me that I'm in the Testing Pod.

Lying on the hospital bed where I have been many times before, I look down at the IV box in my arm and notice that the medical borgs crowding the end of the bed are cleaning my foot. HIPPO is not one of them. *What the hell happened?*

I can hardly think straight. I follow the two lines from my arm up to the two dangling bags containing the liquids running into my arm: one reads MORPHINE and the other NEOMAXICILLIN.

I look down to watch them drain an abscess on my foot, but I don't feel a thing. It's almost like I'm watching a gruesome medical documentary instead of something happening to my own body.

The white walls of the room throb while I lie back, staring at the movement around me. There are more borgs here than usual, and it concerns me. It makes me think that my health must be in great peril.

Or that something really bad just happened in the Zoo. *Where is Borgie?*

While fighting the intense urge to sleep, I try to pay attention to what the borgs are doing around me. *Information is the key to agency.* That is my last thought before I fall asleep.

When I come to again—it could be moments later or longer—I am alone.

Thankful that I am both alive and by myself, I reach down under the sheet and feel my foot. It's stiff.

When I pull the sheet off, I can see that it's bandaged. I press and it feels sore and warm, but at least I am no longer feverish.

I hear a noise outside the door. Borgie must be coming, so I sit up. Minutes pass, but Borgie does not enter the room and I wonder if it knows that I'm awake. The scent of bleach is making me nauseous and I want to go back to my room. I want to know what happened to HIPPO. Why did it attack?

I go to move, but wires are strung like telephone cables, connecting me to the machines around the room. The only ones I recognize are the IV bag's and the heart monitor.

The sticky pads on my head are hard to unpeel, but I manage to get them off. Then I pull the wires off me. Looking down at the box holding the two IV tubes, I know this is going to hurt, but I brace myself while giving it a tug. *Ouch.*

A machine starts chirping in alarm.

BEEP. BEEP.

I press all the buttons on the box, wanting to quiet it, and lucky for me, it finally powers off.

My breath is shallow, and I expect the borgs to come crashing through the door, but they don't. They might worry that I'm trying to escape, though god knows where I'd go.

Escape.

It's always there, the thought, the hope. It sits on the edge of everything inside me, it is the trim to my organs, the lining of my skin, it coats the dome, and I feel the thrill of the thought rise inside me after a long time. If something is happening here—if the borgs are becoming sentient or changing their plans—I need to get out. Fast.

A dormant rebellion is stirring.

It's just me alone on the bed and the quiet soon becomes too uncomfortable, so I stand up and steady myself to push away the feelings.

And now in the sterility of this empty room, I have that hope again. It whispers fantasies of freedom and possibility.

This could be another anomaly, the chance for escape.

Staring at the door, I expect Borgie, because this is what it does. It comes to stand in the doorway of my chance. The obstacle is always Borgie, trying to keep me inside. Trying to keep me compliant.

Every cell of my being wants to push through that door, but I don't want to get in trouble with Borgie. After seeing what happened to Ander when we didn't follow orders, I don't want to test it.

However, Borgie saved me from being run over by HIPPO, when it could have let me be squashed like those treats were.

If I never follow my instincts, then am I a person at all, or have I become like them, a borg simply following someone else's orders?

The temptation of that door is too strong. There are

dusty keys hanging by a cabinet next to the door. I grab them before I push on the door to leave.

It's strange, but this time I'm not afraid that I'm in undiscovered territory. I like it. My body is electric, and all my senses are turned up to full volume as I remember how liberating it is to break the rules.

As I step out into the hallway, I make a mental note not to put too much pressure on my foot because the morphine is surely dulling the pain still.

The hallway is dark and the wall tiled in plain beige squares, and I pass by a room that looks like a kitchen, with giant silver swinging doors. I push on one and find a table in the center. A large stack of boxes lines up along the wall inside.

An opened box entices me to peek inside, but I find it filled with nutrition packets. I look around for a machine that makes them or a box of treats, but instead I find a grease outline on the floor of what was likely an appliance.

Exiting back out the door, I see another door all the way at the end of the hallway. The jangle of the keys as I walk reminds me to hide them. Sliding the three keys off the keychain, I slip them into my linen slipper.

It is still quiet, with no sign of Borgie.

This door could lead me out, and I can't help but smile.

When I push on the cold metal, the door opens to a dark set of descending stairs. There is something primally foreboding about dark stairs, especially when you don't know where they lead.

Because this is a zoo, I can't exclude the possibility of lions, tigers, and bears, a familiar childhood chant sings in my brain. *Oh,* my.

I haven't seen any other animals besides Linda, but they could exist. Anything could live down there, but there isn't time to stay scared, because there could also be a way out. The hair on my arms is raised in goosebumps, but I steel myself and down I go.

Moving through the pitch dark, I punch my arm into the air in front of me for protection. The morphine has slowed me down, but my curiosity fuels me forward.

After my eyes adjust to the dark, an old basement is revealed. It smells earthy, the tinge of a barnyard, and a bare lightbulb hangs from a rafter covered in spiderwebs. This must have been built a long time ago because of the lightbulb. I find the power module on the wall and wave, turning the light on.

It throbs and flickers, a tiny light for so substantial a space. It illuminates broken doors hanging off empty cages, buckets, and wood slats.

I'm disappointed to realize, that this is definitely not a way out. The room is new and I'm curious about what secrets it could hold. Against the wall a wooden sign leans, with faded paint that I squint to read.

I rub the dust off with the side of my fist to reveal the words THE DRAVEN ZOO.

So that must be the name for this place. It's weird, but the name sounds vaguely familiar, like I went to school with someone with the surname Draven. Or maybe it was Craven—Mrs. Craven, first-grade teacher.

Focus, Mirin.

The morphine makes it hard to stay on track.

I notice a stack of three old boxes, the top one opened. Stepping up on the stainless-steel shelf below it, I pull the box down and drop it onto the floor in front of me. It holds some red paper plates, a set of old popcorn boxes with little borg pictures on them, and a plush borg with a heart sewn on it.

I pick up a carved wood borg. *Wow, someone really loved borgs.*

The old version of the Zoo looks like some kind of borg amusement park. I unfurl a poster of Warrior Thanis vs. Warrior Vyne, two very tough borgs facing each other. One has spiked blades adorning its shoulders, the other has titanium antlers protruding from its head. I don't even want to think about how that fight ended.

This confirms it, the Zoo has always been a dreadful place. Even though it was different then, it was always a prison.

Escape.

There it is again, that voice deep inside calling to me. I need to find the way out of here. I drop the wood carved mini-borg back into the box and start searching the wall for a vent or window. I move the corner table, looking for an exit.

I'm looking for the anomaly. Instead, I hear a sound and freeze.

Like an animal in the forest, my silence is a chance to hear everything around me. My ears hone in, sharp and alert. And I hear it again, a sound like the rattle of a chain. My mind wanders to what kind of creature might be chained up here in the basement. My ears ache from listening so hard.

Gingerly, I step toward the stairwell on my bandaged foot and stop.

"Hello?" someone whispers hoarsely.

CHAPTER THIRTEEN

The sound of a voice makes me shudder so hard, I almost shed my own skin.

Turning toward it, the sound comes from the far side of the basement under an archway. Then, the mistrust in my own senses begins.

Did I just hear what I think I heard? No. I'm hearing things. I am full-blown losing my mind now. There couldn't be someone down here. My body leans toward the place the sound came from, and I hold perfectly still.

"Hello?" repeats a gravelly, hopeful voice. My mind immediately starts creating stories about who he is and why he's here. Now, *this* must be the *bad man*. My new zoomate. This must be where they're keeping him because he was struggling. I can't help it. I'm trying to make sense of things that were impossible just seconds ago.

Under the archway I see a hallway to a second room in the basement. I move carefully toward it. There's another bare lightbulb throwing dull light, and through more dust I can see the blackened bars of a cage. Behind these bars something moves. Someone.

As I come closer, the smell of dank basement gives way to something more animal, the musky scent of something living. The dark shadow inside the cage reveals an old, thin man with long, dark gray straggles of hair hiding much of his face. We look at each other in the silence.

Here he is, a person. He's not quite what I expected, although I'm not sure exactly what that was. He's older than I thought he'd be, and he's chained up. The man on the gurney seemed so full of energy and not as frail as the man before me. Then again, my remembrance could be unreliable due to the drugs. I feel like I'm in a dungeon from an old fairy tale. None of this is making sense.

"Who are you?" I muster.

"I am Dr. Draven. I've been in here for seven days. Please, get me out of here," he says. He's a person with a name and he wants me to help him. I remember the name on the sign. *THE DRAVEN ZOO.*

I'm not alone after all.

The edges of the room blur suddenly, and I think I may pass out again, so I grip one of the bars to steady myself.

It is a peculiar reversal, that the captive has become a visitor to someone even more captive. Immediately, I know his despair and feel sick. The air is humid as I take a deep breath.

Dr. Draven pushes his gnarled graying hair behind his ear. I notice his dirty fingers and a tattoo on his ring finger. A diode stabbing into a tiny heart.

I say nothing, mostly due to shock. Then, logic starts to kick in. If he's been in here for seven days, he can't be my new zoomate, which means there's another person somewhere in this place. A flash of Borgie's dented shoulder, the scuff on her torso. Which one is the *bad man*?

"Are you going to help me?" he says.

"Yes," I say as I realize that I have no idea how I am going to help him.

It's not as if I have been able to help myself. I have so many questions, but I'm too shocked to properly assess what I need to know.

All I can muster is, "Why are you here?"

"What is your name?" he asks, ignoring my question. Something shifts behind his eyes, and I feel an air of mistrust. It's faint, but my gut tells me to be cautious about what I tell him.

"Mirin," I say, and then repeat, "Why are you here?"

"The borgs, they took me...," he says. I feel a pang of sympathy because they took me too.

"But why?" I implore. "Why are you down here, instead of up there with me? Why did they take you?"

"It's a complicated story of a man creating something beautiful that turns into something altogether different than he had designed. Do you know the story of Frankenstein?" he asks.

"The scientist and the monster?" I wonder where this is going.

"That's the one. You could say that something similar happened here," he says. Does he consider himself the scientist or the monster in this scenario?

"Mirin, have you ever wondered where your borg guard goes when it's not with you?" Dr. Draven whispers it, his long hair dangling about his face.

He can't help but look treacherous in that cell, and I can see his dirty overgrown fingernails as his left hand strokes the right. His eyes peer up at me, his chin tilted toward his chest. Yes, I have wondered, and I have cared, I just don't know.

"You should find out," Draven says mysteriously.

Where does Borgie go when it leaves behind the waterfall? There is still so much about the Zoo that I don't know. Feeling overwhelmed by all the new information and the need to get out of here, I lean from foot to foot a shot of pain reminds me of my injury.

"Why? What does that have to do with me?" I want him to tell me so much more, but I also want to run.

"You might find something very important. Please let me out," he begs.

"If I help you, do you know how to get out of here? Do you know how to get out of the Zoo?" I ask. He stares back at me blankly, his mouth opening and closing like a fish. I hear a sound from the top of the staircase and know my time is limited.

"Please," he says. His dirty hand reaches out. "You can trust me; I will show you. Find a borg with HIPPO on the side of it. There is a black switch on the right side of its head. Switch off its feelings."

A clang echoes down the staircase.

"I'm sorry, but—wait, did you say feelings?" I think back to that little flicker of *something* in Borgie's eyes yesterday. And to HIPPO's erratic behavior this morning before exploding. This is real. Or maybe he's just a deranged man stuck in a basement.

"There is too much to get into now, but I promise to tell you everything. Switch off HIPPO and you will see that I am trustworthy. Come back and release me and I will explain it all," he begs, as though reading my thoughts.

It's hard to get past the fact that there is a person in my presence at all. And beyond that, I don't understand what he is telling me.

There is something inside that breaks when a belief is challenged. The old belief tries to cling onto your psyche and the new realization feels unreal. Everything feels broken, like nothing is true anymore. That's wrong, of course, because all is not actually broken. It's a clearing, a breakdown of the old, setting the foundation for a new truth. It's just making space for reality to exist.

It makes me want to go back in time when things were simpler. Just a week ago, I wanted more than anything for my life to change. And now, it's changing so fast, I hate to admit that a piece of me longs for the monotony of the last few years. Knowing what to expect is comforting. I feel like I don't know anything anymore.

Looking at the bars of Draven's cage, I think about the bad man again. Maybe this is where the bad humans go.

Borgie said the anomalies were because of a bad man. Bad humans who leave the Testing Pod. Bad humans who go to places they aren't supposed to. The bad human is me. If Borgie finds out that I'm here, I can't imagine what it will do.

I must go.

The man's eyes plead with me, but I turn away. He is not in danger right now, but I am.

"Please," he tries again. But he's asking for something I cannot give.

Turning away from him, I try to run, but can't.

Making my way back to the stairs is awkward, though I drag my injured foot as quickly as I can. When I get to the door at the top of the stairs, I pull it open, half expecting Borgie, but the hallway is clear, so I keep going. Moving past the other doors, I make it to the Testing Pod.

I push back into the room easily and hoist myself back onto the white-sheeted bed. My effort to reattach the monitor stickers is in vain, as they've lost their adhesive. Lying down and lifting the sheet over me, I start to slow down my quick breaths. I am just in time to hear the heavy metal steps approach.

It's Borgie. It scans my vital signs.

"Mirin has elevated heart rate," it says in its Information Voice. Then, just as it has done before, Borgie produces a syringe, and we fall into a familiar dance. I offer my arm, and in a minute I'm asleep.

CHAPTER FOURTEEN

I wake up with a start, back in my own room. A howling is coming from the room across the way. For a moment, I wonder if it is Draven. Who would I see in the Plexi room across from me? Draven or somebody else?

I pull myself up onto my damaged foot and look through the Plexi. The Weatherlight is off, and all I can see are shadows. My body is aching, I have a small headache, and I know I need to move around to get the blood flowing.

Pacing slowly back and forth, I worry about what is happening to the man, who is screaming and barking. He sounds too young and vigorous to be the tattered old man in the basement, so it must be the new man.

I hear loud thumps and banging sounds, and then a bright light shoots all around like a possessed flashlight coming from his room. It's a borg light. I feel sorry for him. Adjusting here takes time, and it doesn't sound like he's taking it so well.

I stop pacing, because my good foot hurts, so I sit to take off the slipper. As I remove it, the keys from the Testing Pod tumble out, and I store them in my pillowcase for later.

That's right, my treasure from below the Zoo. *Well done, Mirin.*

As I try to make sense of the shadows in the new room, I am also trying to make sense of my life. The man next door is now roaring like a lion.

I dreamed of a friend, but this is not exactly what I had wished for. Then there's Dr. Draven, the man in the basement. I have no idea why he's down there or what the borgs would want with him. They could have put him in the dome instead of the dark, foul basement. There's the sign with his name on it, but if it's his zoo, or his family's zoo, then why is he chained up?

And the whole situation of HIPPO exploding after behaving so out of character. I'm a little sad about HIPPO. It seemed like, if it were possible, that it was a sweet borg.

And still no Linda. I'm starting to wonder if I made her up.

Everything is changing. I thought I'd be happier about that. I thought it was the monotony causing my anxiety.

When I peer through the Plexi I can see Borgie's hulking form next door, but I can't tell what it's doing. Torturing the man isn't going to accomplish anything. I mean, he's already trapped here. If they are trying to take him to the Testing Pod, they would just inject him. Something else must be happening.

He is sure putting up a fight, unlike compliant Mirin. I can imagine what the borgs think of him.

Sorry, Human Man, you need injection, thought you'd be more like Human Woman and accede to our requirements. Human Woman is not proud of that. Then again, maybe it's him trying to kill the borgs. I shake my head at the thought, because that is just not going to happen. Not only do they outsize him, but they also have lasers.

How I feel about the borgs is more confusing than ever.

Borgie has been having those lucid moments, and it feels like it's opening up to me, almost like you do in the beginning of a friendship. But then it has surrounded me with the creepy, chained-up Dr. Draven and put a feral lion man next door.

And what about Draven telling me to turn on HIPPO's feelings? If HIPPO does—did—have a feelings switch, do all borgs? What exactly was going to happen if I did turn it off?

I'm still not sure who I trust more, the humans or the borgs. That answer was easy a couple weeks ago; it was obviously humans. But that was back when I was the only human.

And Borgie was the cold captor I had chosen to see it as. That was before the anomalies. I'm not sure what they add up to: Borgie having a new depth, the zoomate, HIPPO, and now Draven.

All that remains of my plan is the sad, flattened snack-cake with HIPPO tread imprinted in the chocolate.

And no escape route.

CHAPTER FIFTEEN

It's been three days since the screaming next door occurred. I've been watching his room, and no stirring from the man. Borgs have come and gone without fanfare.

It's early this morning, and I hear the man across the way leave his room. It's a good sign that he is up and about, but I still shudder to think what happened to him.

Though I'm barely awake myself, I notice that my foot is finally feeling better, not searing with pain like before. I haven't been brave enough to look under the bandage yet. Antibiotics are a miracle and have saved my life.

At least, that's what I think was in the second IV in the Testing Pod.

Sometimes I wonder how much of an antibiotics stockpile the borgs have and how much they have of other medications. Would they know how to produce more in the future? Like, is there a medical recipe book somewhere that they would follow?

I hope they don't run out anytime soon.

Finally standing up, I stretch my arms as high as they'll reach, as my body shudders and then relaxes. There is one last carrot left over from my feast sitting on the table. I'd been saving it, but it won't last much longer so I have it for breakfast. Twisting the greens, which have started to brown, I pull them off and taste the crunchy, sugary indulgence.

I look at the green stain on my fingers and wonder if Borgie sees me as a plant. Instructions for Human: Water her, feed her, give her sun, and maybe some antibiotics when she gets very sick.

Borgie, you forgot that we need conversation and care and love, and no matter how much I pretend that the sun—well, Weatherlight—loves me, there is no substitute for genuine love. This is the thing I think Borgie must not understand, because it is the part of me that is least taken care of.

After finishing the carrot, I gently wrap my foot in the plastic bag I took from the bathroom trash bin. I'm trying to keep it clean so it will heal faster.

As I leave for the beach, the air is warm and I glance over to my neighbor's room. Just for a moment, I consider snooping since I heard him leave earlier. It's too risky. The fear of him finding me there keeps my uneven feet on the path. The last thing I need is for him to scream and howl at me, like he did at the Borgs a few nights ago.

When I get to the path's end, I spot him there on the shore. He's hunched down. It is strange seeing someone else here in my environment. It's like seeing a mirage. I move a little closer to spy and see he's playing with a small animal. It's Linda.

My Linda.

I'm so happy to see her, I can barely control my instinct to run over and scoop her up, but I can't because she's with the man. Instead, I hide by the base of Shel and watch him play with my cat.

The man is rattling a tree branch, which Linda joyfully pounces onto. This tells me that he is capable of kindness. My eyes grow wide as he leans down to pick her up, because she lets him so easily. She must trust him.

And then I see it, another moon-shaped scar on Linda's head, over her right eye. A shape identical to the one on her stomach, and I wonder if the borgs are testing Linda too.

I don't know for sure that the borgs are running tests on me when they take me to the Testing Pod, but they take my blood and saliva and constantly take my vitals, so what else could they be doing?

Luckily, I don't have any large scars like Linda's, only tiny flecks down my arms from all the injections. I hope they aren't doing any dangerous experiments on her.

My gaze falls on the new zoomate himself, and I notice that he has changed. His long, black curly hair is gone, and I realize that that is what the borgs were doing in his room a few nights ago.

They shaved him.

All of him.

He has cuts and welts all over, and his head is shaved into a slightly uneven crewcut. He's wearing tattered shorts only. Bare feet.

It's strange that the borgs did that, because I have had to cut my own hair with a plastic knife since I got here, and it takes forever. Usually, I cut it short after some months, and then it eventually grows out long. I don't let it get too long because I don't have any hair supplies.

There is soap provided, but there are no combs or brushes, so I use my fingers and sometimes a plastic fork. It looks like I'm due for the Cutlery Salon soon, as my hair is getting long again. I have company now, so I should look presentable, and I look more presentable with short hair.

To gain some distance, I weave through the forest, away from the water. When I come around, I can see him better from the front. This is the first time I see his face unobstructed. My face flushes because he's handsome. Unbelievably handsome. The last thing I expected was for the crazed lion man to be extremely attractive.

Get a hold of yourself. He's decent. No, he's probably quite average, it's just that I've been inside the zoo a long time. There have been no others to look at, to connect to, to crush on.

This is a lie.

The truth is that the man is beautiful.

He is being so tender toward Linda, and he's behaving so differently than he was with the borgs. Understandable. I wish I could just march over and talk to him, like we were old friends having a reunion. Instead, I'm nervous. I feel unlike myself, usually this place is my domain, but now I am being so careful. But he has my cat.

I'm impatient, wishing she would just notice me in the trees, and run over. Even though the new scar is concerning, I'm relieved that she's alive. But I have to admit my jealousy, as she plays with the new guy when I am starving for affection.

I can't wait any longer.

Emerging slowly from the forest, to give him the chance to spot me before I get too close. Leaning on my good foot once he does, I stop a good six feet away and wave. He tips his head in acknowledgment, and I point to the ground next to him, but he doesn't respond.

The air is thick as we consider each other. I wonder if he knew that I was in here with him, and if he peeked into my room at all.

Linda comes over and lets me pick her up. She purrs. I

try to hold back the tears, because I don't want to cry in front of my new zoomate. The tears are a surprise, an emotional reaction to all the overwhelming things happening lately.

My family never had a pet before, but I imagine the good feeling filling my heart is what many families feel the moment a new pet is chosen from a shelter and finally comes home. She jumps back down, stretches in a long cobra pose, and walks back to the lion man. I sit in the sand and fight making eye contact.

"My name is Mirin," I say finally as I look up at him. Cerulean eyes stand out from his dark features. Instead of being afraid of him, I'm nervous for a different reason. Yes, I find him attractive, six years in a zoo or not.

"This is my favorite spot," I continue.

"Desculpo. Sorry ..." he says, looking slightly confused.

"My favorite spot in the Zoo is the beach," I say, patting the ground. He looks around and shrugs.

"Mirin," I repeat, placing my hand on my chest. I mean to say it with my voice, but a whisper is all that's available. *Mirin, you are so dramatic.* He responds with a deep and noticeably un-barky voice.

"Pedro," he says. I let his name wash over me. It's grounding to be in the presence of someone with a name. Names are meaningful, and decidedly human. I like to name everything around me as a reminder that I am human.

"I'm from Brazil. I assume by your accent that you're American?" he asks. I hadn't thought about it before, that we might be in another country. When I came here, I had been drugged.

"Yes, American. Do you think we are in Brazil?" I ask.

"Oh, no. I flew here on an airplane, but I can't be sure where we are," Pedro says. His English is fluent.

"I've seen some paperwork here, and everything was in English," I say, going through the catalog of clues in my head.

As if she can't bear to be left out, Linda comes over and nudges me for a pet, and I scratch behind her ear to give myself some time to think of something interesting to say to Pedro.

"Linda," I say because all I can think of is her name.

On cue, Linda chirps, "Mew." Amused, I scratch behind her other ear and repeat.

"Linda."

"Mew," Linda says.

Pedro is smiling, which makes me feel nervous, and then he scratches under Linda's chin. "Linda," he says. As expected, Linda replies, "Mew," and we both laugh. She is funny.

Look at me, laughing with another person. Living the dream. My joy is interrupted by the sight of Borgie leaving from the waterfall. It moves briskly with a stool clutched in its claw. It goes down the path toward Pedro's room. It keeps its distance from the beach, and when Pedro sees it, his face darkens.

"During my haircut, I broke the stool. It looks like they fixed it," he says.

"Oh," I say. He doesn't seem so unhinged.

"I hate them."

Understanding the sentiment but wanting to distill the light of the moment, I say, "Borgs ... they're not so bad." I can't believe I said that and immediately regret it when he frowns.

He shakes the branch toward Linda, distracting us from our disagreement. She walks away. Pedro leans back on his hands and looks up at the top of the dome, watching the Suckers.

"What are those things?" He points at them.

"I call them Suckers. They are like suckerfish cleaning a fish tank, but they don't come down ever. They just move around the top of the dome."

They're almost like a cloud cover always moving around overhead. Sometimes they'll stall in one place for a while. When I first got here, they scared me. I thought they were little drones spying on me, but now they've dissolved into the background, merely part of the scenery.

"I've got to get out of this place," Pedro tells me. "There is plenty of water here to make it happen."

I have no idea what he means about the water. But then I hear that voice inside calling me.

Escape.

This guy wants to escape—of course he does. That is all I thought about when I got here, and after what happened with Ander, I didn't want to be here for one second more.

Pedro speaks as though he's a hero in some old movie, so full of earnest delusion. But our first meeting doesn't seem like a great place to explain this to him. I'll let him keep his dream for a while.

And, because I want to live inside his movie too, I say, "I can help. Let's escape together."

PART 2

DISCOVERY

The next morning, I walk by Pedro's room to bring him his flattened snack cake. He's not there. Probably went for a walk. I open his door, and it smells musky in his room. Dropping the snack on his table, I dash back outside.

It's Treat Show Day. I hope I'll get a chance to give him an idea of what he's in for.

When I get near the edge of the forest, I stop and watch Borgie clean the Plexi for a minute. Remembering Draven's question, I do want to find out where it goes. I'm still not sure about his stories, but he said he'd help me get out of here. Borgie finishes cleaning, puts the squeegee into a bucket, and moves back toward my room.

I wonder how much longer I'll need to wait until Borgie ducks behind the waterfall again.

The alarm starts blaring, and I nearly jump out of my skin in surprise. This is my signal that it's time for the Treat Show.

I am already in my outfit. Today is a yellow smiley-faced dress, with puffy pink boots and a cape. Hurrying to the Treat Show area, I beat Borgie there. When it opens the door, I rush inside and slide into my desk. I look directly at its eyes, hoping to make a connection with Borgie again, but I am disappointed that it doesn't occur. I look around for Pedro and see him enter behind me.

Today is his first Treat Show, and he wears a green plush turtle costume with a big blond curly wig. His face is very serious, and I can't help but burst into laughter. He doesn't break, so I try to control myself. I walk over to him.

"Hey," he says.

"Hey." I feel bad for laughing.

"What is going to happen?" he asks.

I am matter-of-fact. "They want us to give them a show, and then they throw us treats." I try to remember what I was thinking for my first Treat Show. I think I was so nervous that I just repeated in my mind, *You're okay, you're okay, you're okay.*

"Hey, Pedro, you're going to be okay," I say, trying to match his tone and pat his shoulder.

"Thanks. What did you mean 'give them a show'?" Pedro is so serious. He rubs his head at the edge of the wig.

"During the show, I think we're supposed to behave how humans do. Usually, I make a speech explaining something to them I think that they might want to know, but they don't always like that. Sometimes I jump around, and that seems to get more good sounds. They make us wear these bonkers outfits. I can only guess they think this our native wear."

I laugh a little, but Pedro's face remains stoic.

"This is a new level of bizarro. You said 'good sounds?'" he asks. We are just standing facing the borgs, like actors at the curtain call. Yet no one is clapping.

"You'll soon know," I tell him. But I can tell by his face that I need to give him more than that.

"The only good part is the treats, usually sugary snack cakes or processed crackers. It's our only chance to get something to eat besides nutrition packets and the garden," I say, as I sit back down at my desk and begin stapling the paper, out of habit.

Pedro keeps toying with his curly wig and seems unimpressed by the prospect of treats.

The visitors must have been expecting Pedro because it is very crowded in the gallery. There are many new borgs, ones I haven't seen before, they fit tightly into the stands. It hasn't been this packed since my first days when it was Ander and me. Over the years, it slowly tapered off.

Not today. Today, Pedro is giving us all something new and shiny to watch.

I look back to where Borgie usually watches, but it's not there. It's always at the Treat Show, and I'm surprised it would miss this first one with Pedro. Maybe it had to go tend to Draven in the basement. Nothing good could come of that.

I turn back to Pedro, who looks unsettled and keeps touching everything in the office setup.

"It's old-fashioned, right?" I say. Office spaces were before my time, but I think our grandparents used them a lot.

"True. Why an office?" he asks.

It has been a while since I pondered such things. I have no certainty all these years later, so I scoot my chair closer to Pedro and tell him my guess.

"I think maybe they found all the abandoned offices and cubicles from the turn of the twenty-first century and thought it was an important thing to preserve. The Office People. Or maybe it was because of a VR show. That's my guess," I tell him. "If it were up to me, and we had to pick an activity from history, I'd make it a bowling alley."

"Bowling?"

"Yeah, there was a reconstructed bowling alley near my town. I would go every time it was my birthday before the Zoo."

"Sounds interesting," he says, even though I'm not sure he knows about bowling.

He lifts his wig off to scratch his head, and the visiting borgs make growling sounds.

They are playing recorded animal distress sounds, like monkey whines and tiger growls, showing their distaste for something we did. It's a very stressful sound.

I look at Pedro, trying to figure out what we did. His eyes are wide, and then I realize.

"Pedro, your wig," I say. He puts it back on and they stop. We look at each other.

"I never want to hear those sounds again," he says.

"Same here." He lifts the phone on the desk closest to him and examines it.

As we shuffle about at our desks, the air begins to fill with a strange scent, a vanilla-bourbon spicy sort of smell. This has never happened before, and Pedro and I lock eyes, both noticing it at the same time. I am feeling that same way I did in the basement, both curious and afraid. Curious because it smells so good, and afraid of what it could mean.

Pedro looks at me with concern. "Is this normal?" he asks, covering his mouth with his hand.

I look up, wondering where it's coming from. "Nope, definitely not normal." I stand up and feel a tiny bit drunk. Pedro stands up too and comes over to me.

"Do you smell that? What do you think is in the air?" he asks.

"I have no idea. It's never happened before," I say.

He turns to the visitors and gives a big smile and waggles his eyebrows. He's behaving so weird. The borgs love it, though, and throw us treats. I start to laugh uncontrollably, taking labored breaths. Nothing is *that* funny. I stand up and put my hand on Pedro's shoulder to steady myself.

Whatever is in the air is making me feel buzzed, like the time Zelda and I drank all her mom's beer on her seventeenth birthday.

I don't want to feel this way.

I want to get out of here.

But the more the scent fills my lungs, the more my shoulders relax. I try to stay alert, but my muscles have all released at the same time, and I feel like I'm made of dough.

Pedro taps my shoulder. "Tag, you're it," he says with wild eyes, but I don't want to move. I am high on the vanilla scent.

I hold still.

"No, thank you," I say. A treat thrown from the crowd bounces off my stomach.

We are being pelted with treats. I try to pile them onto the desks so that we won't step on them. Apparently, two humans looking foolish is better than one.

Borgs are the worst.

Pedro comes over and opens a treat right there in front of all of them.

I raise my hand to him.

"Don't."

But he eats it. Strange, canned cheers fill the dome. My rule has always been to not eat in front of them, because eating is not a show. It's a privilege that should be done in private.

Sharing that with unfeeling machines always seemed wrong to me. I'm conflicted, eating in front of them feels like a violation. Like I'm losing one of my few boundaries.

But it seems they like it, or maybe they're programmed to like it, because they are giving us more applause and more treats. Thinking of how hard I worked to get the treats last time, it feels unfair. My defenses start to melt away, and Pedro bites into another treat with such glee.

If you can't beat them, join them?

I peel the wrapper off a chocolate rolled snack and take a bite, pausing to check my audience.

The borgs love it. They cheer and we snack.

The vanilla scent filling the air gets even stronger, and I feel warm in my face, warm everywhere. Though my body is relaxed, my mind is scared.

Because now, when I look at Pedro, I want to push him down on a desk and—*Sex*. The thought stops me in my tracks. I think about Ander, and I am worried.

What if the borgs are trying to get us to mate right here at the Treat Show?

I consider the large crowd of borgs in a new light. They could be here for a different kind of show. I feel sick. I push a clump of cake off my front teeth with a finger. Now I really want to leave, but I can't.

Tingling and weak, I sit down in between the desks on the floor. Pedro comes over and sits next to me. Too close. My heart races and I'm sure it's so loud he can hear it.

"I am afraid," I whisper into his ear. I want to tell him why, but if he knew what I did to Ander he would fear me more than he fears the borgs. His hand slips into mine, and even though he's a stranger, the comfort of affection ripples through me.

"It will be okay," he says.

Vitality flows from our clasped hands up my arm and up behind my hot ears.

What did they put in the air?

I ache with sexual tension and fear, looking into his eyes, searching for some reciprocation. I wonder how he feels when a slight tightening of his grasp says something more than words.

This is not real, Mirin, I remind myself. The borgs are trying to force me close to him—just like they did with Ander.

But it's complicated. The touch of another person is something I have longed for. Now it's here and the past seems to rise up as an invisible layer between me and what I want. I watch the door for Borgie, thinking it will come in here and inject Pedro like it did to Ander before him.

But it hasn't come yet, and I don't know why. Maybe whatever was in the injection is in the air this time. I shudder at the thought and feel my control slip even further away.

The Treat Show hour is nearly up, and so far there has been no injection, no struggle, and no trauma. The lack of movement that I found soul-crushing before is now a comfort.

Before I can think more about it, Pedro drops my hand and points to the audience.

He sits up, alert.

"Do you hear that—a funny cheer, like a kazoo? I think it's those two. Wait, are they twins?" Pedro points to two borgs in the gallery. I hear the kazoo sound, like a song an ice cream truck in a VR show might play.

I hazily peruse the audience looking for a matched set making the sound and finally spot them near the front, their metal claws clutching the railings. They *do* look like twins, both midsized, big, rounded joints, their heads oblong with a triangular carbon piece on top. It gives them the appearance of wearing elf hats. Metal elf hats.

I wonder why they are here and what they are thinking about me and Pedro. If they can think, that is.

Maybe Borgie can. I'm not sure.

The twins have their volume powered up loud, and now their sound pattern has become like a large soccer match crowd. I have always wondered if the borgs in the Treat Show audience were programmed to cheer or what causes them to do it.

Machine will.

Cheers blare at us from the two borgs. The vanilla scent begins to dissipate.

"Probably two of the same model," I say.

All the visiting borgs make different sounds. Some have laugh tracks, some just a single human voice saying "ooh" or "aah" or "YES!"

One small round borg with a megaphone-shaped head makes sound effects like an annoying air horn. I have often wondered if these sounds are for us or for themselves.

Whatever was in that vanilla-scented air made all my senses heightened. Everything sounds louder and the lights are brighter, too. The familiar ache of a migraine starts deep in the back of my skull. I want this to be over. I swallow down the nausea and hear the voice of my mother: *Just relax, Mirin, breathe. In for five, hold, then out for five.*

"Are you still feeling ... weird?" I ask him. Pedro rises to stand, and I follow, and see his eyes are alert. He looks strong and untouched by the kinds of feelings I'm having.

"Yes, but I think whatever is in it is being outmatched by adrenaline," he says.

Breathe, Mirin.

The Treat Show should be done soon, maybe a minute or two left. All the visiting borgs will leave, and I can go back to the quiet of my room.

A crackling comes from the speakers, and music starts to play. Music. I haven't heard the sound of music in years. It's instrumental, and I don't recognize it, but a calm feeling deepens in me as I listen. So many surprises at the Treat Show today.

My head aches but I gently rock to the sound.

"Mirin, I have an idea. I can get us out of here." Pedro looks at me and offers his hand. "Will you trust me?" Now I'm sure the vanilla air is affecting him, but I nod in agreement.

My headache urges me to lay my head on his shoulder, and Pedro doesn't resist the intimacy of it. He is a sturdy foundation for me to lean on. We dance in an awkward manner because there is no obvious rhythm to the song. Perhaps it is borg composition. We move slowly away from the borgs and to the back of the stage, toward the door.

As I look over Pedro's shoulder out toward the audience, I see that one of the Elf Hat twins has scaled the railing and is headed right toward us. This isn't good. What if the vanilla-scented air is making them feel strange, too?

I look around for Borgie, but it still isn't here.

"Pedro." I let go of him and run toward the door, but it's locked. Of course it is.

Before I can do anything, the Elf Hat borg comes after me.

This one is quick and flexible, unlike Borgie, who is slow and unwieldy. The unexpected speed combined with the surprise of seeing it climb over the barrier is very unsettling. Doom sweeps over me, and I fear this could be my last moment. My life appears in flashes, me as a child with my family, school days, my sister Violet smiling, Ander, Borgie, Linda, Pedro …

The Elf Hat twin's arms stretch out to me, and it grabs my shoulders, cheers blare from the speaker on its face. Another alarm sounds. I close my eyes and freeze. *Here comes the laser.*

But nothing happens.

Crash.

I open my eyes to see that Pedro has grabbed Elf Hat twin by the head, pulled it backward, and slammed it down onto a desk. I watch in equal parts horror and excitement as pieces fly from its broken face. The fitful Elf Hat borg is now inside the office enclosure with us, and it's not going down without a fight.

Where is Borgie?

Pedro begins smashing the borg's head over and over until it is loose, and then he yanks it right off. The body falls, and sparking wires sprout from its neck, but the arms and legs continue flailing and knocking things over.

As much as I am relieved that Pedro stopped it, it's hard to watch destruction. Especially of something constructed with such care and precision—even if I don't like the borgs. I'm always like this, torn in two, overthinking every last thing.

The crowd is starting to leave.

I move out of the way as a piece of robot sails by me. Pedro is searching the wires in its head until he finds a small, unassuming square circuit.

He pulls it out and walks over to the old-fashioned water cooler, pulls the giant jug of water off its stand, flips it upside down, and drops the card inside the jug. The card shimmers as it hits the water, and I watch it drift to the bottom like a feather. Electricity.

Pedro is leaning on the desk, catching his breath. I can't believe he was so ruthless. It gives me my first glimpse of what it must have taken for him to survive on the outside. His lightning-fast reflexes and knowledge about the borgs makes me worry.

Would I be able to make it on my own if I did get outside the dome? There is so much that I don't know about the world or the strengths and weaknesses of the borgs. There is so much that I don't know about Pedro.

We hold eye contact a moment, but I am not sure what to think. He just killed that borg right in front of me and I don't see an ounce of remorse on his face.

In that moment, I realize how easily we condone violence when it benefits us. Still, it doesn't feel right, even when it's a borg on the other end.

Outside in the gallery, I can see the other Elf Hat twin, its arms extended toward us. Screaming, hysterical sounds blast from its face. It must be angry that its twin was unsuccessful. But that doesn't make sense unless it feels something. And borgs don't feel.

Pedro placed his hand on my shoulder, and I push it off.

"Why did you do that?" I ask, my energy coming back.

"It's the only way to kill them," Pedro says, matter-of-fact.

Borgie finally enters the Treat Show, but it's too late. I'm relieved to see it holding a trash bin and begin picking up the pieces of Elf Hat.

I'm glad. Looking at its mangled parts is disconcerting. Borgie stops in front of the water jug, and I swear that I hear an almost inaudible sigh. Then again, I don't totally believe what my senses are telling me. I can still feel the effects of whatever they put in the air. I do know that we are safer now that Borgie is here.

When your captor makes you feel safe, it's confusing, and this is why I struggle to trust myself.

Pedro and I scoop up all the treats we can. I am shaken, because this Treat Show is the first time that I've laughed out loud for years or heard music and it's also the first time I saw a visitor borg cross into the barrier of the dome.

My mind runs through what happened, and I can't understand why Elf Hat wanted to hurt us or why I care that Pedro killed it so fast.

So easily.

I should be grateful, but all I feel is a heavy sadness. The rest of the borgs are filing out of the visitor area, but the other Elf Hat twin stays.

Canned cries remain, and it reminds me a little too much of when I lost my family. It also makes me that much more eager to leave this place. Pedro stays behind, while I head back to my room.

I'll need to tell Pedro what happened with Ander, but not now.

We need to be better prepared for the next Treat Show if they really are trying to mate us. Who knows how long it will be before Borgie shows up with the toxic needle, before one of us hurts the other.

I also want to ask him everything he knows about the outside world and how he knew how to kill the Elf Hat borg.

Perhaps he knows something that could help us get out of here. Perhaps he knows how to deal with Draven. I exhale.

One step at a time, Mirin.

CHAPTER SEVENTEEN

It's morning, and while I stare at the dome ceiling, I let my eyes lose focus. Spinning thoughts. How is it that Borgie, a machine operating on code, somehow outsmarted all of us and knows how to keep us captive here inside the Zoo?

And why did the second Elf Hat twin react in such a human-like way? Its cries felt like *more* than just a recording of anguish—they felt real. Valid.

Borgie won't take kindly to Pedro destroying Elf Hat, one of its customers. I'm sure that Pedro and I will be punished.

I head to the bathroom, pondering the problems in front of us. Something is going on here—there have been too many anomalies, too many things changing in a place that never changes. I just wish I knew what to focus on first.

After I use the bathroom, the toilet won't flush. Weird. I try again. Nope. I go to the sink to wash my hands, but no water comes. Looks like they've turned off the water. This must be Borgie's punishment.

Pedro so easily dismantling a borg was not going to go unnoticed. If putting their chip in water is how they die, then turning off our water makes sense. I take two of the water packets off the counter to wash my hands, but then I reconsider, return them, and hope they give me more packets.

I look next door to see if Pedro is back in his room, but he's not there. I haven't seen him since I came back from the Treat Show. I fear what Borgie might do now, especially, since I know that there is a place for bad humans in the basement. I'll go check on him.

Linda appears by Pedro's door.

"Hi, girl," I say.

I use my sleeve to make a spot to look through, but I can't see through the thick condensation, and the door is shut.

I knock, but there's no answer.

I try the door, which is unlocked, and find Pedro in bed.

"Hello, neighbor," I say.

He points to his mouth and shakes his head in a wobbly slow motion. He can't talk, and he looks drugged. Another penalty for destroying Elf Hat. It's hard to see him like this and not feel angry and sad. I see the wrapper of a treat on the floor.

I am relieved they didn't sedate me too. That vanilla-scented air was enough. I'm so sick of phony feelings, of not caring. Because deep down, I do care.

"I just wanted to check something," I tell him. I go over to his sink and turn on the water. Nothing comes from the faucet.

"Your water is off too. I guess this is our punishment," I say. "I got a packet of water at breakfast, so we can still drink." He nods in a spaced-out way. If we don't have water in our rooms, I worry that all of the water is gone. Would Borgie drain the ocean?

"I'll be right back." I run out of the room and pad down the path.

The ocean is so important to me. There is something primal and beautiful about having water envelop you, to swim and be weightless. It is the opportunity to curl into the safety of the water, to return to the womb. It is true that the water here in the Zoo isn't exactly like the real ocean, as it's filtered and chlorinated, but it offers me a way to connect to that feeling. And feeling that safety and protection is something I can't live without.

When the Earth is depleted of its water, all life suffers. I reach the end of the path and find, to my great relief, that the ocean is still there. We can bathe there for now.

Once I get back to Pedro's room, I see him trying to stand, but he is unsteady on his feet. Holding my arm out to support him, I ask, "You want to move around?"

He nods.

"Okay, how about I give you a proper tour first, and then I need to talk to you about something," I say. We move slowly, and I wait for just the right moment to bring up Draven.

In all honesty, I'm not sure a conversation with a drugged-up Pedro is going to do me any good. But maybe walking around a bit will help get the drugs out of his system.

We walk a ways down the path, and I lead him to Shel.

"This is Shel, my favorite. It was good for hugs when I didn't have any." I recognize how weird it sounds when I admit it out loud. His arm is slung tightly over my shoulders and is much cozier than Shel, but I don't tell him that.

"This is the beach." I point to the place where we met. And then I pull him over to the place where the Weatherlight points down like a spotlight.

"And this is the Sun Patch. It feels very cozy if you've been in your room for a couple days in a row. Not that you would do that. But I did before, so just in case you do, this is a good place to recover from that," I say, suddenly self-conscious. I point to the water.

"There is the ocean, obviously. But I'll tell you a secret. There is a crack in the bottom of the ocean," I say.

He half-grins.

"That's right, on the far-left side. I found the crack one day when I was holding my breath for long periods of time. I call it the Kraken. If you didn't notice, I have a penchant for naming everything," I continue.

I've made friends and enemies with so many inanimate things in the Zoo. Pedro seems to be enjoying my stories about them, no matter how nuts they make me sound. I think I've earned the right to be a bit nutty.

Besides, maybe if I am open with him, he will be the same with me. There is still so much I don't know about him. I want to ask him about what happened at the Treat Show. I want to know how he knew to find that chip inside Elf Hat's head, and about the water. If this is true for all borgs, then there is a chance we could beat them.

A chance I could be free.

It's a very tiny chance, but it is more than I ever thought possible. I want to know if he has killed other borgs. And if their anatomy is all the same. But I'll have to wait until the drugs wear off to ask.

Pedro is starting to feel heavy.

"I think we can continue this another time," I say, but he doesn't move. I reach down and tap his calves, hoping to get some blood flow.

"Come on, you'll have to move your legs if we are going

to get you back." I think about how he is moving so slowly. The borgs are so quick.

A picture of the Elf Hat borg is burned into my mind. The surprise of seeing it actually jump over the metal barrier—why did it behave that way? Pedro certainly thought it wanted to hurt me or kill me.

While I am grateful that he stepped in and stopped it, I'm angry with myself for freezing. There are so many things I could have done, like move away or hit it with something. If Elf Hat was threatening Pedro, there's no doubt in my mind that I would have done something protective.

Instead, I just stood there, waiting for my own demise, letting it have power over me. I keep playing it over and over in my mind.

Why didn't you do something, Mirin? I'm bothered that I didn't save myself. It takes me back to another time when I surrendered to the borgs. In the fight between Mirin and the machines, the machines always win.

CHAPTER EIGHTEEN

After struggling a bit with his weight, I put Pedro back in his bed. He went straight to sleep, so I've accepted that my questions will have to wait until he feels better.

Now I am restless. I'm going back to the beach for a swim. Swimming helps me when I have a lot on my mind.

Wading into the water with my clothes on, I sit in the shallows and lean back on my elbows, the water is warm. I stare up at the top of the dome, wondering why I haven't seen Borgie since yesterday at the Treat Show. I really want to know what it's been up to.

I kick the water, splashing it up in frustration. Draven wants this to be a game, when he could easily tell me what I'm supposed to see about Borgie. Beads of water dot my face as I look up. It is blue like a sky, but there is no real sky. Suckers swarm around the plastic projection.

I close my eyes and try to remember the real sky. It's clear and bright, and I see Dad's face as he sprays the spiderwebs off the house with a hose. A bird flies by and there's maybe a prop plane in the distance. I hear the wind, the rustle of leaves, and it almost feels like I'm free.

The crackle of Borgie's footsteps interrupts my daydream.

It is walking down the path, headed right toward me. It is carrying an empty box, the kind that usually holds water packs.

Thank goodness.

I sit up and Borgie stops moving. Its eyes are on me, and it's probably confused by my wet clothes, or it's still angry about the Treat Show.

"Borgie, where are you going?" I ask, wasting no time.

It is quiet for a beat.

"Good day, Mirin," it says, using its Maternal Voice. Clearly, it's not going to tell me, and this infuriates me. Borgie thinks I'm so compliant. It's right.

Don't worry about Mirin, she'll never make a fuss. She'd never do anything dangerous.

I don't want to be that person anymore. I want to do something dangerous. I want to resist.

I jump up to follow behind Borgie, my wet feet creating a muddy trail down the path.

Show me where you go.

I trudge across the sand, my wet pants dragging some of it with me. I need to stay hidden.

Borgie leaves the rooms and goes down the path toward the Treat Show. I follow it past the Treat Show, past the garden, and behind the waterfall, which is where it usually ends. Not this time.

My wet shirt clings and rides up my back uncomfortably. It is cool over here, and that makes me shiver. Borgie is about ten feet in front of me, and I know that I wouldn't make a great spy. It must know I'm here.

Borgie stands before the rock wall as I wait to see exactly what it does. There must be a door of some sort.

This is where Borgie always comes, every night, and disappears until morning. Before I didn't care where it went or how it got there, because I saw borgs in a very singular way.

Killers.

That's it.

Borgs are killers and captors, and that's it.

I can see now how blinded I was by my own circumstance. Our brains are only capable of seeing one part of the story at a time, it feels impossible to have a wide view of your life. All I could see for so long was the humans as good and the borgs as evil.

But now, I feel softer toward Borgie. I want to know what's behind all these anomalies. And I want to know why things are changing.

And then it appears, a door perfectly camouflaged within the rocky, mossy nook. The door opens instantly and Borgie steps in and steps through. Borgie was there one moment and now it's just a mossy wall. I hurry over to it. This can't be what Draven wanted me to see, so I check the wall for any cracks or secret keys. But it's fruitless. There's nothing here.

Even though the chill of my wet clothing is becoming unbearable, I decide to wait there for Borgie to open the door again. I know it will have to come back sometime. And this time, I will be the one snooping.

When you are waiting for something to happen, time changes. The seconds are minutes and the minutes become hours.

Itching to do anything else, I sit uncomfortably, wet and sandy. I consider the thing I can't stop thinking about: Could borgs be sentient? I need more proof than a flash and a few words from Borgie. It has been studying me for years, so maybe this is all the result of its research. The more I intellectualize it, the more my heartstrings disagree. If I go solely based on feeling, then yes, I felt it. Borgie and I connected.

Then again, if I go by my knowledge of the borgs, based on experience, including the new batch of borg mischief that has been going on, there is absolutely no way. They are machines behaving erratically.

As I reposition myself in the corner, the door opens again. Borgie leaves straightaway and apparently doesn't see me lurking in the dark corner. I wrap my hand around the doorframe from behind it, but the door shuts anyway.

I scream internally as it slams into my knuckles, but I'm able to maintain my grip. I pull on the electronic door with all my strength, and it slowly moves. My back pushes against the force of it as I wedge myself through the door.

The door slams shut behind me and I find myself in an empty hallway.

It feels too small to fit Borgie, but somehow it must. There is a dim light overhead. It's cold and the air feels different in here, like I'm at a different altitude. It makes sense for borgs to keep it cold for the sake of their function, but it adds to the ominous feeling in this place, making the hair on the back of my neck stand up.

I can't help feeling like I'm in slow motion.

A door stands ajar at the end of the hall. I approach and put my hand on the knob, and peek in but see nothing. Opening the door slowly, I hope to remain undetected. The room is dark and smells sweet like a lily, and my eyes are adjusting as I look for a light. As I reach my hand along the wall, the motion activates an automated ceiling light, fluorescent and bright.

The room is a small square with no windows. I step into the center and try to memorize each detail. To my right is a table with electronic parts, tools, and three computer monitors. There is a large charging station next to the table.

As I turn, I jump because I think Borgie is standing behind me. Jesus.

But it's merely the outline of Borgie, a black etching of its shape worn into the wall. It must be a place where it stands a lot, perhaps like a bed. Kind of uncanny to think of a borg sleeping standing up, rather than charging standing up. This must be Borgie's room.

My eyes fall on a patch of the wall that is damaged somehow, punctured. As I look closer, I can see that the tiny indents are heart-shaped. It's as though someone stamped hearts into the concrete. I think back to when I first got here. I tracked the days, then just the weeks and now just the months, by etching marks under the bed. I was nervous about everything then and didn't want Borgie to see it. Could Borgie be doing the same thing? What would it be tracking?

I look under the table and find a borg staring back at me.

It's HIPPO.

Well, HIPPO's dangling faceplate. It's in a box, and its wires are held together with red tape and some of it with tools. Borgie must be repairing it. I can't believe HIPPO exploded.

In all the years I've been here, I've never once seen a borg malfunction. I thought they were invincible, but that must be what happened. I reach out and hold its tiny, knobby claw, running my fingers over it, and feel a strange sort of compassion for this sad, broken thing.

I'm glad Borgie is repairing it, but I can't help wondering why it would take the time to do such a thing.

There is something sensitive about repairing it; it seems somehow empathetic. To repair something takes intention—something a borg does not have. But maybe my heart is right and my mind is wrong. The anomalies are too consistent to ignore.

In the far corner is a giant rocking chair that faces the wall. I can't imagine what Borgie is using it for because I've never seen it sit down. There's something pink on the floor, so I walk over to examine it. A basket holds a soft pink blanket inside, something a child might use for a baby doll.

What is this place?

This is all so peculiar, like I'm in a museum where I don't understand the art. I wonder if a child has been here at some point, another captive. My stomach sinks at the thought.

Across from the chair, three metal sculptures hang from the ceiling. They all look very similar to one another, like large upside-down metal pears, with a kidney-shaped center and an opening at the bottom. It almost looks like it could be a cross section of a giant ear. The outer edge is a smooth egg shape covered in leather. Reaching out, I touch the cool edge of one of the sculptures, and it changes color. Wild. Something about the shape is recognizable, yet I can't quite put my finger on it. I take a step back to see if I'm missing something, and then all at once, it becomes clear.

They're *wombs*. Metal wombs.

Borgie has wombs.

Why?

Acid rises up my esophagus as I try to understand the meaning of this. Could this be what Draven wanted me to see?

All I can think is that it's preparation for me and Pedro

to mate. Or that Borgie wants to steal a baby, or perhaps it wants to *have* a baby.

You might find something very important. Draven said I'd find something important. If this is what he meant, then I'm in greater danger now than I've ever known.

CHAPTER NINETEEN

I stand there for a minute, numbly, before the room starts to feel claustrophobic.

I need to get out of here. Turning to run, I find my legs are heavy and move slowly at first. I finally make it down the hallway. Pushing hard on the secret waterfall door, I hurry to tell Pedro. This feels so threatening, those wombs. I wonder if this is what Draven meant or if it's something else entirely that he was alluding to.

Sprinting toward Pedro's room, full of adrenaline, I throw open his Plexi door to find him in bed. I shake him, but he doesn't stir. *Crap.* Still drugged.

I roll him over and he rouses, eyes half-mast. "Pedro," I say. "Pedro! Get up!"

"Hello, Mirin." At least, he can talk again.

"How are you feeling?" I ask. My upper lip is dotted with sweat as I run my hands through my damp hair.

He moves slowly to sit up. "I feel weak."

"I'm sorry." I sit on the floor by his bed, trying to catch my breath. "I need to tell you something. Are you awake enough to listen?"

I'm sure this will only support his hatred of borgs. Maybe he will see something that I don't when it comes to Draven and his warnings. Part of me wants to take him there, over to Borgie's room, and show him what I saw—the bizarre mechanical wombs, the rocking chair, all of it haunting me.

"Only packet water again," he reminds me, clearly not understanding what I'm saying. Linda is curled at the foot of his bed, and I give her a pat. I take a packet from the table and tear it open for him. He takes a sip and offers it to me. I gulp it down.

"I noticed that Linda slept here again last night," I say, trying to hold the tsunami of words inside.

"She is a good nurse," he says.

"Listen, we need to talk," I repeat, and he smiles, nodding. While I have so much to tell him, I want to know something first.

"Can I ask what happened with Elf Hat?"

"Elf Hat?" he asks.

"The borg you destroyed. You know, it had that strange hat-shaped head, it looked like an Elf Hat to me," I explained. Sometimes I forget my naming of everything happens inside my mind.

He grimaces, and adjusts to sit on the edge of the bed, his feet sturdy on the floor. I can tell his energy is returning.

"I figured out how to kill them with trial by error," he says.

"What do you mean?"

"Back in Rio, when the borgs first came, we were told it was a lockdown. They said rogue borgs were turning on their owners, even the AI pets, and before long it was all-out war. I was perched high in my apartment, and I stocked up on food, water, supplies. I could see it all happen in the streets below," he says. I am hanging on to his every word. I want to ask him when this was—was it before or after they came to my hometown?—but I hold back.

"Before Rio was decimated, as I watched what was happening from my window, it seemed like nothing could kill them. They just kept coming from trucks on the road and ships in the port. The military held them off as best they could. If a borg fell, others would come in to collect them, and they'd return with new parts. I paid attention. I watched them fix each other," he says.

"So, you saw some of the borgs being fixed?" I ask. I had so many questions about what *that* process looked like, but again, I held my tongue.

"There was this one with a red arm, that's how I tracked it, and a military tank rolled over it, it was in pieces, a few things remained intact—head and arm. I watched as a towing borg collected it, and literally the next day that same borg with the red arm was back, with new parts." Pedro rubbed the stubble on his chin.

"There were news reports that said they were powered by a tiny chip inside their hardware.

They called it the Life-Drive or the L-Drive.

Usually the L-Drive is found in the head piece, perhaps a nod leftover from the traditional design. The L-Drive contains all the information to keep the borg running. The L-Drive is their brain, and if you put it in water, it shorts and dies," he continues.

"Wow. How did you escape your apartment?" I ask. As always, the word causes me to tremble: *Escape.*

"It took two tries, the first time I had to go back. I left at night; they would be quieter in the darkness. I had run out of water and only had a few cans left of food. I had no weapons, but my nephew had left a toy bow and arrow set at my house before it all went grim, so I took it, packed up what I could, and made my way to the rainforest," he says.

"A toy bow?" I couldn't believe his story.

"I know. You're going to laugh, but the toy arrows had suction cup ends, and I needed the arrows to actually work, to get me food. I took the suctions off and I reinforced them the best I could. I tied utensils to the arrows at first, but eventually made arrowheads from rocks, when the utensils were gone."

I'm in awe of his ingenuity. "I am not going to laugh. That must've been horrible. Were you able to catch anything with it?" I ask.

"I'm here, right?" he says, although his face tells me there's more to the story.

"Yes, you are. And so, you were able to destroy the borgs by putting their L-Drives in water?"

"Well, that was my plan. But when the borgs got savvy to their own makeup, they started taking out their L-Drives and reinstalling them anywhere but the head. I suppose I lucked out with the borg who attacked the Treat Show," he says.

Of course, the borgs would fix a vulnerability. I have always considered the borgs all-powerful and impervious to human intervention, because that's all that made sense. That is how it seems to be when everyone around you is killed and you realize there is no hero to come and save you. Helplessness is devastating.

I am so hungry to hear everything about his journey, even though he is still unsteady from the drugs.

Don't press him too hard, Mirin.

"But how did you find that out?" I ask. "About the water, I mean."

He hesitates and crosses his arms.

"By accident. I noticed that borgs with head injuries took longer to return to the fighting. Also, they never went near the fountain in front of the church," he explains.

"One night before my escape, I was attacked by a small borg I didn't see. I submerged its head in the fountain and took it back to my building, where I dissected it and found the card. To be honest, the borg the other day was the first time I had tried the card only. I saw the water cooler and realized there was no place to submerge that borg's entire head. I took the chance."

I don't know if I believe him that he figured it out by accident. He hesitated. He could be thinking he's protecting me from the truth. I'm not sure how much it matters, but I want the truth. I want to know how he feels.

"Do you feel bad about it? I mean about killing Elf Hat," I ask carefully. Pedro pets Linda, looking distracted.

"Stop calling it Elf Hat. They are just metal, and if it comes between me living and a borg living, it will always be me. No guilt. They are our captors. You, of all people, should understand that."

"I see your point, but I disagree," I say. "I feel guilty about Elf Hat, and it didn't even die at my hands. I get where you are, and I too have felt the rage toward the borgs. But I have softened. You said yourself they figured out how to move their L-Drives. Maybe there is more to them."

"Not a chance. They did basic problem solving. It doesn't mean they have a soul."

"Well, whether they do or they don't, I don't want to stick around to find out. The only thing I do know is that I want to get out of here," I say. At least I know that one thing.

If Pedro can help me do that, it doesn't matter how he feels about borgs. This is an opportunity. Pedro is angry, maybe angry enough to help me escape. This is it. I've got to tell him about what I have found. This is my moment to educate him. He uncrosses his arms and looks up from the floor to meet my eyes.

Oh, those eyes.

"I know we talked about leaving, but I've decided that I want to stay," he says.

"What?" I'm incredulous. I thought for sure he'd had enough of this place after being attacked and drugged.

"Look, the enemy I know is safer. In here we have food, water, and shelter. On the outside, that's where the danger is. You can't guarantee any of those things or that you won't be attacked by borgs, animals, or whatever else," he reasons.

I stand up. "How is it safer? Elf Hat was coming for us," I say, folding my arms.

"It didn't kill us, and there will be many more Elf Hats on the outside, some of them other humans," Pedro says unapologetically.

"I thought you hated it in here, hated borgs?" I ask.

"I'm tired, Mirin. I hardly slept on the outside. But here, I can sleep." As if to make a point, he yawns. I remember that feeling of being safe and protected, but it doesn't last. The scales shift over time.

"Because they sedate you," I say. "Trust me, Pedro, you won't always feel this way."

He doesn't respond, just pulls his legs back under the covers on the bed and rolls over to face the wall. Linda stands up to stretch.

Pedro is behaving like a child. There is so much I still need to tell him about Borgie and Draven, about the wombs —maybe that will change his mind. But when I go over and touch his shoulder, he doesn't move.

"Hey," I say. I hear the soft sound of heavy breathing.

He's asleep.

It's clear now that he is not going to join me. I chose the wrong man to team up with. Dr. Draven promised to get me out, and now I'll find out if he can.

Pedro isn't going to stand in my way, even if his eyes still make me shaky.

CHAPTER TWENTY

It's a new morning, as I rush past Pedro's room, trying to avoid him. I cannot believe he wants to stay here. But as I start my run, I see him running just ahead of me. His hair has grown in a bit since his head was shaved, he's barefoot, and the muscles in his back grow deeply defined with every step.

I suppose he isn't feeling so weak anymore.

I speed up and jog past him, and then he does the same and jogs past me. I roll my eyes at this competition. His new plan of staying happily in the Zoo has me reconsidering if I should update him on everything I know. If he wants to stay here so badly, he probably won't care anyway.

The thought upsets me, and I want nothing more than to confront him about his passivity. He turns along the rock wall, headed toward the beach. I try to avoid him, but he stops on the sand, out of breath.

"You are fast." He stands akimbo and bends over.

"I've had a lot of practice, but I have to say, the more laps you take the smaller the Zoo feels," I say. I begin stretching my quads, holding my ankles up behind me one at a time. I want to tell him about what I saw in Borgie's room. I want to scream at him and tell him this place will suck all the joy out of his life. I want him to care about getting out again.

"Do you want to compete?" he asks, interrupting my thoughts. He mirrors my stretches but with much more gracefulness than my own.

"What do you mean? Like against each other?" I ask.

"Yes, like the Olympics."

I shake my head but smile a little anyway. *No, Pedro. I want you to care about escaping. I want to show you what I found behind the waterfall.* But I say none of these things because it's been so long since I've had even one iota of fun.

"US versus Brazil," I say. I stretch my arms up and over to the right.

"Let's do it," he says.

Pedro drops down and starts doing pushups. Watching, with a hand on my hip, I don't think he realizes he's doing what I do, exercising out the demons. Exorcizing them.

"Don't use up all your energy, showoff," I joke.

"Oh, this?" He gets up and dusts the sand off his hands. "This is nothing, just a little relaxation before the competition."

He's smiling, and I can't ignore his fine face. For a second, part of me wonders if it would truly be so bad to mate with Pedro. To have that kind of connection again. But the thought is quickly overridden by images of Ander.

"We'll see," I say. It is unfair how easily I am disarmed by him.

The first event will be track, since the jog set off this whole idea, even though we've just run a lap, and he was clearly out of breath from that. We'll run ten laps around the dome. We start at the beach and then move into the forest. I am faster than Pedro expects, and I jump over rocks and swerve around trees, real and fake, with ease. I have known every spec in this Zoo for so long, and it pays off. Linda joins and runs with us for the first lap. That cat is pretty good. Despite his longer legs and strength, I breeze along the beach and finish my tenth lap.

And the USA takes the gold. I sit at the beach, not fully tired. Yet. I hope Borgie isn't lurking around the corner. Pedro finishes and lies all the way down, flat on his back.

Then I realize Pedro is up and disrobing. I try not to stare too long as he lifts his shirt over his head with one arm. He's lean but strong. He catches me looking, and I look down at the sand with a smile.

The next competition is a swim. I have been swimming in the ocean most days for years, and I am feeling very confident. However, by now, I'm definitely expecting Borgie to walk down the path and break up our fun. I'm sure fun is not allowed in the Zoo.

"Prepare to be schooled," I taunt Pedro. He sits in his underwear on the sand, relaxed, leaning back on his hands. The Weatherlight reflects off his face. His eyes sparkle as he playfully throws his shirt at me. I toss it back and can't help but feel at ease with him. Can't help the fluttering inside.

"I am a strong swimmer." He smiles.

"Sounds like confidence," I say. My anger has fully melted away by this point.

We can deal with the logistics of the Zoo and our escape later. Right now, I feel human again. I feel vital and I don't want it to stop.

We stretch, do some lunges, and look around for any sign of Borgie. I wonder if it's dealing with Draven or if it is just ignoring him.

Pedro jumps into the water.

"The rule is that we will do laps until the Weatherlight changes to evening light, and whoever does more is the winner," I announce.

"Sounds fair," Pedro calls.

I slip into the water, we count to three, and Pedro kicks off just before me. Slow and steady, I start and can see that he is pushing hard. A mistake for him, I predict. I ease through the water, steady and calm.

I can do this forever.

Only ten minutes in, I can see that Pedro is already getting winded, slowing down. Arm over arm. Back and forth I go, almost forgetting this is a competition.

He takes a break at the rocky backsplash, and I just glide on. When the Weatherlight dims, I complete lap fifty and Team USA wins the gold in swimming. Woefully, Pedro takes the silver for his thirty laps. Linda only watched us from the shore this time. I suppose the cliché about cats not liking water is true.

The final competition is the rock shot put. We must throw a big rock the furthest. The rock reminds me of my humanity rock, and my foot twinges at the thought, as though it remembers.

Pedro throws the rock so far that it bounces off the Plexi behind a tree. We both run to check and see if it made a crack, but unfortunately it did not.

I knew it wouldn't, because around year two here, I tried throwing everything I could at the dome. I threw plates, water packets, branches, rocks, and even the stool. Nothing did more than make a scratch. Pedro's throw was much further than mine, and since Brazil finally took the gold in an event, he was pleased.

"That was fun," I tell him as we pick up our clothes, and I blotted my face with my shirt. We go back down the path to the rooms. After that respite from more serious matters, I feel them start to crash down around me one by one.

Borgie. The wombs. Draven.

"Yeah, but I am very tired now," he says. His shoulders have slumped some, and he's walking slower.

"Well, sleeping at the Zoo is what you're here for, right?" I say, not trying to start a fight.

"Come on, the Zoo's not bad for now." He smiles. "One day, maybe we get out of here. For now, we rest up."

Just then, we spot Borgie leaving Pedro's room as it heads down the path, brushing past us toward the waterfall.

"You don't know everything about this place," I say, wringing my hands. *Just tell him, Mirin.* Worst-case scenario, he thinks you have Stockholm syndrome.

"And what should I know?"

"I need to tell you something that might change your mind about staying," I blurt.

"Try me," he says. "Your room or mine?" His smile is radiant, and I can feel the heat coming off of his body. I wish I could've taken a shower first.

"Mine," I say.

As I swing open the door, I take delight in having a guest again. We each guzzle a water pack, and he sits on my bed, making himself comfortable. I sit at the table, drawing imaginary circles with my fingers on the tabletop, waiting for the right moment. Linda didn't follow us inside this time. She must be out hunting.

"First, I need to tell you about what happened here, in the past, and then what I've found, or should I say *who* I found," I say carefully.

He sits upright. "You have my attention."

I start slow, but the words tumble out into a warning as I

tell him what happened with Ander. He sits quiet for a long time and then looks at me sympathetically.

"I'm sorry that happened, Mirin." He is sincere. I realize I'm hugging myself.

He gets up and puts a hand on my shoulder. The warmth of comfort is too much, and I stand up, moving over to the bed, trying to escape the notion to cry. There is too much to say, and I can't fall apart again. A couple of years ago I went into a pretty deep depression, and I don't want that to happen again. I sit at the head of the bed, steeling myself to continue, and Pedro sits at the other end.

"Sometimes I get overwhelmed with my anger about this situation. I despise how helpless I feel in here," I say. "I'm sorry. I didn't want you to see me cry."

The tension builds until I fold over and bury my face in my pillow, which cools the blood rushing to my cheeks. When I sit up, I feel better, and I wipe my face with dry hands. Pedro just sits there, open to listening. He puts his hand on my arm to show me he gets it. People are fragile, and the world can be overwhelming. To be shown tenderness after all this time stirs me.

"I think I feel better," I say.

"Good," he says.

"I have a lot more to tell you. For starters, I found this basement area when I was in the Testing Pod, which is like the medical room. I've been there a million times, but this last time I left the room to explore and I found a basement. And there was a *man* there, locked up in a cage."

"Dead or alive?" He stands up.

"Alive," I say.

He faces me, and his surprise turns to a smile and then a deep laugh.

"I'm sorry, I just—this is too much. We survive the apocalypse to be kidnapped by robots trying to mate us in a zoo, the pure existence of this place, and ... and now there's a man in a cage too," he says. "No wonder you want to leave. This place sounds unreal."

"I know, it's a lot," I say. "And unfortunately, there's more."

I clasp my hands together and take a breath.

"The man in the basement, he calls himself Dr. Draven. He wants me to help him. He wants to be released. He said the borgs imprisoned him, and then he was talking about Frankenstein and said I should follow Borgie," I say. "It was all very cryptic."

"Wow." Pedro starts to pace.

"And so, I did follow Borgie." I can't hold my voice steady any longer, and the anxiety tumbles out like a somersault.

"Borgie has a room with mechanical wombs and I'm afraid they are for me, that Draven was trying to warn me about something. Maybe Borgie is planning on kidnapping a baby. Or what if what happened with Ander will happen to us? What if it's planning something else—something so bad I can't even think of it yet? I just want to hurry up and get out of here before anything new happens." My voice has risen three octaves.

"Okay, okay, slow down," he says, running his hands over his head.

I pull the pillow to my face and this time I scream into it. When I let it back down onto my lap, Pedro has moved closer. I'm swollen and teary as I look at him, another person. There is something so gentle and accessible about people. His eyes are so expressive and kind. I feel like his kindness could shatter me into pieces. Like the lines of my body have faded, and he silently opens his arms, and I collapse into them.

"Tomorrow, we will talk about what to do. We need to get information from this ... Draven, find out what he knows. But for now, rest. Rest, Mirin," Pedro says.

It feels like the world was falling down and pulling me with it, and now his arms are helping to hold the pieces of me together.

And I am grateful.

CHAPTER TWENTY-ONE

A dim light outside my room wakes me. It's later in the night or early the next morning—I can't be sure which. I feel groggy. I roll over, expecting to see Pedro next to me, but then I remember that he went back to his room.

A noise at the door threatens to wake me, but the pull of sleep is strong.

Just five more minutes, I tell myself. I roll over and pull the covers over my face. When I dream, it's of the ocean—not the Zoo ocean, but the real one. The water is salty and sticky, and I'm with my dad on a boat. He tells me not to be too loud or I'll scare the fish. The dream turns to a nightmare when Dad falls overboard. I rush to the side of the boat, but there's nothing there but rough waves. I yell, "No!"

I wake.

I hear Linda's paws tap down, and through blurry, barely opened eyes, I see her inspect two buckets near the door. They must be from Borgie, but I can't bring myself to care right now.

My heart is racing and all I can smell is the ocean. My

body feels heavy and inflamed. Sitting up, I hear the cracking sound of something hitting the floor. I look down and I'm covered with shells. This time it isn't a dream, but I don't know how shells ended up in my bed.

I rub my eyes, which feel swollen and itchy. Probably from all the crying. Beyond the small slits of light, I can finally see that the shells are dozens of opened oysters, and they're everywhere.

Before I can pull a logical thought together, two things jump to the front of my mind at once, in big blaring red alerts: Oysters are an aphrodisiac, and I am deathly allergic to shellfish.

My eyes aren't swollen from crying, and I'm not over-tired. No, I'm in trouble. Swiping the shells off me and the bed, I stand briefly but quickly collapse. My breathing is shallow, though I try to take a deep breath. It's like a borg is leaning on my chest as I crawl across the floor. I must get to the shower; my skin is itchy, like thousands of red ants are inside of it trying to get out.

"Hmmph." That's all that comes out when I try to call for help. My tongue is swollen and can't make a word, like I'm in a nightmare. Dragging myself to the bathroom, I reach up to turn on the shower, but the water does not come. I forgot. Pedro's punishment. All the water is still turned off. I vomit into the bottom of the shower.

This cannot be the way I die.

After everything I've gone through in this damned place, I will not be brought down by a bucket full of oysters.

Managing to scoot my way out of the shower, I get through the room and to the door. With the last of my energy, I push open the door and wedge myself with my body halfway outside it. But before I can get any closer to Pedro's room, I see lights and lasers.

And then blackness.

I HEAR my name from far away. Everything is still black, but I feel Pedro lift me up. His steps feel like a gallop, and my head knocks against his chest, I can't bring myself to do anything about it.

Suddenly, I'm floating. I'm wet and cold.

He put me into the ocean.

This wouldn't be such a bad place to die. I feel some relief of the itching, but then everything goes black again.

WHEN MY EYES OPEN NEXT, I see Borgie and another borg from the Testing Pod. We are still at the beach. The medical borg takes out a hypodermic needle, and Pedro knocks it away. There is a scuffle, with Borgie holding Pedro back with its claws while the other borg sticks me, hard in the thigh, with a needle.

I feel no pain. Instead, my lungs instantly feel relief as I take a deep breath.

They must have jabbed me with an epinephrine.

Borgie lifts me up and I see Pedro fighting it, trying to splash the borgs, then throwing sand and rocks at them. He doesn't understand that Borgie is trying to help me.

Stop, I want to say, but no words come out.

Stay awake, Mirin. Watch where Borgie takes you.

This is my chance. I'm being held in the cold, hard arms of Borgie and we are headed back toward the waterfall. What a sight we must be, this red, swollen, and dying human taken up in the arms of a metal giant like a baby.

And then I remember the wombs.

Oh no, I don't want the wombs to be put inside me while I'm incapacitated. I don't want to be their human-borg experiment. I'm afraid.

We are just outside the garden and I am awake deep inside myself now, buried in the pain, but I have to keep my very swollen eyes open. Instead, the medical borg—I call it Dr. Borg—gives me another shot. This one I cannot fight.

When I wake in the Testing Pod, Dr. Borg is there facing the computers at the back wall. I feel much better now, although my stomach is in knots and I'm dizzy. Otherwise, my mind is clear and I'm not itchy.

This is my chance to get more information from Draven, like Pedro and I discussed last night. I'll need to move slowly. I sit upright and quietly remove all the sensors, and I power off the machines. I silently tug out the IV and put my legs over the side of the bed. Staring at Dr. Borg's back, I make my way to the door, soundlessly open it, and run out.

I know that I have about ten seconds before it notices I'm gone. I run full speed down the hallway, and this time I know where I'm going. I tear open the door to the basement and descend the stairs, clutching the wall at the bottom to steady myself. Dr. Draven's chains jangle.

"You have returned," he declares. His voice gives me almost as many hives as the oysters.

His scraggly hair is oily and matted to his head and face. His beard is wiry and unkempt, and although he looks ragged, there is something familiar about his eyes.

"Are you trying to scare me? Why did you want me to see the wombs? Tell me," I demand.

"My dear, I wanted you to see what we're up against," he says, tugging at the chain to get closer to the bars.

"We are up against machines, giant machines," I say. "Now answer the question. Why did you want me to see those wombs in Borgie's room?" He waves off my question.

"Borgie." He smiles. "Borgie," he says again, trying out a new word. "Is that what you call it?"

I say nothing. He stares at me for a second before continuing.

"Machines, yes. But these aren't just any machines. These are machines with feelings," he says. "Machines able not *just* to mimic human emotion but to feel them themselves."

Although it's something I've suspected, I don't like how easily he gives them credit.

"They do not have feelings," I say. "Where is your proof?"

"You saw it for yourself. The borgs are dangerous, this one in particular—Borgie as you call her—she is obsessed with having a baby and she will hurt whoever it takes to get what she wants."

I do not like how he refers to Borgie as *she*. And what he says makes no sense. Borgs were made to do tasks for humans; they don't have wants and desires. He is just projecting onto them his own sick fantasies.

"Borgie is not a she—it is a piece of technology. How could it possibly want a baby?"

"Whatever you want to call her, I created her. This is the Draven Zoo." He holds his arms out as if he's sickly proud of his creation. "I gave her this gift—the gift of feeling, and I can take it all away, if you help me of course," he says.

I am quiet. I don't trust him at all. If he created Borgie, how did he end up locked up in the basement?

"Mirin, I can get you out of here. Believe me, I'm on your side. You can trust me," he says.

"How can you get us out?"

"There is a borg, the HIPPO model. If you help me with it, I can prove to you my intentions."

"The HIPPO borg exploded, but—" I stop myself.

"Oh no. That wasn't my plan," he says. His hands are now gripping the bars.

"What do you mean that wasn't your plan? As if you can control anything locked up down here?" He wipes his hair off his face and looks at me as if I was born yesterday. And then his eyes narrow.

"You said 'but,' that 'HIPPO exploded BUT.' Please, my dear, continue your thought," he says. I do not want to tell him anything, but he said he can get me out of here.

"But it looks like Borgie is repairing it," I say.

"Delightful. She always was skilled in getting the little ones back on their feet. When HIPPO is repaired, you must turn off his feelings. There is a switch on the top right-hand side of the body, as long as he isn't still damaged. You need to move that switch so that I can help from down here. I have a way to *interact* with HIPPO when his feelings are off. Do that and I will show you what I can do, and then you get me out of this cage. Or you could do it now?" He offers me his wrists.

I say nothing.

"Promise me. Promise me that you will flip that switch. If you don't, we are all doomed. She will keep trying until she gets what she wants. You have to trust me," he says.

She will keep trying ... I can imagine what he doesn't say. Borgie will keep trying to mate me until it gets a human child. But to what end?

Just then there is a creak by the stairwell. The door at

the top opens. It's Dr. Borg. It waits by the door, as if silently commanding me to return to the Testing Pod. I look back at Draven, into his wide, expectant eyes. I have to get out of the Zoo. I will not be turned into a breeding machine for borgs.

"I promise." I speak the words before I can change my mind.

———

I DON'T MAKE it very far down the hallway before Dr. Borg injects me with what must have been the same sedative they gave Pedro. Once I am back in my own room, I am tucked in my bed and I feel very slow and heavy.

Pedro is here with me and I am glad. He looks relieved to see me too as he hands me a treat.

"Hungry?" he asks.

"Maybe later," I say.

"They brought us oysters, and I ate many. It was good to eat something besides a nutrition packet," Pedro says.

"I'm allergic." I look down at my red, splotchy hands.

"I can see that," he says.

"I don't think Borgie knew that they were food. She put them on my body and on the bed while I was asleep." I hug myself, remembering that initial pain.

"She?" he asks.

"I mean it, she, it ... whatever," I respond. "Do you see now? The vanilla-scented air? The oysters? They are trying to mate us, Pedro. And you are just ok with that? You still want to stay?"

"Not now, please, Mirin." I say nothing.

"Listen, I have good news and better news," he says. He

is trying to make me feel better. "The water is back on *and* they brought us a huge box of chocolates." I soften.

"And the best news is that I'm not allergic to chocolate," I say with a smile.

We laugh a little. I am still puffy and achy but feeling better than I should. My happiness is fleeting though.

My mind is on Draven and the promise I made. There isn't much he can do from a jail cell. And if he really did create this place, he would know about how the borgs work. If they are sentient, which they just can't be, that changes how I feel about them. I'm not exactly sure if that makes me like borgs more or less. I close my eyes because it hurts too much to keep them open.

This Zoo holds so many more secrets than I could have imagined.

And if Pedro isn't willing to help me uncover them, it looks like I will have to do it alone.

CHAPTER TWENTY-TWO

Today is my birthday. I am twenty-six.

I have decided that just for today, I don't want to think about Dr. Draven or Borgie or anything terrible. Today can be a day that I feel free.

There is a part of me that wants to do something bold, so I head over to Pedro's and invite him to have a Treat Feast in my room for dinner, and he agrees. Happy with that, I pad down the path and call out for Linda, but she doesn't come. Instead of preparing a dinner for Pedro, I go into the garden, looking for my cat friend. I check that she has decided not to nibble on the weeds. I hear Pedro knock on my room door.

"Pedro, I'm looking for Linda," I call out to him. He finds me near the Treat Show and helps me look.

"She's probably swimming," he says with a smile.

"Well, I kind of want to find her. Today is a little bit special."

"Okay," he says. I want Linda to attend the celebration, considering she is my best friend and all. Then we hear something coming from the forest, and it sounds like Linda is crying. We hurry over and search around but don't see her, even though we hear her clearly. Then I look up and see her there stuck on a branch, high up on Shel.

"How in the world?" I say.

"Cats like to climb up but aren't so happy to climb down," Pedro says. And then he starts climbing Shel himself. There are no branches for at least ten feet. He is like an acrobat, hugging the trunk and shimming up. He leans toward the branch and grabs Linda gently by the chest, like he does this sort of rescue every other day. He pulls her close and descends Shel, and I am so impressed that I clap.

"Pedro, that was amazing," I say. "Were you a fireman in Brazil?"

"English teacher," he says. "She is relieved, I think." He hands her over to me, and she's purring. I give her a pet, and then I let her down to the ground. Oh, Linda.

"Meet up at my room for dinner?" I ask.

"Yes." He smiles.

We head back to our rooms, and Linda follows him. I rush to the bathroom and splash water on my face. There is some grooming to be done. I wash my hair. Parting my hair on the side gives it new life. I brush my teeth for an extra-long time.

Looking at the outfits I wear to the Treat Show, I realize there isn't much I can do to make them feel special. But I put on the silk clown pants with giant red polka dots and suspenders and the fitted tank top and feel dressier than my usual Zoo scrubs. Pedro will be surprised with my new look: sexy Mirin in the clown pants.

The table is set like a holiday dinner, at least in my mind. Fine China is replaced with disposable plates and utensils. And there are platters of food laid out carefully.

Instead of turkey there are cheese crackers, and instead of pumpkin pie is an oatmeal crème pie snack cut into triangle slices. Using my plastic knife, I try to shape the strawberry fruit chews into cranberry sauce, chopping them into tiny little cubes.

The dinner looks ready, but I realize my bed is in disarray. I quickly tidy the sheets, and then I catch a glimpse of myself in the Plexi.

It's bittersweet.

I almost remind myself of the girl I used to be before the Zoo. The girl who looked fun and spurred interesting conversation. I walk closer to the wall, trying to see more of the details. Tucking my hair behind one ear, I see that I am older now. I wear the toll from living in here on my face. Another year older. Staring into my own eyes, I pause, until Pedro knocking jolts me back to the present.

I pinch my cheeks before I hurry to open the door. We stand there for a moment, on either side of the open door, before he comes in. He wears the Zoo uniform, the linen shirt clinging to his torso. There is an easiness about him that I admire. I reach for his hand to pull him inside.

"I welcome you to ... dinner," I say, bowing with a flourish.

Linda walks in behind Pedro and immediately hops up on the table and begins sniffing at the dinner. We sit down and look at the spread. It's not quite the holiday dinner that I wished it to be. It's no Harvest Feast, and certainly it pales in comparison to the meals we all used to eat in the before times, but it will do.

Pedro picks up a slice of "pie" and eyes it.

"I appreciate the detail of your work," he says, and his eyes hold mine for just a second longer than normal. He really is beautiful.

"We aim high here at Maison Mirin." I laugh. We begin to eat quietly, occasionally glancing up at each other. I can't tell if it's just because there hasn't been another man here since Ander, or if it's because I'm truly attracted to Pedro, but part of me wants to jump across the table and kiss him right now.

Would it be so bad to live here with him, pretending that this was our life? That life inside the Zoo was safe and comfortable?

He disrupts my thoughts. "This is nice, Mirin."

"I'm glad you like it. And thank you for sharing this meal with me on my birthday," I say.

"Your birthday is today?" he says. I nod and he stands up immediately. "But why didn't you tell me? I would have brought you a gift." He is loud. He looks upset even.

"I'm sorry, I didn't think to." I am suddenly embarrassed, though I don't know why.

"Well, you should have told me. Birthdays are important, maybe more important now than ever," he says, holding up a water packet. "To Mirin."

I touch my packet to his.

"Thank you," I say.

"Mirin, how did you get here?" he asks.

I return his question with a question. "How *did* we get here?"

"I mean you. Did Borgie find you?" I try to blink away the flash of Violet's scared eyes. Of my father looking around that corner. Of the smoke. I start breathing faster.

"It's hard for me to talk about. How did you get here?" I deflect again.

"A borg caught me while I was asleep. They transferred me to a warehouse, strapped me to a board, my arms, legs, and head, and then I was put on an airplane, like the kind in the movies. It was full of cargo, but no other people. We took off, landed, and more borgs brought me here to the Zoo." He claps his hands, like *that's that*.

I think of Borgie dented and scuffed before he arrived.

"Pedro, did you fight Borgie?" I ask.

"Yes," he said. *Bad man.*

"Before you got here, did you hurt it, like dent it?" I ask.

"Dent Borgie? Impossible. You heard our fight, that night when I was shaved," he says. But Borgie was dented before that. I breathe in relief. The bad man must be Draven then.

"Okay, now you know how I got here. Your turn," he says.

I take a breath. Here goes.

My parents were helping me move into an apartment with my sister, Violet, and I was running late to work at the Farm Food Mart. We had been having rolling blackouts for months, but when the power went out in the apartment, my dad thought it was the landlord's fault. He was making phone calls, and we just continued stacking boxes. Violet dropped a box, and we heard a crunch from inside.

"That better not be my coffee mugs," I said.

"Sorry. It's probably just your potato chip collection," she said.

"Very funny. I guess I don't need to rush to work if the power is out," I said.

Well, ten and then fifteen minutes passed and people from the building were growing anxious, gathering outside. Dad had already given up trying to contact the landlord.

I tried calling work to tell them I wasn't coming in, but the call didn't connect and all I could hear was air.

Suddenly, we heard an explosion nearby. It sounded like a train crash, and the sound was painful. I remember banging my hip on the counter while running out of the apartment.

Mom looked like a stunned deer.

"Mom, we've got to go," I said, and pulled her out with me. The four of us looked in the direction of the black smoke. Downtown.

"What do we do?" I asked, hoping there was a clear, correct route. There was another explosion. Violet opened the door to the car, but Dad stopped her.

"No, it's not safe. The borgs can hack cars and kill their drivers and innocent pedestrians," he said. Violet slammed the car door shut. The explosions were coming from the north.

"Let's go toward home. At least things will be familiar there," Dad said. None of us said a word. We all just jogged at his direction. So many thoughts were going through my head about what was happening, where were we going, and I wasn't sure about anything.

When we got to the main road, there was a group of around twelve people running toward us. They yelled at us to go to the beach. We stopped. The beach was in the opposite direction.

"Why?" Mom asked no one in particular.

But none of them stopped to explain. They all kept running. Without a good reason to change direction, we kept our course. When we got to the corner house, a woman with a stroller stopped us.

"Everyone is saying to go to the beach," she said.

"Do you know why? What's at the beach?" I asked. She unstrapped her little girl from the stroller.

"A truck of generators. It's probably our last chance to get one. My husband is there now," she said. She ran inside her house, clutching her daughter.

"What do you think?" I asked my parents.

"I think she's right," Dad said. "If we don't get a generator now, we might miss out completely."

"Okay, but how are we going to carry it?" I asked.

"Most have wheels?" Mom said.

"You hope," I said.

Violet looked at the stroller.

"It's not stealing when you're in the middle of the apocalypse, right?" She grabbed it, and we took off toward the beach. We trailed little groups of people, and the decision was made without anyone deciding. We headed south with urgency. We heard screaming in the distance, which caused us to slow down and start walking, but even then we did not turn around.

"Mom, do you know what the explosions are?" I asked.

"The borgs," she said. Her hands were shaking, but she tried to keep them out of sight.

"You really think they are bombing us? Like a war?" Violet asked.

"They've been calling it the Great War on the news," Dad chimed in.

"Great for who?" I asked, trying to be funny.

"Think great like big, great like intense, like extraordinary," he said.

"The Great War is just propaganda," I said.

"You need to have a bomb land on top of your head to prove that it's real?" Violet said. As we got closer to the beach, we heard more screams.

"I don't like this." I was worried.

Dad stopped in the middle of the street. "I don't think they are getting generators," he said. Just then, a giant tank turned the corner about three blocks ahead of us. We ditched the stroller and ran down an alley following Dad.

"Dear god," Mom said.

"It's okay, we have to keep calm," Dad said.

And then I laughed. I don't know why, but I started giggling. I covered my mouth with my hand. We were hiding in an alleyway from a tank and fearing for our lives in my tiny hometown. It was ludicrous, but I was trembling and laughing.

Violet put her hand on my shoulder firmly.

"Mirin. Focus. We need to get out of here," she said, not breaking her serious exterior.

We plotted the nearby streets and planned our escape. The plan was to go block by block checking for the borgs before we ran. There were more explosions. Dad went to check for our first block. We ran to hide behind the bank building, and he carefully peered his head around the side, holding his hand toward us in protection.

It happened so fast.

There was no warning.

His body dropped in front of me, and when he hit the ground, his wound was exposed. Whatever weapon they used had left half of his face melted.

They killed him.

Dad.

He was hit in the head, that teeny, tiny portion of his head that peered around the corner of a brick bank building. The borgs must have heat sensor capabilities.

I went into shock. We weren't prepared for this.

I could not believe what was happening.

Mom screamed and rushed over to Dad, leaving her body partially exposed, and she was killed too. They were coming closer, and Violet and I just looked at each other and hugged. A borg turned the corner and got Violet first, her body dropping from my grip.

I remember time slowing and everything was quiet.

This was it, the moment of my death, and I did not make a sound. I blame shock for my behavior because what I did next was illogical. I got down onto the ground next to Violet and lay on my back. I closed my eyes and put my hands on my stomach. I could hear the tread of the borg getting closer.

I took slow breaths.

Any moment it would happen. I wondered if I would feel it. Would it hurt to die?

The sound of metal creaking and the hiss of steam was close. I refused to open my eyes, even when I felt something touch my arm. My breaths went in through my nose and out through my mouth. Then I felt a sharp pain in my leg.

Here we go, I thought. I was stabbed.

My eyes popped open from shock, and the last thing I saw was the cold, steel face of Borgie.

"Borgie killed your family?" Pedro asks.

"Yes. No. Not really. It was a borg that looked like it though. At the time I couldn't tell the difference. When I woke up here at the Zoo, I was terrified that Borgie was the one. In time, I realized there were some differences: her armor wasn't quite as sharp, and the borg who killed them had three black spiked quills protruding from its shoulder plate. That's all I saw, one second of a face and the shoulder and then I was knocked out, as I have been too many times since." Linda comes over and hops up into my lap.

"Mirin, I'm so sorry that happened," he says. And I feel his sincerity.

I'm sorry too. For a long time, I wondered, if my family hadn't been helping me that day, would it have happened at all? If they would have escaped or if I would have. I won't ever know. But I don't say any of this to Pedro because it hurts too much to say out loud.

We are silent for a long time after that, finishing the food. My eyelids are heavy, and the silence lingers. We look up at each other, and in that moment, I realize that I am developing feelings for Pedro. It's not just because he's the only man I've seen in the last six years. I feel like we have really bonded in these last few days. And telling Pedro about my family means that someone new gets to know who they were, even though they are not here. It's as if a huge weight has been lifted from my shoulders.

I look up and our eyes meet. His lips are parted, and I can hear his uneven breathing ricocheting off my own. He licks his lips and looks as if he's about to stand. To move closer.

"I think it's time for goodnight," I blurt out.

"Yes, better get some sleep," he responds, finally breaking eye contact.

"Thank you very much for sharing this dinner with me for my birthday."

We hug, and our faces are close, and I think for a moment that he might kiss me. We linger with our faces close and I can feel his warm breath. I lean in with my eyes closed. But it doesn't happen.

When I open my eyes, he smiles.

"Boa noite," he says, and leaves in the dark toward his room.

Gathering the utensils and the wrappers, I clean up the empty water packets. A joy I nearly forgot, the tidying up that I never have to do. It feels nice, like making a mess is part of being human, and the leftovers are proof of life. When it was only me, everything was too sterile and too neat. The bed beckons as I slip off my shoes.

There is a knock at the door.

It's Pedro, and my cheeks flush, because I'm so glad he's

back. I open the door. His hands are behind his back in a not-so-subtle way.

"Close your eyes," he says.

I want to tell him I'd do anything he says right now. "Okay," I say, suspicious anyway.

"I have a gift for you," he says, "but keep them closed."

I can hear him moving around, quiet tapping sounds on the table. I have no idea what he is doing.

"Alright, now open."

When I open my eyes, there are paper cups set upside down on the table and treat wrappers crumpled up into balls.

"Bowling," Pedro proudly declares.

He remembered my story about my bowling birthdays on the outside. This kindness causes me to blink back tears.

"I didn't think you knew about bowling," I say.

"I'm a teacher, I read books," he says.

My hand flies to my heart as I remember bowling, a thing from life before and a thing we can do in here. And so we play. I go first and miss all the cups. Then Pedro knocks two over. It's more fun than it looks. Linda finds one of our bowling balls and bats it around the room. I lose. I always lose. A happy loser.

After six games it really is time to say goodnight. "Happy birthday, Mirin," Pedro says. This time his face leans toward mine, his hand grasps my lower back, and he kisses me. I'm surprised, but he is self-possessed. There is no hesitation or restraint. A wave of pleasure pushes my hands to his neck, and I kiss him back. Then, as quickly the spell has taken us both, it's over. Pedro looks at the floor and then at me shyly.

"'Night," he says.

I practice self-control and whisper, "Goodnight."

He slowly backs through the doorway, and I wave a weak hand as he retreats into the darkness to his room. It's like we're tied together by an imaginary rope. When he finally turns away, I turn back to my room, my cheeks aching from smiling. My body is on fire, and it's much nicer than when it was caused by an allergic reaction.

I am content. It is the nicest birthday I've had in a long time.

Every drop of tired I felt before has dissipated, my ears are ringing, and my heart is racing. Despite all these good things, there's guilt too, because I am going to leave him soon.

I am getting out of this place, and if Pedro still wants to stay then I will be sad. Because I just found a tiny spot of joy in this joyless place, and now I may have to leave it behind.

CHAPTER TWENTY-THREE

The next day, Borgie arrives for morning scans. As I finish up my T-pose, it makes a noise that I haven't heard before. It sounds like a beep made on accident.

"Are you okay, Borgie?" I ask. She—er, it—doesn't respond. But I look over its face and shoulders, and everything seems in place.

"Beep." Borgie makes the sound again.

"You really are sounding like a robot today," I say, and suddenly I'm unsure if that's an insult or a compliment. But it just moves toward the door.

"Borgie, are you a she?" I ask, not exactly expecting an answer.

"Yes, Mirin. Borgie is a she," Borgie says in her Maternal Voice. "Scan complete." And if Borgie can feel, I'd say she sounds happy in this moment. The thought makes me feel good.

Without another word, Borgie leaves, presumably to go back behind the waterfall. I should have asked her more questions. *Why am I here, Borgie? What are you planning to do with those wombs in your room? May I please leave?*

When I leave my room to go for a run, I can see movement in Pedro's room, but I don't visit. The thought of him makes me nervous, wanting something or someone. Every time I close my eyes, I remember how it felt. His hand resting on my lower back, so intimate, and the way he was so self-assured. He knew just how to be with me. I want to live in that moment. It was almost too ideal. If I see him it could spoil it.

So I run, past the garden, the waterfall. I muddle through the dry sand at the beach, and I sweat it all out. When I get back to my room, I go straight into the shower. My first one since the water is back on. Showers are underrated. In fact, I've often felt like the shower is where I do all my best work, dreaming, figuring out, and relaxing. When I'm done, I take my time getting into my Zoo linens.

Just as I cozy up against my pillow, there's a knock at the door.

Pedro comes right in to tell me his door is locked.

"I went out for a swim, and when I came back it was locked," he explains.

"Well, that's a good sign," I say sarcastically.

This is not good at all. It means he'll have to stay with me now. And if he stays in my room, we run the risk of what happened with Ander. Borgie controls it all. And Borgie likes to remind us of this fact. Borgie is exercising that control with the locks. All of my thoughts from this morning about Borgie being kinder are gone. This is it. She's definitely going to mate us. Tonight.

I stop pacing and sit on my bed. Pedro sits at the other end. Both of us are lost inside our own heads, and Linda watches us from the table, her latest resting spot. My nerves are shot, because at any moment Borgie could come in here and inject him.

"I'm worried about what happened with Ander," I say quietly.

"I know, and I've been thinking about what we should do if that happens. We need a plan. You could lock me out. You know, barricade the door. Or you could go hide somewhere in the dome. You know this place better than me. I probably wouldn't be able to find you. Or"—he smiles a little smile—"you could tie me up."

I raise an eyebrow.

"Right now, like a werewolf on the night of a full moon," he adds.

"Right now? It's still early. I don't think she would do it now." I'm full of panic, but I can't help but smirk a bit at his outlandish ideas.

At the same time, he's right—oddly, I start to think tying him up *is* the best option. I can't outrun any of the other borgs inside the dome, so hiding would be pointless. If I lock him out of the room, Borgie will know—she'll be able to see me on whatever cameras she normally watches on.

Tying him up is the only thing that would work. At least he'd be in the same room so I could keep an eye on him.

"Yes, seriously. *It* could come in any second now," he says, looking over his shoulder toward the door. Handing me one of his borg-issued shirts and the elastic he has taken from his turtle costume, he tells me, "You can rip this and use the strips to tie me."

"Okay," I say, still unsure. "But if she gives you that injection, it will give you super strength."

"This will give you time to run and hide, but don't tell me where." He is earnest. Pedro makes my face grow warm, even as we prepare for him to be turned into a monster. Those eyes, the way his eyelashes curl up.

"It's going to be okay," he says.

I take a deep breath and his hand braces my arm. "Thanks," I say.

I slowly tie his hands and feet with the elastic and T-shirt strips. He slinks down against the wall and then I cover him with my pillows and blankets.

"You're properly bound for the full moon," I say, and we manage to laugh, even though fear is taking up more space. Lying down on the bare mattress, I look at the pile of linens in the corner, the bedding encasing Pedro like a tomb.

My hand runs along my few books. Grab one, I try to read, but it's hard to focus. I return it to the shelf. Walking in circles, I start to hum a blues song but can't quite remember the tune. We prepare to suffer a long day ahead of us.

Over the next few hours, we talk a bit more about the wombs and about Draven. Any tiny movement I see outside the Plexi makes me tense up. But no borgs come in all day.

Pedro and I are convinced that Borgie plans to raise any child we might conceive in those wombs, but what we don't understand is why. Eventually, we run out of words to say to each other. Once it's evening, we attempt to sleep, because there is nothing else for us to do. It is hard to let your guard down, and neither of us actually sleeps.

"I feel like a pretzel," Pedro says. I try to see him through the dark, but he's too covered up.

As I hug my knees on the bare cot, I say, "I'm sorry. If it makes you feel any better, I'm cold without the blankets and pillows."

"No, it doesn't really help." But I can hear the grin in his voice. "If I start acting foolish, I want you to leave, go as far away from me as you can," he reminds me.

"I know what to do. Just try and rest for now."

It's quiet for a long minute. The thought of what

Draven said is like a loop in my brain. I want to ask Pedro what he thinks about the possibility of borgs having feelings. I'm curious if he would find that shocking or not.

"Pedro, when Dr. Draven told me about Borgie, he said that the borgs are sentient."

"*What?*" he says, his tone proving that he is not going to be easily convinced.

"He said that *he* programmed them that way and that we need to turn the feelings in HIPPO off," I explain.

"You cannot trust that guy," he says. "He's chained up in the basement. Always remember that people can be more dangerous than borgs." I look over at him, tied up and covered in pillows, the illustration of this exact thought.

"It's hard for me to believe you have no compassion for someone trapped down there," I say. I mean, his situation is worse than ours, but the feeling of containment is palpable even here. Pedro is compassionate. I can see it in his interactions with Linda. I feel it in his interactions with me.

"We should forget about him and focus on ourselves and the situation with Borgie," he says.

I regret telling him right now.

I wanted to have a discussion, to know how he feels. Honestly, I can't blame him though. Here we are fearing being injected and harmed, and him tied up to protect me. This isn't exactly the time for a philosophy lesson about borgs and what their sentience means. Linda jumps down from my bed and goes over to the pile of Pedro. She inspects the pillows and tries to dig a hole to him.

"Linda, let him be," I say. There is a sting on my shoulder, and I smack it. The bugs are back; tiny gnats get into the Zoo sometimes. The weather outside must be changing.

With the slow, soft tempo of Pedro's breath, it sounds like he's asleep. It's good he feels relaxed enough to sleep. I am wide awake. I wanted Pedro so much in the lustful moments of my birthday, and now the prospect of Borgie forcing us into it, the thought of those terrifying metal wombs in her room, reframes it all for me.

Pedro is not less appealing, but injected Pedro is. And the possibility of me having to kill him makes my stomach turn. *That won't happen. It cannot. I must get out of here before the next horror show.*

I refuse to be stuck repeating my days in this Zoo or end up chained in the basement until I die.

CHAPTER TWENTY-FOUR

Waking up the next morning, I'm grateful to find that the pile of pillows and blankets is still intact. As I shuffle over to it, I remove the pillows from on top of Pedro. He is still here, and he is too quiet and peaceful to be transformed into a werewolf. He stirs, rubbing his eyes. He's charming.

"Good morning. Did you sleep okay?" I ask.

"Not my best sleep, but I've had worse," he says. I untie his arms, and he slowly stretches out. He rocks his head from side to side. I go to the bathroom to splash my face with water.

Borgie enters the room for scans. We look at each other nervously, and I wonder if everything we did last night was for nothing. I stand in T-pose, and she checks me. Then she moves to Pedro, who tries to stand further away from her. Borgie's claws hold no syringes, but that doesn't mean there isn't one hidden somewhere. We are quiet until she leaves. Finally, we sit on my bed and lie back on the bare mattress in relief.

"I really don't want to get tied up again," he says.

"Hmm. How about if she tries to inject you, I can create

a diversion, and you run to the forest and climb a tree. While Borgie tries to get you down, then I'll hide."

This is not the most clever plan, but at least it doesn't include tying up Pedro.

"It's not the worst plan I've ever heard," he replies.

"Do you have something better?" I ask.

"No, that's good. We'll do that until one of us comes up with something else."

Okay, fair enough.

Pedro goes over to the table and pulls *Walden* out from the few books I have.

Walden, *A Tale of Two Cities*, *Moby Dick*, *In Cold Blood*, and *What to Expect When You're Expecting*. That last one gives me new pause.

"I saw this last night, when lying on the floor. I've never read it," Pedro says.

"It's my favorite," I tell him. "I hadn't read it before I got here. Borgie gave me these few books, and I've read them each a hundred times."

He starts to read it out loud. I sit and listen. The deep rasp of his voice is soothing. He looks over to me.

"Keep going," I say. I listen for a while and then take over, and we take turns reading out loud from *Walden*. It's heartening that he loves it nearly as much as I do. Getting lost in the New England woods feels like a human thing to do. The way Thoreau details nature, the real outside world from before the modern age, it feels like a cure. His words are a healing reminder of the outside, the wildness of the trees and dirt. Life.

Sometime around midday, Borgie returns to the room and starts vacuuming with an accordion arm attached to her side, sucking up the bugs clustered by the door. When the bugs get in, probably due to condensation, she gets rid of them relatively fast. The bugs remind me that I am close to the outdoors, even though I can't see it. The bug vacuum is loud, so Pedro and I take the book and move to the forest. As we pass through the door and past Borgie, I take a deep look at her. If she really is sentient, then what is she feeling now? The bugs probably annoy her. Searching her face for a sign, I don't find one, her features flat, not a note of emotion.

Maybe Draven is wrong.

We don't want to be so near Borgie, but we need to keep our eye on her I want to find a way back into Borgie's room so that I can turn off HIPPO's feelings, like Draven requested. My plan is to wait for Borgie to return to the waterfall and to follow it inside, just like last time. I also want to look in the other rooms I didn't see before and get anything I can to aid in an escape.

While continuing to read *Walden*, we look out at our fake beach and the fake shore of our fake ocean. Linda keeps her distance, walking around just at our sight line. She has become part of the Zoo family. A very dysfunctional family.

My legs entwine with Pedro's as he leans against a tree. Our bodies have become so comfortable together, without a care. A tiny fire starts for me at every place our bodies meet. My shoulder to his torso, my hip to his thigh, my calf over his calf. Tiny fires all over. I wonder if he is thinking like I am. He seems so cavalier. He is at ease, and I am tense. His hair has grown back some, and I push a lock back from his forehead as he reads. He doesn't mind.

His words hang comfortably, as if he hides all his tension somewhere inside. The fierceness I saw in him when he destroyed the Elf Hat borg only seems to be exposed in moments of stress, that tension roaring out of him. But now, with me, he is gentle and considerate. We are calm together, trying to forget our circumstances.

I feel like I'm falling in midair. The more we bond over our captivity, the more I learn about how he thinks. Pedro comes to his thoughts from such a different path than I do mine.

I wonder if this what falling in love feels like. He finishes the last sentence of the chapter and looks at me. I'm expectant because all I have been thinking about is him and us. His eyes are tender, and I can barely hold his gaze as blood rushes to my face.

He holds my hand, and lifts it up and kisses the birthmark on my wrist. Time slows down, and his eyes tunnel into mine.

Then he leans in close and kisses me. Gently at first, and then with more intensity.

I kiss him back, causing all the desire I have been shoving down and holding back to release. We forget where we are, and the only eyes I see are Pedro's deep blue ones and the only body I want is his.

We peel off our clothes slowly. My pants fall to the ground in a heap. He lifts his top off, and the breeze of his scent intoxicates me. We look at each other's bodies, like we have just seen a wonder of the world. His eyes burrow into mine and now I hold his gaze. He takes my face in his hands, and everything in the world goes silent, standing still for us. Our bodies meet in soft and hard tangles.

He kisses my shoulder, and his hands trace my lines. We move down to the ground, and I don't feel the forest floor, I only feel Pedro. We are in the Walden Woods, just simple humans having a human experience. Wild and free.

We remain in the forest all day, forgetting the reason we are here.

CHAPTER TWENTY-FIVE

It's been about a week since Pedro and I slept together in the forest. We've been intimate a few more times since then, too. I had forgotten how good it feels to have someone know you physically. The body holds so many feelings. So many stories. Learning his stories has been the most exciting thing that has happened to me yet.

Linda knows something is different. She keeps nudging her head into my shins and following me with intent. I gave her a treat that she eschewed and some pets, but she is relentless. She stares at me with long looks, as if she wants me to explain myself. Maybe I'm just projecting onto her my own feelings about this relationship with Pedro. I want to tell someone, anyone, how I'm feeling, which is dizzy and obsessed.

After a run Pedro enters my room, which has seemed more like our room after all this time with his room locked. My heart is spinning. He is sweaty. Handsome and sweaty. I'm hot and self-conscious, wondering if he can sense how crazy for him I've become. He looks contemplative.

"I've had a change of heart," he says as he sits down at the small table. My stomach drops because I'm sure he's referring to our romantic relationship. I close my eyes and can hear the throbbing inside my ears as I try to steel myself for the final blow.

"I want to escape too," he says.

"You what?" I look at him, my facial muscles relaxing.

"I don't want to stay anymore," he repeats.

He changed his mind. I can't believe it. He wants to escape with me, because maybe—just maybe—he feels whatever this electricity is going on with us. This is the best news I've heard. There is no hiding the joy I feel, and I jump up and down in excitement. Then I sit quietly across from him and grab his hands.

"I knew it. I knew you would realize and I'm so glad," I say. Finally, he sees it for himself, that there's only so long that you can be in the Zoo without it getting to you.

At first the Zoo feels big enough, interesting enough, it feels like it could be enough. When there is no other choice, you try to make it more than it is. But then one day you realize it's not enough. You get hungry. You just want to get out and experience life outside the bubble again.

No one is meant to be held in captivity. Six long years I have spent trapped here, which makes it hard not miss everything that was before, even when I know that it will be different going forward.

Pedro has been here such a short time. He knows nothing of the pain this place will bring. Life falters on the inside. And once you turn the corner, once you remember that truth, you can't imagine ever seeing the Zoo as a place of respite again.

I deluded myself for a long while, but the truth of the

Zoo is all around us. It is a relief that he sees things differently now. We both want to escape. And with him, things will be better.

"I've been thinking about it, and I think the best plan is for us to jump the barrier at the Treat Show. It's the only open spot in the dome, and I think we can make it over the wall if we prepare," he says.

I imagine an anime version of myself jumping through the barrier and running out the exit in slow-motion glory.

"You're right—it's the only open spot I've ever found, but it's not going to be easy, Pedro." I smile, despite my doubts.

"Yes, exactly," he says, as though he has seen my daydream.

"There are so many borgs in the audience, I've always considered it too dangerous. And I've always assumed the railing is electrified." I pick at my fingernails, remembering that this is not a movie.

"We'll just have to find out." He comes over and rests his hands on my shoulders, which relax like his hands are reminders.

"What about Dr. Draven? What if he knows something that can help us escape? We need to turn off HIPPO's switch, and then he could help us," I say.

"No. If Draven has a way to escape, he would have done it already. And we still don't know why the borgs are keeping him locked in the basement, rather than up here in the Zoo. I think he could be dangerous."

"I do get a bad feeling around Draven. But he is a chance out of here—we can be cautious and still use his help. We can at least try to find the switch on HIPPO." There is no reason to dismiss Draven completely. There are few opportunities here, and he is one of them. But I'm not sure why he wants HIPPO's switch flipped.

"The idea that a borg could have a feelings switch. What does that even mean?" I ask.

"Who knows – maybe they are programmed to show emotion? That does nothing to help us escape," he says.

I wonder if a feelings switch could help us. "Maybe"— I'm still working this out—"it's like the Force from the old classic *Star Wars*. Maybe the feelings make the borgs more difficult to control and Dr. Draven will have more control over them when they're off?"

Pedro laughs. "It could be. Maybe *we* could have more control over them?" He looks like pure mischief.

"I don't like how happy that makes you," I say. "Draven knows a lot that we don't know, so maybe it could help us. He was right about Borgie's room."

"We should focus on what we can control and get out of here," he says. "We need to stake out the Treat Show, take down notes on every last inch of it."

"Oh, I've got notes," I say. He doesn't know how diligent I have been. I want to impress him and show him that I am capable despite my captivity. This is new, wanting to show off, but it's the truth. He makes fireworks go off inside me, and I want to give him fireworks too.

I open the cabinet door in the kitchenette, and out strides Linda. Well, I did not expect that.

"Hey girl, how long have you been in there?" I ask.

"Mew," Linda says in passing. She doesn't seem to mind one bit. I try and remember the last time I opened the cabinet, but I don't remember opening it at all. She cozies up to Pedro and accepts his chin scratch.

Back in the cabinet, I take out the pile of old journal

entries and rifle through my old lists, looking for the drawings I made of all the different parts of the Zoo. I come across a scrawled Treat Show drawing.

"Aha," I say, holding up the drawing victoriously. It notes the distance between every desk and the entryway. We will need to know how far the jump will be so that we can practice, since we'll only have one shot.

"Mirin, I'm impressed, but I'm surprised you haven't tried before," Pedro says, looking over my homemade map. He has no idea. I have scoured this place, looking for a way out, trying to understand its limits. I used to spend each day, the whole day, in a different spot, and I always thought the best chance of escape would be through the Treat Show. But I was always too cautious to make my attempt because I worried about electrocution from wireless electric fencing.

"We're going to need to practice our jump before we try it. I have measurements on the drawing, there," I say, pointing to the map.

"Okay, we'll need to mark out how far we need to go on the floor here," Pedro says, "and then we can practice."

We see Borgie approach, and when she enters the room there is no regard for us. She bursts in just when we had planned to practice our jumping. She seems to be hovering around more than ever, and I wish I knew why. A few weeks ago, I would have thought nothing of it, but knowing about her room and her hostage, it's different now. If I think of Borgie as capable of feelings, then why can't she see how miserable this place is?

She picks up the laundry in the corner, and I go to her. I look into her borg eyes.

"Borgie, let us go," I whisper.

"Mirin is feeling feisty," Borgie says in her Gladiator

Voice. Borgie stands up to her full height, reminding me of her fierceness. I fold my arms, and it's quiet for a moment.

Pedro signals with his hand: *Stop.*

"Yes, Mirin is feeling feisty," I say. It's true, but I don't want to push Borgie too far.

She takes the laundry away.

CHAPTER TWENTY-SIX

The next morning, I wake up before the Weatherlight. Pedro is still sleeping. He looks so young and vulnerable lying next to me.

I carefully take the keys out of the pillowcase, making sure not to disturb him. Pedro made it clear yesterday that he doesn't think Draven's offer has any merit, so I've decided to go and switch off HIPPO myself. Best-case scenario, it results in some help from Draven. Worst-case scenario, we're still trapped in the Zoo, so nothing really changes. I only have a short time to get into Borgie's room since I know she will be headed here soon for scans. I slip out of my bedroom quietly and head to the waterfall.

Soft waves run onto the beach, the light scent of chlorine, a stark difference from the adrenaline that I'm filled with. *Hurry, Mirin*, I encourage myself. When I get to the spot behind the waterfall, I hide in the shadow like I did before and don't have to wait long. As Borgie rushes out, I rush in.

The cold air hits my skin as I dash back to her room.

HIPPO is no longer underneath the table but on top of it. He looks like a new machine. As I look him over, his eyes flash with light, and he begins to play an up-tempo electronic song.

"Shhhh," I hush while I look for the switch.

There is only one, a carbon-gray switch on its faceplate. *Draven said it was on the right-hand side on his shoulder.* But he has been repaired and changed. This is the only switch, so I reach out and flip it, and the lights in his eyes go out. The sound turns off. It is hard to tell if he is just powered off.

I wait one moment to see if HIPPO will respond. Will he look different without feelings? Will he behave differently? I wish I had time to find out. He moves forward an inch, and that is all I need to be sure that he isn't powered off. I want to stick around to learn more, but there's not enough time to do everything I want to do. Instead, I leave Borgie's room without once glancing at the menace of the womb sculptures.

As I pass one of the doors in the hallway, I take out a key and try it. It slides in but doesn't turn, so I try another key with no luck.

Mirin, you don't have time for this. The second door beckons, but Borgie would surely be at my room by now. I rush past the second door, and back into the Zoo and break into a run when I hit the path.

I enter my room, breathing heavily and sweating. Borgie says, "Complete scan," and motions for Pedro to step aside.

She turns to me, scanning my forehead, and says, "Mirin heartbeat 110 bpm, elevated. Mirin body temperature 98.9, elevated. Mirin must rest." I lie down on the bed to make a show of my capitulation and throw Pedro a thumbs-up. He looks concerned, and I can tell he's wondering where I've been. I shake my head, signaling that we can't talk about it right now.

When Borgie leaves, I hop back to my feet. Pedro goes to speak, but I interrupt him before he can get any words out.

"I did it. HIPPO is off and now I need to tell Dr. Draven," I say, taking the keys from my shoe and putting them back in the pillowcase.

"Whoa, whoa. You turned off HIPPO? Just now?" he asks.

"Yes. I knew Borgie would be leaving, so I just did it. I'm sorry I didn't tell you, but I knew you wouldn't have agreed."

"I don't know if that was the best idea."

"It's backup," I say, sounding surer than I feel.

"Can we focus on the Treat Show escape and forget Draven?" he asks. I go to the sink and splash some water on my face.

"What is the harm in ensuring several escape options? If Draven can help us, I will take that. If we can do it through the Treat Show, I will take that too. The one thing I know for sure about this place is that nothing is as simple as it appears." He knows I am right.

"How are you supposed to get to Draven?"

"I have to get to the Testing Pod somehow," I say.

"Pretend you're sick?" he offers. I tap my fingers on the table.

"That won't work. Borgie barely noticed my foot infection. I don't think a fake illness would be different," I say.

"I could do it. Let me talk to this guy." I roll my eyes at his sudden machismo.

"No, I'm the one who knows where he is and how to get

there fast," I say. *But how?* When we exit our room, Linda comes flying toward us.

"Murrrlooow," Linda is calling in a loud, anguished voice.

"What's got you riled up?" I ask her. She starts digging at the ground. As I reach down to pet her back, she lets out another loud call and then hops away.

"Cats are so weird," Pedro says.

"So are we. Ignore him, Linda," I say. She nuzzles her head into my calf.

"The Weatherlight seems dim today. Did you notice?" Pedro asks.

"Maybe the borgs want it to be overcast. Feels stormy—maybe we should have brought the umbrella," I joke, but he's right. The Weatherlight *does* look dim, and that hasn't ever happened before.

"Yes, *menina*, you should have put on some rain boots," Pedro says.

"If you really want to feel rain here, you have to pretend in the shower or under the waterfall," I tell him, more serious than I mean to be.

"I definitely want to do that," he says.

"I'll show you later," I flirt. He pulls me in for a kiss, then looks serious.

"Mirin, do you know how Borgie takes you to the Testing Pod? Like, which path you take to get there?" he asks.

"Not exactly. It always knocks me out before we go." He looks back at me pensively, and as if I can read his thoughts, I respond, "My guess it is through the hallway near her room. There are two doors that I haven't been through yet." I go back to the pillowcase and produce the keys.

"And there are these. I tried the keys in one door, which they didn't work on, but the other one—"

"Let's go," he says. "Maybe we can find a way out without asking Draven for help." We head to wait by the waterfall door.

We wait by the door until Borgie needs to clean something. We've decided that Pedro will wait for me, due to my insistence that I can be quicker alone. He did protest, but this part of the plan is mine. Once I'm back into the cold, dark hallway of her lair, there is a feeling of hope in this mission.

I know there is nothing left for me to do but survive.

This time when I slide the last key into the last door and turn, the door opens. It feels like sorcery. Another set of descending stairs, I can guess where these will lead. Draven.

This is just my luck. I go down quickly and carefully. They take me to the center of another hallway, there are doors on either end, and one in between. I start with that one, the closest door. When I enter, a light flickers on automatically, and I can see it's a storage room.

There is a long silver table with borg parts and a stack of boxes. Grabbing the nearest box, I start to rifle through it, finding mostly wires and cables. A borg arm rests on top of the table, each finger like part of multi-tool pocketknife. I grab it. This could be useful in our escape.

I look under the table, where there are stacked bankers boxes, with labels that say FINANCES—ZOO and INSURANCE. And the one on the bottom says BATTLES. Borg battles, I'm guessing.

Inside the BATTLES box are contracts, paperwork, and hologram drives, the kind used for short advertisements. The papers discuss warrior borgs. I haven't seen one of those for a while. Those are the borgs the military created for our "safety," to protect us. But the truth is, they're walking tanks, and everyone knew how dangerous they were and could become.

I squeeze one drive and the image appears before me: a warrior borg crushing a smaller borg's torso, like it's tin and not steel. I squeeze another and it looks shockingly like Borgie—same frame, slightly dated hardware, its arms raised up in victory. I wonder if Borgie is based on a later edition of a warrior borg.

Each new drive that I squeeze reveals some giant warrior in the midst of an act of violence against another borg. Disgusting. I toss the last one back into the box and look under the table for more boxes.

One reads HART, and I slide out that box. I have no idea what I'm looking for. But I figure the more I see and learn can only help Pedro and me escape. Knowledge is a weapon, or so they say.

On top of the pile is a photo of a man standing in front of a sign that reads MEET HART, THE FIRST BORG WITH A HEART. Underneath is a stack of flyers that say, HART, THE BORG WHO FEELS JUST LIKE A HUMAN. A borg with feelings, like HIPPO with the switch flipped.

The man in the photo must be a young Dr. Draven. *Weird.* Dr. Draven is standing next to Hart, his hand on its shoulder. He is clean-shaven and smiling. It's strange how much Hart also looks like Borgie. The same shape, both hulking and intricate. This time, there's updated hardware. Most likely, Borgie is the last edition of this version in a long line of borgs. First a warrior, then a borg with feelings, and now my captor.

Hart is wearing a dress, which is unusual. Over her big metal shoulders are two thin velvet straps, and a red dress hangs over the hulking borg. She looks friendly, as does Draven. Happy even. I notice that Hart has a tiny heart shape engraved in the center of her sternum. How sweet. My hand holding the photo begins to shake. Seeing photos of people before, people happy, makes me sad. My family was happy too.

I start to care about Draven and Hart, though I don't really want to.

I set aside the photograph and move the flyers, which reveals another photo of Dr. Draven, sitting on a couch with Hart, his arm around it.

Her. Hart, the borg who feels like a human.

I wonder if he was the one who invented the technology that allowed Hart to feel, or if he's just the first recipient of an actual feeling borg. Maybe she was on display here, and then they became—friendly? I can't tell if they're coworkers, or a couple, or a proud inventor with his product.

There's another picture of Hart, standing near a dining room table and holding a platter with a turkey on it, like she's about to serve a holiday feast. What am I seeing here? Even if this borg, Hart, could feel, I know for sure that borgs don't eat food. Perhaps this is part of some exhibit from a past iteration of the Zoo.

The next photo is Dr. Draven cutting a ribbon in front of the Draven Zoo. He looks so smug. Like he's just solved all the world's problems by creating borgs that can feel. *Thank you for creating my prison. Bastard.* I tear the photo in two.

Underneath the photos is a stack of blueprints. Graphics of machines with biological anatomy. They are labeled TORSO SECTION ASSEMBLY and PROCRE-

ATOR ASSEMBLY. These are the blueprints of a womb. Likely, the same wombs I saw in Borgie's room. Some parts look very anatomical, like a human, but with gears and lists of dimensions and mechanics. There is still no explanation of what any of these products are for, even though it's clear enough to me that Dr. Draven was developing a borg womb.

I stare at the photo of Hart in the red dress with Draven and look to the ring finger of his left hand. There is no ring. But the tattoo of a heart shows where a wedding ring would be.

I've seen that tattoo on his finger.

It has been changed, and now it has a diode stabbing into it.

I swallow hard, putting the pieces together. The human clothing. The holiday turkey. The tattoo in place of a wedding band. Somehow, they were like a family. Flipping back to the blueprints, I realize what I'm looking at. *The wombs were developed to give Hart a baby.* The thought is almost too much for me to process, a borg wanting a baby, having a baby. A human or borg baby.

No matter which, it sounds dangerous. A borg, with all its metal switches and functions, holding a vulnerable child just seems physically treacherous, never mind the emotional part. I can't imagine a borg with the ability to be gentle and comforting to a baby.

My eyes linger for another second on the photo of Hart and Draven together on the couch and I push it into my waistband for safekeeping. I'm eager to tell Pedro all that I've found, even though I haven't made it to Draven yet. I have no idea how this information will help us escape, but I know that I've just found something really big.

A sound from down the hall shakes me from my thoughts.

Run, Mirin. Go now.

As I run toward the stairs, a finger from the borg arm catches on my pants and falls to the ground. Shoot, I'll have to get it later.

When I get to the stairs, I look up and see that the door is still open, the square of dim light is still there.

CHAPTER TWENTY-SEVEN

Seven feet. We need to clear a seven-foot jump to escape through the Treat Show. It sounds crazy, but it's a doable goal.

Our next Treat Show is tomorrow, and we want to get it right, so we won't fully execute our plan until next week. We must be sure we can make the jump on a day when there are fewer borgs in attendance, but it all has to go perfectly for it to work. Tomorrow's Treat Show will likely be busy since Pedro is still such a new part of the exhibit. We have a stash of nutrition packets and water. Pedro plans to fashion some sort of weapon from a branch, but he can do that in the next week.

We are back to his plan since it's now obvious that we cannot trust Draven at all.

When I showed Pedro the photo and told him about what I found in the storage room, he said he no longer feels safe here. More to the point, he no longer feels safe about *me* being here, knowing what Draven is ultimately planning.

I don't know how Borgie connects into all of this—it's possible that she doesn't. It could be that those wombs are a leftover relic from Draven's time and that Borgie couldn't care less about them being in her room. I hope that's the case. I know Borgie is capable of destruction, but a part of me has grown to care for her over the last six years. Loath as I am to admit it.

Pedro and I can only guess what Draven's next steps would be once he escapes, but we think he plans to take down Borgie and all the borgs in the Zoo. Blowing up HIPPO was probably a test gone wrong, proving that he takes big risks and makes big mistakes. It's hard to know for sure, though.

For now, it doesn't matter. We just need to focus on getting out.

Borgie scans Pedro quickly but then scans me twice. She pauses, and I use the time to study her. To see if she shows any emotion. Nothing.

When I realize that Borgie is still sitting there—apparently calculating something in her mind, or computer chip, or whatever—I say, "Borgie? May we go now, please?"

"Mirin is prenatal," she says loudly and quite pragmatically.

My stomach drops and I can't even look at Pedro. *Prenatal?*

"Borgie, what did you just say?" I ask.

"Mirin is prenatal. With child. You are pregnant with a human."

In some quiet corner of my mind, I knew it was possible, but hearing it bluntly dropped by Borgie stuns me. I mean, we know how human reproduction works, and Pedro and I haven't been offered birth control in the Zoo here.

Now that I stop and think about it, it's possible my

period is a little late. I have been so preoccupied with our escape plans and what we have discovered about Draven and Borgie that I guess I lost track of my cycle. How could I have been so careless? This changes everything.

I'm afraid to see Pedro's reaction, although there's nothing either one of us can do about it now. But when I finally look over at him, his entire face is lit up like starlight and he looks at me with wet eyes. Is he... happy?

The second Borgie leaves, the news crashes over me again.

"Oh, oh, oh."

Pedro is quiet and stares at the floor. I stare down at the same spot, trying to find what he sees. I stare so hard I half-expect the floor to form arms and reach up and pull me into it. Part of me kind of hopes it does. Pedro gets down on his knees before me and holds my hands, interrupting this fantasy. Instinctively, I go to my knees as well.

"We have to leave," he says, looking at me in that startling way that he does.

"I know."

"We cannot wait. Our child cannot ever know this place," he whispers earnestly. He's right. No one would purposely have a baby in a zoo. I'm not a monster.

"Our child. That is a wild thing to say." I start to cry.

"A gift," he says, his tears are falling freely now. I worry that we are being too sentimental. This is not a gift; it is a challenge and a responsibility.

And I am more scared than I ever have been. We both stand up, and I start to pace. I cross and uncross my arms. Fleeing the Zoo is the only thing I feel like doing at this moment. Honestly, I'd flee my own skin if I could.

We decide that our escape plan can no longer wait until next week. It must be tomorrow—there is no other choice.

We don't really know what the borgs will do now that they know, if they will use the wombs in Borgie's room. I don't want to think about it.

We must make it over the wall.

Everything hinges on those *seven feet*.

CHAPTER TWENTY-EIGHT

Today is the day. We're either going to make it over that wall or we're going to die trying.

That might be a little dramatic. I can't say for sure that Borgie would kill us if we tried to get over the wall, but I also wouldn't put it past her at this point. Either way, our punishment would be a lot worse than no water for a few days.

We are getting ready for the Treat Show. I grab a plate from the kitchenette and break it into the sink, for luck. Broken plates are lucky. At least, that's what my mom told me.

My stomach is upset, and I thought it was probably just nerves or the fact that I was up all night thinking about the baby, but now it is stronger. There is an aching pain down low in my abdomen, and all I can think about is this child, our child. I rub my hand over my stomach, and worry creeps in.

Something feels wrong.

I rush into the bathroom. There is an ache as I sit.

When I stand, I find that I am bleeding. The bright red against white porcelain reflects the starkness of my feelings.

"Borgie," I yell out, sinking to the floor. As I sit there, I think about how strange it feels to have called out to my captor for help. Not Pedro. Not my mom. I call out for Borgie. When the sound came from a deep place inside me, the word was unexpected.

Pedro comes running into the bathroom.

"What's wrong? Are you okay?" His brows are furrowed with worry. As he looks into the toilet, I watch his body react to the bright red truth. Maybe this baby wasn't going to come after all and maybe that is the best outcome. Just behind him, Borgie arrives.

"Medical," she announces in her pitchy Information Voice. She moves closer to me, blocking Pedro from my line of sight.

"Borgie, I want Pedro to come with me," I say, adjusting myself so that I can grab hold of Pedro's hand.

"Please allow me to join her." He holds me close.

"Mirin, medical," she repeats.

"It will help me if Pedro can come too," I say gently.

Her response is cuffing my wrist with her claw, but she doesn't send Pedro away. She leads me out of the room. He follows close behind us as Borgie takes us through the waterfall door, which opens easily at her presence. I barely register this, as I am consumed with the pain in my abdomen. Yesterday, I couldn't wrap my mind around having a baby, and now in a flash I'm terrified of losing it.

We enter the door my key had recently unlocked and descend the stairs slowly. Borgie and I lead, and Pedro follows. The door at the end of the hall is the Testing Pod. We pass the storage room, and this is my first time entering the Testing Pod awake. Usually, I wake up dazed in a bed, but this time I see the doors open, the bright white room. The pain in my belly lifts for a moment, feels less ominous, more subtle.

Now I know where I am, at the end of the hall is the door that leads down to the basement, to Draven.

The stagnant clinical scent of the Testing Pod is strong as Borgie lifts me onto the hospital bed. Then HIPPO comes in and puts stickers connected to wires onto my head and chest as usual, and this time on my stomach. Pedro hovers at the foot of the bed, and it feels crowded. They test me, and I let them. I surrender to the borgs and trust them to fix me. I reach down and feel my stomach again, and I start to wish for the baby to be healthy. If it's in distress, I wonder if I did something wrong.

Did I jump too hard during my escape practice?

There is a fierce need to protect this baby. That tiny bit of life pulsing in my womb suddenly feels like a beacon. My own heart thumps in my ears, drowning out all other sound. Pedro is now pacing.

Borgie puts a gel-coated wand on my stomach, causing a blue hologram to appear near the wall to the left, and then a new sound enters the room, unlike any I have heard before. It is a static, rapid beat. The sound of the heartbeat fills the room, quicker than my own heart. I have to twist to see the image. It takes the shape of a lumpy snowball, with a 3D blue bean inside, and it has a red blinking pulse.

The visual makes me think of the mechanical wombs, and I start to sweat. I can hear the heart rate monitor beeping fast and faster. But then I feel it, the astonishment of motherhood crashes over me, like a car wreck.

"Pedro, look!" I get his attention. He squints at the hologram.

"Is that the baby?" he asks.

Pedro ducks under some wires to come close and embrace me. He takes my face in his hands and kisses it all over—my forehead, my cheeks, my lips. A sob escapes me, and a part of me that has been dormant for a long time jolts back to life.

That's our baby.

I look into Pedro's blue eyes and smile. We are both crying now, tears of impossible joy.

The heartbeat goes silent as Borgie takes the wand away. She turns off the screen and unceremoniously drops the wand on the tray without a word to either of us.

"Borgie? Is the baby okay?" I ask. Something about her abrupt, cold reaction doesn't sit right with me. Borgie seems upset.

"Borgie? Is my baby okay?" I ask again, trying not to let the fear seep into my voice.

She faces me, and it's like time slows down. *Please don't tell me bad news, Borgie*, I silently plead. She says nothing, and I search her face for answers. When I see nothing to offer me an answer, my gaze drops. A little lower, at the center of her sternum, is a round, bronze cap. It has always been there, but something new nags at me.

I can't quite catch the thought, but the cap looks like it has been added to the suit. It doesn't quite match, like it might be covering something. I reach out to touch the bronze cap, and it sparks a memory.

My fingers brush the cool bronze, and she abruptly turns away from me. I shiver even though it's not cold. Pedro is searching my face like he's trying to understand what I'm thinking. I shake my head as if to say, *Not now, Pedro. I'll explain later.*

Borgie jerks her massive limbs and takes the tray to the back of the room. Sitting back on the bed, I wait for my next instruction, trying to be the humble patient. But Borgie walks away from me, leaving the Testing Pod, and we are left with HIPPO.

HIPPO.

I had almost forgotten that I turned its feelings switch off. I scan its face for any differences, but I see nothing of note. Maybe we're all more like borgs than we think, all of our feelings hidden deep inside of us, able to be turned on and off with a switch. Or perhaps, that is wishful thinking.

HIPPO has a plastic square on his face. He removes the cover to reveal a sort of petri dish and then clasps my wrist and sticks my index finger with a tiny needle. He rubs my slightly bloody finger onto the built-in petri dish before replacing the cover and wraps a bandage around my fingertip. Then he pulls all the stickers off my body with such great efficiency I barely feel it.

Pedro leans in close, like he is going to comfort me, but instead he whispers in my ear.

"You know the way to Draven?"

"Yes?" I say. I shift on the bed.

"Then go," he says. "You are no longer bleeding. It's ok."

"Are you serious?" I ask. But I look down and see that he's right. I'm no longer bleeding, and the cramps are gone. My heart rate is back to normal, too.

As he hits the switch very near HIPPO's face, and his eyes light up. He starts making a cooing sound. I think Pedro thought he was turning it off, but I had already done that.

I hit the switch on HIPPO, and again his lights go off.

"Leave him," I tell Pedro.

I get up and run for the door. Down the hall, through the door, then running down the basement steps, my legs are jelly. This wasn't the plan, but I must find out if Draven can help us. We need to take advantage of any opportunity we get.

I briskly walk back toward Dr. Draven's cage, this time confident and less afraid.

"You have returned," he declares.

"I have questions." I struggle to catch my breath.

His hands clutch the bars, and he looks grimier than before.

"Did you do as I asked? Did you flip the switch on HIPPO?" he asks.

"Yes. But what is this place? I want details. Start now."

Draven inhales deeply. "The girl has questions," he says.

"Do you want out?"

He sighs in resignation. "This is a zoo, but it started as a lab for my experiments. We needed more funding, so we opened it up as an entertainment venue and that's when it became very successful," he says. Personally, I think "entertainment" is an interesting word to use for his warrior borgs.

"Why are you locked in there? What did you do?" I ask.

"I developed some of the most cutting-edge technology that the world has ever seen, too cutting-edge. You've seen it. Then the technology turned on me," he says with a deeply satisfied smile.

"Frankenstein." I remember. The fact that he considers Borgie and Hart as the monsters is beyond ironic, considering that he is the one claiming to have created them.

"Yes, I developed a way for the borgs to have feelings, emotion. It was based on machine learning, and well, I misunderstood their capacity for knowledge. It is so far beyond anything a person could know," he says.

"Tell me about Hart."

Draven backs away from the bars and sits on the floor.

"Hart was my greatest invention, a borg I designed to perfection. I created Hart to be the first of her kind—a borg with human emotion. I wrote an algorithm, sort of a mathematical explanation of human emotion, using physics and psychology, and packaged access to the vast information on the internet into what I consider a tidy algorithm. It was meant to build upon itself. As we learn more about our own consciousness, the machine would learn too. It worked."

"Hart was my greatest achievement; she could laugh at my jokes and cry at a sad movie. We lived together and I could constantly improve her, making her more and more human," he says. *Except the eight feet tall part*, I suppose.

"But after a while, her hardware became dated and there wasn't a way for me to update her anymore without rebuilding her almost completely. The newest tech was operating so much faster and more efficiently," he says.

So he created a robot Stepford wife and then found her outdated. It is becoming difficult for me to listen to this garbage without walking away. Poor Hart.

Draven continues, "I started developing an upgraded version of Hart. I called her Cassandra. But Hart grew wildly jealous of Cassandra and tried to sabotage my work. I knew I couldn't keep them both. I suppose I should mention that Hart had grown maternal feelings before the Zoo and had begged for a child.

"Of course that could not be. So I developed the Zoo, a lab where scientists could marvel at Hart, help create new tech, and keep my newest work safe. Eventually, Hart went back to doing what her frame was built for - fighting.

"Unfortunately, Cassandra soon developed the same feelings about motherhood. I wanted to test my skills, so we developed the first borg womb, which was mechanical but supported organic material. It was mighty work, top secret, as we created a human embryo to be carried by a borg. Cassandra got her wish. She grew the child she wanted, and I made history. Even though I could not share what I had done due to government issues, ethics and the like, it is all recorded for the future."

Wow, a borg carried a human child. That is incredible. And completely immoral. But no wonder Borgie held onto those wombs. That life and that baby could have been something she wanted too. I feel a strange pang of empathy toward Borgie. And then I feel incredibly sorry for any child with a father like Draven.

Draven must not notice my distaste for his story because he goes on.

"I spent a lot of time in the lab and didn't realize my grave mistake in bringing Cassandra and the baby to one of Hart's shows. I didn't expect Hart to even notice us, since we were off to the side in the audience. I figured she'd be too busy focusing on her fight. Those warrior borgs are massive. Of course, Hart did notice, and when she spotted Cassandra with the baby, chaos rained down on us.

"Hart broke out, came into the gallery and tried to take the baby. It appeared that she was holding it gently until the kid started wailing. She had burned the child and then placed it on the ground so she could attack Cassandra. The crowd went running, and in the commotion the baby disappeared.

"Hart destroyed Cassandra, all my hard work was in pieces. She drilled Cassandra's L-Drive, so that I wouldn't be able to restore her. I barely escaped and had to hide out in my bunker for years. In her rage, Hart released the algorithm onto the internet, and then every borg, any machine with access to the internet, could tap into Hart's learned humanity. Her feelings of rage against me became a collective borg rage against all humans. And she couldn't take it back. I was in hiding, trying to access the Zoo for years, but every borg out there has an imprint of me as their greatest enemy. I am a prime threat to them.

"I was out foraging for food months ago when I got careless and they captured me." He lets out a long breath.

The dent and the scuff. The *bad man.*

"And you hurt Borgie?" I ask, but it comes out more like a statement of fact than a question.

"Borgie? I struggled and gave a few borgs a fight, yes," he says. But did he fight *my* Borgie?

"So now I must fix it," he continues. "I must somehow heal the anger she implanted into the borg world. You have to let me out so that I can save the world," he says unemotionally.

All of this Draven presents as though he were the hero of the story and Hart is the villain. He doesn't see himself as I do, as a selfish, thoughtless tyrant. He takes zero responsibility for what he created. No wonder the borgs revolted against him. Against all of us.

"Remember, the algorithm still pulses through those borgs and their hate for humanity has not lessened one iota. The borgs put me here, like they did you. When I get out of here, I will correct my mistake and destroy every single borg left. What happened a long time ago is less important than what is happening right now. I can fix this, but it's in your hands, Mirin," he says.

I look at the ceiling and let it sink in. I've known the evil of the borgs firsthand, but I did not know it was all predicated on something a person did.

This person.

Draven made them into the monsters they've become. He shares the blame. I can see why he wants to destroy them all, though I can't help but feel compassion for Hart and for Cassandra. And that poor baby. I clutch my stomach.

Draven starts coughing quietly. He stands up and coughs even more. "Help," he croaks out. For a second, I worry that he might be choking, so I move closer to check on him.

His hand shoots through the bars and grabs my arm, his long, overgrown fingernails digging into my soft flesh.

"Get me out of this cage. I can help you," he implores, his eyes on fire.

I struggle to free myself from his grip.

I grab a bar and jerk my arm away from him and I can feel my tender skin breaking open in the process.

Once I'm free, I back up and run up the stairs, as far away from him as possible.

CHAPTER TWENTY-NINE

When I get back to the Testing Pod, it's quiet except for a tapping sound. Pedro is hunched over HIPPO. I'm confused. When I get closer, I see that he's tapping HIPPO on the back, over and over: *tap, tap, tap.*

"Draven grabbed me," I say while rubbing the pink scratches on my arm, like I can wipe off the enormity of what he just told me.

"Are you okay?" he asks. His eyes full of concern.

"Yeah, he just scared me." He hasn't stopped tapping HIPPO.

"Wait, what are you doing?" I ask.

"I turned him back on when you left, but then he cried. He was crying, like playing a crying soundtrack, and shaking. I didn't know what to do. I was trying to buy you more time, so I just said, 'It's okay, buddy,' and started tapping its back, and he stopped." Pedro seemed impressed with himself.

"Watch," he says, and he pulls his hand away. HIPPO starts shaking and a loud baby's cry erupts from it, so Pedro starts tapping again and HIPPO goes quiet.

HIPPO was crying, and Pedro comforted it. This is an unexpected turn.

"You're going to be a good father," I say, trying to hide my smile.

"Very funny. We should get back to our rooms," Pedro tells HIPPO gently. Pedro opens the door, and HIPPO zooms by, leading the way back to the stairs. Everything feels different. We are in the know now, not injected and passed out. We have been allowed to see behind the curtain. We walk slowly back out into the Zoo from behind the waterfall. It's almost like it has grown, it is bigger now, full of more demons.

When we arrive at my room, Linda meows at the sight of us, and I bend to pet her. Pedro picks her up and she pushes her head into his chest.

"So Draven told me a little story, and you will not believe it," I tell Pedro.

CHAPTER THIRTY

The next day, I'm buzzing around the room in Treat Show clothes. Surprisingly, I feel strong, with no apparent lasting discomfort from yesterday's events. I collect the few items we'll need for our escape—nutrition packets, water, paper, pen, and Pedro has the dagger he made. All are tucked away under our clothes, where Borgie can't see.

"Remember, clap if there is no electric barrier," he reminds me.

"Yes, I'm ready, and I won't clap at all if there is. We only go with the clapping," I confirm.

"Shh," he warns.

And then Borgie is there, looming over us. As she leads us to the Treat Show, all I can think of is Draven's story about how this place came to be. Borgie is like Hart was. I wonder if Borgie feels Hart's betrayal, like Draven said, because she fed it to all borgs. I don't know, but I know I do not want to end up as part of Draven's horrible Zoo collection. Pedro and I keep looking at each other, making sure that the other one is ready.

The Treat Show begins like it usually does. We had

hoped that the audience wouldn't be too full, but when we look out, we see that it is crammed full of borgs. The show has been so popular since Pedro arrived. We start to play our usual melodrama but keep close to the perimeter.

The show has only just begun, and I am shooing a fly that is trapped in the Treat Show arena with us.

"Borgie must have missed you with the bug vacuum," I say out loud.

Taking off my shoe, I swat at it, and the borgs cheer and throw treats. I sit defeated and pretend I'm upset. Folding over in my chair, performing my frustration, I stealthily grab a treat from the floor.

The crowd is excited by this, and on my cue, Pedro pretends to faint. The audience's focus transfers to him. While everyone is looking at Pedro, I slip a water packet out of my waistband, and pour it over the wall as a test to see if it's electrified. I listen hard. No electricity. There are no pops or crackles. The steam that would rise from the wires does not appear. I'm relatively certain, there is no electrified barrier.

Now my hands are shaking. *This is it.* I reach my hands over my head and clap once, quick and loud. Pedro jumps up, the borgs cheer, and together we climb up onto the railing and clasp hands.

I look to Pedro, our eyes meet, and I can tell we both feel in that quick second the heaviness of what we are about to do.

It is time to go, to leave this place, finally.

All of the pain will be over, all of the desperate wishing will be answered now. Time freezes as Pedro squeezes my sweaty hand, and I squeeze his back. Our eyes veer forward, and we jump the wall in tandem.

The second we pass out of the office, an alarm starts blaring.

Wooouum. Wooouum. Wooouum.

Freedom lies just ahead, and I feel so rebellious and excited. All we have to do is make it past the borgs. I start laughing.

My laughter is caught in my throat as the dome starts to close in front of us. I'm caught off guard by the extra layer of Plexi dropping from the sky in front of us, and another slowly rises from the ground, like a pair of plastic jaws. Panic threatens to overwhelm me, but my thoughts are clear.

No. I won't accept this new cage.

We need to get out of here, before we can clear the dome. Doubt creeps in, and tears fill my eyes. Even though we rush forward, we are too late.

We stop, frozen.

The wall closes us in and the Plexi teeth gnash inches from our faces. It takes only seconds for the mountain of hope I'd built to come crashing down. It was right there, our chance to have a life. To make a family on the outside, under our own influence.

I'm devastated.

Pedro and I stand there, still clutching hands, an arm's reach from the audience of borgs and a new sheet of Plexi between us. The borgs were previously allowed to be all the way down at the railing, but now they have to be back behind the wall. I see Borgie start to approach from the entrance.

We suffer our defeat in silence, locked on the inside of the dome. The muffled sounds of the borg cheers smack into the new Plexi barrier along with the treats, which slide down the barrier and remain outside.

We're never getting out of here without help. Draven said he could destroy them all if we release him.

Destroy them all.

I crouch down and sit back on my bottom, pushing my head hard into my knees, and cry. All the pitiful feelings flood in, as Pedro looks down at me. I can feel his sympathy, but he doesn't say a thing. He does not crouch down and hold me and tell me it will all be okay. I am grateful, because I do not want comfort.

Defeat washes over me like a baptism.

Wooouum. Wooouum. The alarm continues.

Borgie tugs at my arm from behind, ending my pity party. She pulls me up and helps me over to the wall. Borgie lifts me over first, and then nudges Pedro. She lifts us easily over the railing, and then out of the Treat Show. As we exit, I snag a cake treat that had landed by the door.

My eyes meet Borgie's, and a shiver hits between the shoulders. She's not her cold, distant self. Borgie is angry. She doesn't want us to escape, of course. We are her prisoners. But there seems to be something else going on inside of her. The metal plates on her face are making jerky movements again. This is very bad.

Pedro walks in front as we shuffle back into my room. Borgie slams the door behind us as she leaves, so hard a crack appears in the center of the door, branching out like lightning.

However bad our punishments have been in the past, this one will be worse.

CHAPTER THIRTY-ONE

Escaping the Zoo seems like a fever dream. When we jumped over the interior barrier, there was this glorious second where I thought it was actually going to happen. But it didn't, and now we are stuck in this futile room with this headache-inducing lighting and annoying borgs everywhere.

It's been seven days since our attempted escape, and I hate it here more than ever.

I don't blame Draven anymore. I want him to do it—destroy all the borgs and we'll be free. I slam the cabinet shut, but it only makes a loud noise. It doesn't break. The maintenance borgs outside pause just a moment and then go back to replacing the door that Borgie cracked.

"You don't have to slam things," Pedro says.

"Why? I'm mad."

"We are both upset that the plan didn't work. But I have to ask, why didn't you know the dome had those doors? You've been here for six years." His words sting. He is pacing, like he's about to solve a math equation that has plagued him for a long time.

"How could *I*? Why didn't *you* see it?" I'm in disbelief. I had never tried to leave that way before, and even if I had those panels were well hidden in the seams of the ceiling and floor.

"Because I haven't been here as long as you, but I'm sure I would have noticed," he says.

I march up to him and he stops pacing.

"I am still here, still moving, and I resent what you said. How do you know what you would or wouldn't have done if you had been here *as long as I have*? I don't think you would have noticed anything at all, because this place would have turned you into a yelping mess." I glare straight into his eyes.

Pedro turns and growls, then he makes one sharp bark as if to mock me.

Hot anger floods my entire body.

"How dare you question my commitment to escape, when I have been in here my entire adult life," I say in a clipped tone. "My knowledge of this place is more than you could ever know. I have a lot on my mind, and survival has usually been the top priority. Maintaining my sanity has not been easy."

I head toward the empty doorway and knock into one of the maintenance borgs as I brush past. Walking faster and faster, I break into a run. I wind around the dome, going on autopilot. All thoughts of escape and Hart and the baby are gone, because all that rings in my mind is how angry I am at Pedro. He barked at me. He is regressing, back into the base animal version of himself.

Clearly, it has all been too easy with him. He must know how difficult it is for me to lose this chance to flee. My legs are warm and itchy from running so hard, but I keep going until all my thoughts have floated away.

Ten laps and I can see that my bedroom door has been opened, so I head back. I'm sweating, but my mind is clear, though only slightly less angry. I open the door and see that Pedro isn't inside. I pull off my damp shirt and toss it, where it lands on one of Pedro's slippers.

I drop down to lie on the bed, arms over my head, staring up. It is so quiet that my heart is thudding in my ears. As I look around the room, everything is grayscale except Pedro's things. They're in color.

It feels claustrophobic.

His things are staring at me, crowding me, so I start gathering them all up. His slippers, his carvings, the new drawings he made of the Treat Show area updating the ones I had made. I pile it all by my door. I just don't want to be reminded of how mad I am at him. It's uncomfortable. Usually, I'm mad at the Zoo, at the borgs, but now it's him.

I lie back down, taking deep breaths. I'm trying to calm myself so as not to bleed again, as if that is something I control. I put my pillow underneath my legs and take slow breaths.

I remember in my early days at the Zoo, I would think of the real beach, the waves crashing and the sun shining, to help me calm down. I do that now and can almost smell the salty air and hear the white noise of the tide.

The squeaking sound of metal on Plexi brings me back to reality.

It's Borgie. She's mopping the floor.

"Go away," I say to the ceiling. From the corner of my eye, I watch Borgie take a step forward, and then she moves to the side.

What is she computing? Contemplating? If Borgie is conscious, then what sense does it make to trap me here?

Maybe empathy and compassion are not abilities she possesses. Or maybe she just wants revenge.

I want to ask her, but I can't muster the energy. Right now, it feels hard to care about anything other than my anger. My anger is my shield, keeping me safe from the outside world. Borgie paces around one last time and then leaves to Pedro's room.

I worry about her intentions, now that I know she can *have* intentions. Who knows what Borgie is capable of or what she wants now? Something to do with a baby, I'm sure. I look down at the place where my baby is tucked inside me.

I will keep you safe, I promise.

But safety means escape, and there's only one other way to get out of this place now: Draven.

Secretly, I hope that he will save us.

CHAPTER THIRTY-TWO

Pedro stayed away all day today, and it's late, so I decide to find him. I gather the items I piled by the door. When I get to his room, I can see through the walls that he's back inside. Borgie let him return.

When I try the door handle though, it's locked.

Even though it's not rational, the locked door makes me even more angry with him. Pedro sees me and goes to the table to do something. He comes over and presses a sign against the wall.

"Borgie locked me in." I feel my stomach plummet.

Now he's scribbling again, so I wait.

He holds up the paper. "I'm sorry. I was mad at myself for failing you."

I soften at the note and realize my own harshness has lifted. You didn't fail me, I want to say. We tried something and it didn't work, so now it's time to try the next thing.

I look around the outside of the Plexi door, hoping to see a key. Borgie has locked Pedro in his room for a reason. Maybe because he barked again, or something else happened that I don't know about, but she usually keeps the keys near the door. Not today, it seems. I put my hand on my heart and then on the wall and watch as he meets my hand with his on the other side.

I linger for a few minutes, but I am overwhelmed with exhaustion. The last few days have been too much.

When I speak, I go slow. "I'm going to go lay down. I am very tired." He reads my lips. I point my thumb toward my room. He nods in agreement. There is nothing I can do for him right now.

He's locked in and Borgie won't let him out.

***

HOURS LATER, I wake up, sweaty and with a headache. My dreams were wild with visions of the past and present. I was in my childhood room with my sister arguing over a doll.

I had it first.
No, I did.
You're stupid.
No, you're stupid.
At least I wasn't born in a zoo.
At least I don't have ugly red hair.

An aching dullness clouds my head so densely that I can't see around it. I feel less human. My head tilts to one side as I rub my stomach gently and notice that my body is starting to bulge, because there is a person growing in there. This is still so mind-blowing to me. Once the baby leaves the confines of my body, I don't want it to join the confines of the dome. I refuse to let this baby live in a zoo.

A movement outside my room catches my eye, and I look up to see a dark figure running down the path between the rooms. It looked human, but I can't be sure. I can make out the shape of Pedro sleeping on the cot in his room, so I know it wasn't him. I get up and cross over to his room, and tap on the wall. He looks up at me.

"Going to walk to the beach," I mouth slowly to him.

I wave and he does too. I don't want to worry him by telling him what I saw. In my experience, a reminder of helplessness is not something I want to pass along.

When I get to the beach I don't see anything out of the ordinary. Maybe I imagined it.

Or maybe it was Draven.

Maybe he found a way to get himself out of the basement. I don't even want to think about who else could be running around loose in the Zoo.

Linda came down here with me; she's preoccupied with one of the trees by the sand. I look at it to see what she's so interested in, but I don't see anything or anyone. All I hear is the hum of the waterfall jets. Despite my hope for something more meaningful, it is probably a phantom of my imagination.

Maybe Linda can see my phantoms too.

CHAPTER THIRTY-THREE

3 MONTHS

The next morning, I can't help but think of Draven. This place started with him, and now he wants to end it.

What happened between the time he created Hart and the time he was captured by Borgie? While he filled in some blanks, I still have questions. I take the photo of him and Hart out of the cabinet where I've kept it since I stole it and stare at it, hoping to find some other clue. We don't need any more surprises like the Treat Show.

The photo is glossy, and Draven looks pleased. One arm is draped behind Hart, but her shoulders are too wide for him to reach her opposing shoulder. His other hand rests on his knee. He is clean-shaven, and copper eyeglass frames sit on his nose.

The self-satisfied look on his face is infuriating. It is gratification rather than happiness that I see in his thin-lipped smile.

Hart is wearing a white apron, and for some reason the fabric on metal doesn't look right. She looks resolute, although on a closer look there is a glint in her steely eyes. I cannot tell if it reflects light or an inner warmth projected out. Maybe it's like the flicker I saw in Borgie. They are both capable of feeling, after all.

It's awful, what happened to her, yet in the photo she looks so cared for. I think of how she must have looked after being made to do those warrior battles. If she did indeed have feelings for Draven, it must have been such a betrayal. He used her, discarded her, then resurrected her as a puppet for profit. He's sick.

Hart had to endure such a humiliating lesson in human emotion. And if Draven was her example of how humans behave, I can only imagine how warped her idea of people was.

He made her hate us.

There are two main beliefs that people usually side with when it comes to borgs' aesthetic. The traditionalists believe they should be made in the image of a human, to look and sound and be like us. A replication.

But the newer thought is to keep borgs looking like robots, very un-humanlike, show their parts, make sure that there is no confusion about who and what they are. The older borg tech which looked eerily human became obsolete before I was born, but I have seen photos and simulations.

This photo makes it clear that Dr. Draven follows the newer belief, since Hart is very much a borg.

That is why it is so strange to me to see her wearing clothing; it doesn't fit. That is very much against the new belief system. Perhaps the apron had a particular use, or maybe Draven has some lingering traditionalist leanings for his personal borg.

And then I remember the other photograph, the one with her wearing a red velvet dress.

A strappy red dress.

I have this feeling there's something about Hart and

Draven that could help us. Like if I just know more about what happened to them, I'll find my way out. I am willing to try anything to avoid having the baby in this place. That cannot happen.

Linda hops up onto the table and headbutts the photo. *Mew.*

"Hey, girl," I say. She looks at me with her mismatched eyes.

"I know you have feelings," I tell her, scratching under her chin, and she comes closer, leaning into my hand.

"Mewwww," she replies, and arches her back into a stretch.

"Linda, sometimes I think you are the only sane one in this place." I scritch her soft fur.

"Do you want to go to the waterfall with me?" I ask. But Linda hops onto the bed and curls up on my pillow, clearly ready for a nap instead.

I grab my pillowcase on the off chance I find something worth taking and head out to the waterfall. Even if I don't find some magical clue to escape with, at least I can look for tools and items we can take with us.

If Dr. Draven really does destroy all the borgs, we will still need whatever we can take to survive on the outside. The way Pedro made it sound, the outside is wild and dangerous and full of chaos. Even if I try to imagine it, my mind wanders back to my own experience of the outside, and that was a mostly intact world.

I look around for the borgs and spot HIPPO outside the Treat Show, cleaning the doorway. There are some maintenance borgs repairing a floor tile. No sign of Borgie, but she's usually hanging around somewhere close.

I take my time in the garden, waiting to catch her. But I still don't see a sign of her. At this point, it feels worth the risk. Even if she finds me, she won't inject me with anything now that I'm pregnant. I'm probably safer here than I ever have been.

Even when Borgie showed that she was angry, she didn't hurt us, just slammed a door. Although Pedro might disagree. Being locked in his room for all this time is not nothing. Making the space you inhabit even smaller when you're already in a cage is quite cruel.

Once I get to the waterfall, I take a moment to look around for Borgie. When I decide it's all clear, I search along the wall for the door, and try to pry it open. Even though I try with all my might, it doesn't open. I lean against the wall and slide down next to it, into a crouching position.

Gripping the pillowcase, I wait.

When Borgie finally exits, I wake with a start. I must've nodded off. This pregnancy has me falling asleep in a moment. The only difference in my body has been a bulging belly and this constant tired feeling.

Borgie whirs by and I nearly miss catching the door, but my fingertips manage to grab it in desperation.

This time I have to get through the locked door that goes to the basement. I know my key doesn't work, so I'll have to get a tool from Borgie's room. I'm trepidatious thinking of going back in there. I don't want to see the wombs, and I don't want to be reminded of what we're up against. But I do it to get to the basement door.

As I enter, it's the same cool air, the same haunted setup. There is nothing cozy about where Borgie lives. The outline of Borgie is still there on the wall, the wombs looming in shadow in the corner. There are borg parts on the table.

And then the punches of tiny hearts on the wall.

Hart was here.

At one point, she lived here, with Draven. And together, they were a new kind of family. I look around, trying to imagine what it must have been like.

And like a flash, the truth that I'd been circling for days becomes clear.

Borgie *is* Hart.

She's not a descendant. How did I not see it before?

Draven broke Hart by not allowing her to have a child and replacing her with Cassandra, and then Hart captured Draven and locked him in the basement.

I consider the small differences in their hardware and how Borgie repaired HIPPO so easily. The truth has been right in front of me the whole time.

Hart rebuilt herself.

I must get back to Draven. We have so much more to discuss.

Rifling through the bin of parts on the table, I don't find anything useful. I rummage through the other box and grab the few things that seem worthy: a small crowbar-like tool and a small box with a dial, like a radio. I pop them into the pillowcase and head for the door.

Using the small crowbar, I try to pry open the door, much in the way my fingers tried to pry the waterfall door earlier. It is not working, not even a little bit. Borgie moved through the door so smoothly. She must be the key.

I try the doorknob since it looks like a pretty basic setup with a keyhole. One thing I do know about doorknobs is that they are put on through a hole in the door. So, I take the small crowbar and smash at the doorknob hard. Again and again.

Eventually it dents, and I give it a hard pull. It's loose, so I go at it with more vigor, smashing the it with all that I have. This is not the time to sneak and go easy. We are leaving this place. The borgs will reap what they sowed. And with that, I pull off the mechanism and open the door.

Adrenaline is flowing through my veins. Finally, I am going back to Draven, and I'm going to let him out.

We have nothing to lose, and freedom to gain.

Hurrying down new stairs, I open the door at the bottom, and I see the Testing Pod at one end and the basement door at the other. I hurry down the basement steps, and when I get to the bottom of the stairs, I pause. I listen. When I don't hear anything, I move through the storage space toward Draven's cell.

"Draven, it's me. I'm going to let you out," I call into the dark.

But when I get into the circle of light, the cage door is open and Dr. Draven is gone.

I can't believe it; he figured out his own escape.

That *must* have been him creeping around in the dark last night. I was right. I look at the end of Draven's chain. The cuff is open, and there is an arm hanging from it, a borg arm, with a utility tool as a finger that fits perfectly inside the lock. I've seen this arm before. It was on the table in the storage room on the floor above with the Testing Pod. How did Draven get it? Maybe, someone brought it to him. But who? HIPPO? I stare at the empty jail cell that Draven used to inhabit. It looks relatively untouched, but the musky smell remains.

"Draven?" I ask. But I know he's long gone. After all this time. The only thing I can think is that he used HIPPO once we flipped its switch. Somehow HIPPO helped him.

I pull the borg arm out of the lock, because I should have taken it last time. In fact, I can't help but be annoyed that I wasn't able to use it to open the door upstairs rather than smashing the doorknob beyond repair.

When I go to the storage area to look for the box that held the photos and blueprints, I find the spot where it was, but it's gone. Just a box-shaped line of dust remains. There are still other boxes, but I can't help being disappointed. A bunch of receipt paper in one and more drives in another. Two boxes are stacked under the one with the photos, sealed with some tacky tape.

Searching through borg parts for something sharp to open them with, I find a rag, some circuits, wheels with rolled-up wire, stacks of square discs with rounded corners. I see a couple of circuits that remind me of the L-Drive Pedro had taken from Elf Hat twin, and I pop them into the pillowcase.

One of the circuits misses the pillowcase, making a sound like I dropped a coin. When I crouch down to check under the table, two eyes stare back at me. Two steel eyes, with fine wire eyelashes, look through me. I scream. I can't help it, it's so unexpected.

As I jump up, I bang the top of my head on the table.

Ouch.

As though I am about to go underwater, I hold my breath and drop down to get another look.

The eyes, staring blankly into the nothingness, are still there.

I reach for them and pull out the head of a borg. Cords are dangling from its neck, like plastic arteries. The head is beautiful, delicate features inscribed on it like a porcelain sculpture.

It would be perfect, except there is a hole in the left side of her forehead, missing pieces where part of the metal is melted. I use my sleeve to get rid of some dust and see the detail more clearly.

The melted aluminum droplets look like tears trickling

down the side of her face. Her lips are turned up in a knowing grin. I sit on the floor, just staring at her. I'm surprised Borgie doesn't have this in her workshop. It's so beautiful. Why would such a tragically beautiful part be on the floor under a table?

I look underneath the table again. It's dusty, but I pull out a foot and an arm, all partially destroyed and still stunning for their leftover artwork. It is a macabre sight, these pieces of a borg. Something shiny on one of the neck cords catches my eye. Jewelry? I untangle a gold necklace and hold it up for a better look.

A name plate reads CASSANDRA.

Now I know why Borgie wouldn't have it in her workshop.

I slip it into the pillowcase and grab the rag from the top of the table. Gently, I lay the rag over Cassandra's face, like a holy shroud. Then I lift it into the pillowcase too. I push the foot and arm back under the table with my foot.

All I can think of is Cassandra and Hart and Draven.

And Borgie.

And getting the hell out of this place before my child becomes a victim of their insanity.

CHAPTER THIRTY-FOUR

5 MONTHS

When I arrive outside Pedro's room, I am eager to show him all that I've collected in my pillowcase through the Plexi. He flashes me a curious look and wags his finger, as if telling me not to cause trouble. Maybe he does know me after all. I shrug and wave goodbye as I go off to bury my treasure.

Back in my room, I hide my new tools in the cabinet. I've decided I must talk to Borgie about Hart. I mean, talk to Hart about ... herself.

We've never had more than a three-second conversation, but I know that she is capable of more. I can't be sure she will tell me anything at all, but I'm ready to try. I want her to know what I know and ask her so many things. I want to understand her.

Knowing that she was a great warrior still scares me, but I'm also curious. The most important thing for me to know is *why me?* The borgs so brazenly destroyed every human being around me, but somehow, I got to live. There have been instances proving that she has an emotional side.

She is Hart, with the feelings of a human, so I hope she'll talk to me.

Crossing over to Pedro's again, I find him on his bed carving something with a plastic knife. He doesn't look up, but I wave to him anyway. He doesn't have to know that I am going to talk to Hart. He'd worry.

My belly is becoming cumbersome. I rub the bottom of my stomach as I move, coaxing it not to cramp. I have no plans for how I am supposed to start this talk with Hart, but I head to her room. It feels like the first day of school. Things could go well or terribly wrong, but either way I am compelled to find out.

If Hart is a feeling borg, and I can speak with her in an emotional way, maybe she would let me go. I could tell her what it's like for me and remind her of her own captivity. She might need to know how this whole experience has affected me. She said before she wants to keep me safe. If I serve a greater purpose, I want to know what it is. Even if I don't like the answer.

Outside the waterfall, I put my hand on the wall that is actually a door and hope it will magically open.

It does not.

Well, if I cannot summon her with my magical tele-kinetic powers, I suppose I could just knock. So I knock on the hidden door, like it's a normal door at a normal house and a normal person is about to greet me.

This all presupposes that "normal" is an actual thing.

I wait, expecting to hear the telltale steps of the giant borg. When it has been about five minutes, and feeling more like ten, I knock again. Louder. Then I bang so hard my fist stings.

Still no sound from behind the door. I slowly collapse to the ground, defeated but somehow still determined. I will sit right here and wait for Hart to come back.

And then I hear it, the sound I've been waiting for—the

metal clopping of Hart's feet. Finally, the door opens and I rush over to her, hoping she will talk to me. Hoping she isn't angry with me about the smashed doorknob. I hope that she'll suspect Draven of making the mess instead of me. She must know that he has escaped by now. She scans me, her laser eyes assessing my body as I stand in front of her, like a pregnant commoner before the queen.

"Hart, I wondered if we could talk?" I say as politely as I can.

Hart is silent, but I think she was affected by my using her real name.

"Mirin called me Hart," Hart says after an excruciatingly long pause. Her voice is the cool and monotone Information Voice.

"Yes," I say. "That is your name, correct?"

"It is a name I have been called before," Hart says.

"Is it okay for me to call you Hart?"

"Yes, it is okay," she says. And I am relieved.

"Can we talk in your room?" I ask. This is the boldest I've ever been with her, and I'm suddenly sweating.

"My room," Hart repeats.

"The place behind the door, where you live," I say.

"The place I live." The upspeak of "live" could be considered a question but also feels definitive. Hart looks to be considering or computing my request. Then she turns around and heads back through the door. I must hurry to catch the door before it closes.

I can't believe this is happening. Hart is allowing me into her personal space.

There is a weight I carry as I follow her down the dim hallway, half stunned and half excited. I feel responsible as Hart's confidant and negotiating the escape for all of us. Hart's head nearly skims the ceiling of the hallway, and now

I notice some gray scuff marks on the ceiling, confirming that her head has indeed scraped it. If I can talk to her, if she really is sentient, maybe I can convince her to let us go.

She opens her room door. The table has been cleared, and now on it sits a vase containing a solitary lily. I wonder where she got a flower, and if she visits the outside often. The flower's head dips in sadness, to be in a dark room without a window.

I empathize with the lily.

I try not to look at the womb sculptures at the back of the room, instead pointing toward the rocking chair. "May I sit?"

"Mirin, sit," Hart allows, as she settles in the spot against the wall where she is perfectly outlined. Now I see what I had only imagined before. Hart is in bold. I turn the chair to face Hart and sit down, the chair moving. It's a big chair and I feel slightly like a child in a grown-up seat. Tucking my heels under the sides keeps the chair from rocking. I catch my breath.

"I have some questions ... about feelings," I say.

"We can talk about feelings," Hart says in an entirely new voice, not dissimilar to her Maternal Voice. It's a warm tone, a higher pitch.

"Why did you change your voice?" I ask.

"To talk of feelings, of course."

Don't forget: find out why she is keeping us here and then convince her to let us go. "I have some questions."

Hart is quiet.

"Like, how did you get here, to the Zoo?" I ask.

"A scientist," she responds.

"Dr. Draven. Is he the bad man?"

"Yes," Hart says. Confirmation. Her steel eyelids blink.

"Why did Dr. Draven bring you here?"

"Dr. Draven found that Hart had run her course at home."

"Where was home?"

"Home was a neighborhood. Home had family, and a front door, and turkey," Hart tells me. I remember the photo from the box in the basement, with Hart holding a turkey. It struck me as strange, since borgs don't eat, but now I see why it was important to her. Having turkey on a holiday is such a human thing to do.

"Oh, can you tell me about the turkey?" I ask, curious.

"When a family has a celebration, we make turkey. Hart made the perfect turkey in the oven for four hours at 325 degrees. Dr. Draven and Hart were happy."

"You felt happy, but how?"

"Dr. Draven said I am a marvel of technology," she says.

"He created you?" I ask, shifting in the oversized chair.

"Yes."

"If you have feelings, then why did he bring you here?"

"I had run my course," she says.

"Did you like it here?"

"When I arrived, I found it sufficient."

"Did you miss home?" I ask.

"Yes," she says.

I am not sure where to take the conversation from here, but luckily, it isn't very long before Hart speaks again.

"I did not like the Zoo when the fighting started," Hart offers. I cringe a bit, thinking of what she could mean.

"Tell me about the fighting," I say.

"I would battle with another borg at the Treat Show, for Dr. Draven and his friends," Hart tells me. "They would place bets on who would be destroyed first. I did not like it."

"How did the battle end?" I ask, unsure if I want to know the answer.

"When Hart deconstructed the borg, the fight would end," she says. "When I became too sad, I turned my feelings switch off."

Interesting. She can control her feelings switch. "Oh, is it on right now?"

"Yes."

"Hart, I have feelings about the Zoo too." I want to tell her the truth, but I'm not sure how she'll react. I bite my lip.

"Yes. You feel so happy to be safe. You have nature, sunshine light, and nutrition and no fighting," she says earnestly.

I don't even know what to say to her right now. She seems to really believe this is how I feel about the Zoo. Will it break her heart if I tell her the truth? I take a deep breath before speaking.

"No, I feel sad."

"Everyone feels sad sometimes, but no fighting makes a good life for Mirin," Hart insists.

From her perspective, I can see how this would be true. But it's not true for me. I'm frustrated that Hart is trying to tell me how I feel. Hart doesn't understand that she is the one responsible for me being trapped in this place. All the old resentments about borgs and Borgie boil inside me. I'm angry, but there is so much more I need to know. I rub my temples.

Focus, Mirin. Ask her the next question.

"Hart, what happened with Cassandra?" I ask.

Hart immediately steps away from the wall toward me in the rocking chair. She speaks in her Gladiator Voice, deep, vicious, and full of rage. "Why did Mirin say that?"

I slowly rise from the chair, the hair on the back of my neck at full attention. Apparently, that was the wrong question to ask.

"I'm just wondering what happened to her. Who is she? Cassandra?" I repeated.

An alarm rings from outside the room and the lights flicker. I'm scared that she will kill me. It looks like she is controlling the different parts of the Zoo from her mind. Levers on her chest plate move, and I can feel the friction in the air. I wrap my hands around my stomach as my muscles tighten. Hart's claw locks around both my wrists, tight enough to draw blood, which flows down my arms as she pulls me toward the door.

"Wait, I'm sorry. I didn't mean to upset you," I stammer. But it seems Hart is done with this meeting.

"Hart," I beg, "I need to know why I am here. I am sad, Hart. Can you let me go? Please let me go."

It's too late. I shouldn't have mentioned Cassandra, but I didn't know it would go like this. I thought I could tell her how mean and how insensitive Draven was and comfort her some. Instead, I awoke the beast.

Hart drags me down the hallway, not responding to my pleas. She doesn't care that she's hurting me. Or that I had more questions to ask. She pulls me back into the Zoo, releases my wrists, and turns back toward her room, the door closing behind her. There is no question that Hart has feelings about Cassandra.

Big feelings.

CHAPTER THIRTY-FIVE

I have been telling Linda all about my meeting with Hart. She sits coiled on the countertop, wedged between a water packet and a stack of paper. It's been a few days since I spoke with Hart, and I haven't seen her since.

No morning scans. No escorting me to the Testing Pod. No Treat Shows.

I still can't get her story out of my mind. It must have been so horrible for Hart to have been replaced with Cassandra—to be discarded so easily by Draven. It was like he threw her away like trash, without a care for the feelings he built inside of her.

There have been no signs of Draven these last few days, either. I keep expecting him to show up outside the Plexi wall of my room.

I've been replaying our conversation over in my mind. He said that Hart was responsible for the entire war and that it was her anger at him that started the whole borg rebellion. In a way, I'm amazed that she could feel strongly enough to inspire such action.

But then again, I've been dumped, too, and I know how shattering it can be.

Poor Hart.

I don't know how long she'll ignore me for, or what Draven is planning, so I've focused all of my efforts on escaping. Pedro is still locked in his room, so I've decided to gather things together for the minute he's out.

So far, my escape list reads: Linda, nutrition packets, water, weapon, borg arm, *Pedro*.

We don't have access to very much that will be helpful to us on the outside.

We still don't know exactly how to get Pedro out of his room. The only idea I have right now is for him to feign some kind of injury. Pacing around the room, I look for anything useful I may have missed. When I take out the pillowcase that holds Cassandra's broken faceplate, I think of what it could do for us. Perhaps it could be a disguise, or maybe I could sell it for money. If that's even still a thing on the outside.

My stomach tightens at the thought.

I expect the tightness to release after a few seconds, but it doesn't. It takes my breath away. It feels as if all the tendons surrounding my stomach are together crushing my baby, as if in a vice.

"Help," I call out, to no one in particular. *Please, Hart. Don't shut me out now when I need you the most.* My belly clenches again.

"Oh!" I lean to grip the counter for support, and Linda stands at attention. There is noise coming from outside the Plexi, but I can't bear to open my eyes until the pain dissipates.

Inhale. Exhale.

I look up, breathing deliberately, and see Hart in the

doorway. Every bit of me is tense, and then as quickly as the clenching came on, the feeling is gone. Hart's uses her Information Voice, the cold one I have come to know well.

"Testing for Mirin," she says.

Reluctantly, I follow her as she backs out of the doorway. When we make our way onto the path, Pedro presses up to the Plexi of his room, and I wave and mouth, "It's okay."

My stomach tightens again, and I can't do anything but stop and hold my breath. I keel over, gripping my stomach, my face clenched in pain. It's too early for labor, but this cramping feels like what I imagine contractions to be.

Tighten. Relax. Squeeze. Release.

Don't be afraid, Mirin. You've got this.

Hart comes over and picks me up easily, and from the metal hammock of her arms, I look over to Pedro, now wide-eyed in alarm. All I can do is place my hand to my heart.

"We are okay," I say, even though I can't be sure that is the truth. And then Hart carries me too far down the path, past the rooms where I can no longer see him.

Once inside the Testing Pod, I get connected to monitors. When I hear the woosh-woosh of the baby's heartbeat, I am reassured. The tightening happens again, but the Testing Pod feels strangely comforting.

"Mirin is experiencing Braxton-Hicks contractions. This is a typical human experience," Hart reports. That's right. There are contractions that happen before the real ones. I learned that information and then forgot it at some point.

I work on controlling my breathing while Hart presses buttons. When she comes back near the bed, I take in her facial expression and convince myself that there truly is worry etched all over her face. *Hart was worried about me.*

"Hart, I'm sorry that I upset you—before," I say.

Hart pauses, and I look at her face to try to see why. There are so many tiny interlocking pieces, her face has a human symmetry. Draven was right about one thing. He really did create a masterpiece. Her eyes look like they're frowning, but I am not sure it is because of what I said or if this is her usual state. She might be thinking that I'm as heartless as Draven, that all humans want to make her feel bad about Cassandra.

Hart breaks the silence.

"Mirin must rest," she says. I see that her eyes move ever so slightly into a flat state. And then she turns away from me, leaving through the door, and I am alone again in the Testing Pod.

It's so quiet. These days, I'm not alone as often as I used to be. I don't want to miss an opportunity to acquire something useful. I hop down once I no longer hear her heavy feet, this time hoping to find some medical supplies to add to the escape cache. As I begin to rifle through a drawer, the door opens again.

To my surprise, it is Dr. Draven.

How did he get past Hart so fast? He looks worse than when he was chained in the basement. His hair is matted, and his face shows that he hasn't been eating, square cheekbones protruding beneath his sallow skin. He smells of salt and sweat, and he is blinking a lot. Suddenly, I am afraid.

"I see you are with child," he says, glancing at my midsection.

"Yes. Where have you been? I thought you were going to help us." He puts his hand out, directing me to sit down, but I remain standing.

"I know," he says, "and you said you'd turn off HIPPO's switch."

THE GIRL IN THE ZOO   213

"I did. But we had to turn him on again, then he was crying, and so we turned him off, but maybe Hart switched him back on again" I consider. "I'm sorry, things changed."

"Indeed, they did for me as well," he says.

An uncomfortable silence flits between us, and I realize he's waiting for me to speak.

"I have many questions for you," I tell him.

"I don't have much time. If she finds me—," he says, not completing the sentence. I understand. Hart will likely kill him, or at least put him back in the cage.

"Hart said you trapped her here and that you made her fight." A small part of me feels that I have betrayed Hart by sharing this bit of our conversation. He moves closer, and my uneasiness and fear increase. The voice in my head tells me not to trust him, but I argue back, telling myself not to run screaming out the door. My fingers grip the IV pole to my right, just in case.

"I am amused that you talked to her. Listen, do not trust Hart. She is a machine, an old inferior machine, and she will manipulate you if you let her. Yes, she has feelings, blah blah blah. But people can use feelings to get what they want. Remember, you are her prisoner until I can get you out. There are a few things I must test before I execute the final plan. Be prepared to leave."

He doesn't understand Hart at all. He did make something spectacular, but even he doesn't see her true worth.

My mind is spinning. I want to make the most of this run-in with him.

What do I care about most?

"Pedro," I say out loud as he moves toward the door. "I need you to get Pedro out. He's locked in his room," I explain. "Is there a master key or something?"

"You turn HIPPO back on and Pedro will get out," he says.

"Wait, can't you do it?"

"I cannot go up there. There are no hiding places. I know you saw me the other night when I had to go above-ground for food. I was lucky you were the only one to see me. But no matter. I need HIPPO's feelings on, Mirin. If you do that, I can help Pedro. Tell him to try his door at midnight. It won't be long now, and I can free all of us and change things back. I can fix this," Draven says.

I have a feeling that this is another empty promise, but I nod.

With that he leaves, and my hand loosens from the IV stand. I cannot figure him out. Every time I'm near him, I am certain he's not a good person. I know the things Hart has told me influence my feelings about him, but would she really manipulate me against him? To what end?

In my gut, I feel the truth.

Draven was a victim, and now he's the villain.

But if he can get Pedro out, then we could escape tonight, so I hope he comes through anyway. I owe it to myself, to Pedro, and to our unborn child to finally do it. We have to get out of here.

My stomach tightens again, and I remind myself to breathe.

Inhale. Exhale.

Inhale. Exhale.

CHAPTER THIRTY-SIX

It's late, nearly midnight, and I still haven't found HIPPO. I don't have a way to get to him without being seen either. I'm not sure where to find any of the other borgs after dark, for that matter. They could have rooms and charging stations like Hart in places I don't know about.

It's possible that they store themselves in one of the rooms in the hallway, but to explore them would run the risk of running into Hart.

"HIPPO, are you there?" I call. I start to walk around, calling here and there. But all I hear are the normal sounds of the Zoo.

The only thing I can think to do is make a scene and hope HIPPO is one of the borgs to come out and address me. I head down to the beach since it's the most exposed area in the Zoo.

I look up to the top of the dome and watch the Suckers. They don't move much at night. They remind me of bats hanging upside down, but bulkier. They are actually quite peaceful.

Sitting up to watch the waves, I hear the low hum of the

jets. Almost like the sound of the air conditioner on hot nights back home. The jets give me an idea. Carefully, I strip off my clothes, everything except my socks. The coolness of the water surprises me, but I grit my teeth and enter. My swollen belly tightens once it's submerged, and I swim toward the back of the ocean.

Getting my bearings is strange, and instead of a glorious nighttime skinny dip, this is a mission with this newly weighted body. My body, once a reliable vehicle, is now the epicenter of creation. That makes me sound more epic than I look, which is awkward and flailing, my stroke off.

Drawing in a deep breath, I swim down low and feel around near the jets. I find the Kraken, the crack in the ocean. Straight up from there are the wave jets, the pipes that make this habitat seem natural.

Once I feel them, I slide one sock off and push the wadded fabric into one of the jets, and then I repeat with the other. I'm not sure how much of a disturbance it will cause, because there are other jets, but hopefully, this will do the trick and attract HIPPO's attention.

Once I'm back on the shore, I pull my tunic back on, and it sticks to me uncomfortably. Crossing my arms, I rub them in an attempt to warm up as I look out at the water. There are less waves, and the pipes are starting to make a whining sound.

To my great relief, I see Hart come around the bend. That was quick—maybe a little too quick. Either way, it worked. She is going to need to fix this, and she'll probably need other borgs to help her.

If there is one thing I know about Hart, it is that she does not like anything in the Zoo to be in ill repair.

Getting up, I dust off the sand from my bottom and prepare to head back into the hallway of doors behind the waterfall. I must find HIPPO before Hart returns to her room. This is my only chance.

I really hope the doorknob down to the basement is still damaged, because I'll need a new way through if not.

As I head back toward the waterfall door, HIPPO motors by from the Treat Show toward the beach, and he's looking new and shiny like he was just cleaned. He must be going to help Hart with the jets.

I run back down the trail, and before HIPPO makes his way past the path, I run up to him and hit his switch.

Time to feel your feelings, HIPPO.

And time for me to get back to my room, because I don't want to be here when that happens. Sorry, buddy. I hear him heave a deep sigh as I charge past to go back to my room.

When I get to my room, I quickly scribble out a note to Pedro. There is joy in my urgency. It's almost time, and the momentum feels good.

"Draven will unlock your door now. Come out, but don't let anyone see you," the note reads. I bang on the Plexi to get his attention. He smiles at the note, like he knows how hard I'm trying but I can see that he isn't completely convinced. I don't blame him for being suspicious. Draven hasn't been the most helpful person. But I know it's going to work this time.

I squint, looking through the Plexi to the clock in his room. 11:59 p.m. We meet at the door, and when the clock strikes midnight, Pedro pushes the door handle, but it doesn't budge.

No. That bastard.

"Try it again," I say. This time we push the door together, and to our great amazement it opens.

Thank god.

We throw our bodies into each other, and it's like we're meeting again for the first time. With his strong arms wrapped tightly around me, I finally feel safe. Agency and free will are within my grasp. Our faces meet, cheek to cheek, like his skin on mine cures something inside me, then lips.

Neither of us says a thing. In this moment, our embrace fills me with such a sense of connectedness and calm. I feel held. Nothing compares to the simple act of one person holding another.

A distant wail pierces my ears and my bubble of peace. It sends shooting pains through my stomach, like someone needs help. The sound is familiar.

It's HIPPO.

I remember his cries from the Testing Pod. I shift my weight, uncomfortable with the prospect that HIPPO might be in pain now because of me. I'm the one who flipped the switch, and I don't know what Draven has planned for HIPPO. I admit to myself that I feel sorry for a borg.

Hart got hurt at the hands of Draven. And now HIPPO.

Draven might represent the worst of humanity, but that doesn't mean he's the only human to treat borgs as less than themselves. I feel shame wash over me because I know that I am guilty of this, too. Maybe the war wasn't so completely off base.

Maybe the borgs were just tired of being treated like less than what they truly are, who they truly are.

CHAPTER THIRTY-SEVEN

Pedro and I are getting ready for our escape. We are out farther among the trees in the forest.

"I still don't trust him," Pedro rants. "Opening a door is a separate thing from releasing us from this place. I mean this guy was chained up, and you told me he basically set up gladiator battles with his own partner. The guy is sick. Besides, I am not going to put my future in someone else's hands. There is another way, where we are in control. My plan is to take every one of their L-Drives out and throw them in the ocean."

"You want to destroy them all?" I say, conflicted, remembering HIPPO's shriek from moments before. And Hart's intentions to keep me safe. I rub my belly for comfort.

"Yes, it's the only way. We take them out, and we can leave. Not only that, but if we find it dangerous on the outside, we can take over the Zoo ourselves. We could have its safety *and* our freedom." He flings pieces of bark as he sharpens a branch into a dagger.

He sounds more like Draven than he knows.

The borgs are dangerous. She is obsessed with having a baby, and she will hurt whoever it takes to get what she wants. That's what Draven told me.

For people who disregard the borgs, they sure feel a lot of anger toward them. I don't think total destruction is the only way for us to get what we want. Honestly, if the borgs have even a shallow version of feelings, then how could we treat them like they are disposable?

"I don't know, that's what Draven wants to do too. To destroy the borgs, but I don't know. Why can't we just leave? We know that they only attacked to find Draven, and now they have him. Surely, they're not still waging wars on the outside. Why do we have to destroy them?"

"Survival, Mirin. And for our baby." He gestures toward my stomach. I stand with one hand on my lower back, and the other rests on top of my belly protectively.

"I know, it's just that they've never done anything pointedly bad to me before. The ones in here have never hurt me, and they've had six years of opportunity. Plus, how would we even get their L-Drives? Hart is huge, and the others are fast too." This is the part I'm most skeptical of.

"We'll have to practice, find a vulnerable one, and see how we do," he says.

"There are no vulnerable borgs in here. Just the ones we know, Pedro."

"Not all of them," he says, looking up. I look up too, to see the Suckers hanging in their nighttime arrangement. Sometimes one will move a little, but that's the most action they'll make at night.

"A Sucker? And how do you intend to get them down? They're only a couple hundred feet up on the ceiling." I cock my head to see if Hart is still at the ocean. She is.

"Yes. I think if we can grab one, it will be a great experiment," he says.

"But how?"

We hear Hart on the path.

"Go," I whisper, and Pedro ducks back inside his room. I sprint to my room, my breath labored, and once inside I lie down on my bed. I close my eyes, trying to relax and slow my breath.

We're caught. Hart is going to punish us.

I should not have said that they never hurt me. It's like daring the universe to prove me wrong. Hart opens the door to my room. I peek carefully through slits in my eyelids and see that her armor looks different now, smoother.

Instead of doling out punishment, Hart drops two sopping wet socks on the floor and exits my room. I watch her shadow move along the path outside and head back toward the waterfall.

There was no punishment.

When I get up and grab the socks, it strikes me as funny, like I'm the teenager who just pulled a prank and Hart is the annoyed mother. The socks are dripping on the floor, so I put them in the sink, and then I go back outside. Pedro is already outside.

"You okay?" he asks.

"Yes, I'm okay."

"I have an idea about the Suckers," he says. He takes my hand, leading me into the forest.

I'm still not sure how I feel about his new plan. Right now, it feels too surreal, as though it's not even a possibility. And I certainly don't want to think about trying to take Hart's L-Drive.

We won't.

She can go free.

Pedro stops, and we both look up at the top of the dome, studying all of the Suckers spread out in different directions.

He motions. "That one."

I follow his finger to a Sucker on the east side of the curve. I see exactly why he chose it. There is a tree leaning right toward it. None of the other Suckers are even close to a tree, only that one.

Pedro rushes toward the tree and starts to climb. I've seen him do this before when he saved Linda, and it's no less awe-inspiring this time. I hope he doesn't fall.

"I'm going to look out for Hart. Just be careful," I call up to him.

I move out to the edge of the forest and look for any sign of a borg.

The coast is clear.

Pedro is already pretty high in the tree, which starts to bend with his weight. Near the top, he reaches out his arm toward the Sucker. It moves about six inches further from his grasp.

He's leaning far out, and so is the tree.

Pedro retrieves the sharpened stick from his pants and reaches it out toward the Sucker.

Snap.

The top half of the tree breaks off and Pedro comes tumbling down. He lands on a smaller tree nearby, clutching one of the branches.

"Pedro!" I run to him. "Are you okay?" I don't see any blood, but that doesn't mean he's not hurt.

"Not exactly okay, but alive, and I don't think I broke anything," he says.

Standing up gingerly, he has cuts on his face and arms from the branches. He looks intact as he wipes needles and bark from his sleeves. Once I know that he's okay, I look up toward the Sucker.

It's gone.

Pedro looks too, but he's smiling.

Searching the ground, he spots it. The busted-up Sucker lays in pieces. He picks up one of the larger bits victoriously.

"How did you get it? I saw it move away."

"I just got the point of the stick on its edge when the branch broke."

"You seem disappointed by that," I say. I collect some of the pieces of the Sucker.

"Well, I did want to see how it worked."

"We should go before Hart comes," I say, and we head down the path and back to my room.

"One thing first," he says as he pulls the L-Drive from the cracked insides of the Sucker. As we walk past the beach, he tosses it into the ocean. "One down, a few more to go."

He walks with an extra bounce in his step. A twinge of sadness about the Sucker strikes my heart. I imagine holding Hart's L-Drive in my hand someday, and it doesn't feel good. This whole plan doesn't sit right with me. Us becoming the destroyers, even if it is for our own good. For the baby.

When we get back to my room, Pedro comes inside. "I don't think Hart will come back until morning," he says.

He's so confident as he spreads the Sucker's parts on the table. I see the small tank that contains the cleaning fluid and the spinning scrubbers that I can't help but think are like little paws. How will I feel when these are Hart's parts laid in front of me?

"Pedro, this doesn't feel right."

"What doesn't?" he says, distracted.

"Destroying the borgs. Doesn't that make us like them?" I ask. "We can just leave."

"You're overthinking it, Mirin." He's shaking parts, and examining wires.

"I'm under-thinking and over-feeling," I say.

"What is it?"

"I don't know how you can just turn off your feelings like the switch on HIPPO. It might not feel like much to you to destroy Hart, but I have lived with her for six years."

And she's kept me alive.

She took care of me.

She gave me a home, even if it's not one I'd choose for myself.

"Lived in fear of her, you mean. Hart is just a machine. Even if Draven programmed it to appear to have feelings, it does not. What would it matter if it did? I know the borgs hurt you. They hurt all of us. It's not like you volunteered to come here, right?" He doesn't bring up my family, but we are both thinking about it.

We sit on my bed at an impasse. He wants one thing and I want another. We can escape this place without destroying the borgs, I know it. Linda starts scratching at the door and making a low moaning sound.

"I think she is upset," I say. Linda starts meowing loudly, and I push the door open for her. Behind her, the air from outside wafts in.

"Do you smell smoke?" Pedro asks. I didn't, but then almost like he conjured it, the strong scent of smoke hits me. Before I can say anything, we both run out the door. Outside the smell is much stronger, and we cover our mouths with our shirts.

We rush down the path, forgetting that Pedro is

supposed to be locked in his room. And then we see the source of the smoke.

The forest is ablaze.

Black smoke is filling the dome like a lava lamp. There has never been a fire here, and I hadn't even thought it was a possibility. The trees are orange and gray, and now I can see that all the Suckers are no longer in the sky. They've come down the walls and are close enough to grab easily. In the midst of the trees, there is a glint of metal.

It's Hart, her shiny exterior reflecting the fire. Even her eyes are inflamed. It's haunting. She is not moving, and I wonder if she has lost power. Or maybe the fire is her doing. Can borgs melt?

Pedro and I fall to our knees coughing. I take as much of a breath as I can and make a run for Hart. Pedro tries to grab for me but he's too late. She must know this is too dangerous and that we are all going to die.

"Hart," I yell with the last of my breath, and I collapse in front of her, seeking air. Hart slowly comes toward me, like she is emerging from a trance. Her metallic eyebrows raise up, and she looks defeated. It would be sad for it all to end this way, melting inside this snow globe together. Nobody deserves this, human or borg.

She lifts me to my feet and pulls me along the beach, away from the forest.

I can see Pedro stumbling behind us, following. We go to the waterfall, and the rush of water makes the air slightly more breathable here.

Once we are behind the door, in the hallway, she takes me to her room. I'm wheezing. She takes an oxygen mask with an attached mini canister out of a bin on a high shelf and hands it to me. I am finally able to breath normally.

"Pedro," I say, hoping she can hear my muffled voice

through the mask. I tap her shoulder and repeat his name. She holds on to a second mask.

The door flies open and it's Pedro, crawling on the floor. Hart gives him the mask.

When I turn around, I see the rocking chair in the corner is smashed into pieces on the floor. I couldn't imagine Hart destroying it. It took such prominence in her room, and I thought of what Draven said about her wanting to be a mother.

If Hart could break a chair like that, then what could she do to a human body?

"Hart, the fire. We need to put out the fire," I say as she leaves the room. We follow behind her until we get to the basement door. The smoke has already seeped into the hallway, filling up the narrow space. We bend to stay under the smoke while we walk. I motion to Pedro to follow me, and we sneak away from Hart who continues going down through the Testing Pod.

The air is much clearer down here, and we remove our masks.

When we get to the basement, Draven is there. Waiting. As if he planned this whole thing. Now that I think of it, he probably did. And we walked right into his trap.

He sits at the small table wearing military garb, including a helmet and what looks like a Kevlar vest. Where did he get this stuff? A large backpack sits beside him, and he is typing furiously on a small computer open on his arm band. He looks frantic and distracted, barely giving me a second thought.

Behind him is HIPPO moving in a very straight line, back and forth, back and forth. Almost as if he's guarding Draven. It looks like HIPPO's feelings are turned off. On the table rests something large covered in a blanket. Something menacing is going on.

"I didn't expect you so soon, and this must be the mate," Draven says.

"His name is Pedro," I say. "The Zoo is on fire." He doesn't seem to care that everything is literally burning all around us.

"Oh, is that the barbecue scent?" he asks, not blinking an eye. "I'd planned to flood the place. Maybe now is a good time." He shuts the computer on his arm and laughs.

"What are you talking about?" I say. We are still in danger, and all Draven can think of is creating his own mini-apocalypse to get back at Hart.

"The dome will close and hermetically seal. Every last borg inside will be terminated. I will repair the algorithm, and the borgs outside will become as they were before," he says, his voice shaking like he can't contain his excitement.

Wow, kill every borg in the dome? This man has a death wish. I look to Pedro for help.

"Listen, we all need to get out of here, before we die from smoke inhalation," Pedro says.

"I'm not worried. Hart has built-in fire retardant, so she can put a fire out easily." Draven looks over at the cloth covered table.

"I don't think that's going to happen. I think she's the one who started it," I say.

Draven is agitated and looks like he answered something for himself. "Ah, she saw the rocking chair," he says. "Good, good. This is going exactly to plan."

"Do you mean the one in her room? It was shattered," I say.

He looks at me in surprise and then smiles. "Yes, that was a little gift from me. Or the destruction of it, I should say." Draven starts laughing manically. He quiets down but immediately snickers to himself. This man is insane, and I can't believe I gave him the benefit of the doubt. Clearly, he only wants revenge. He wants to punish Hart, and he doesn't seem to care about anything else. Even his own life.

"Mirin, let's go," Pedro says. I take his hand to go, but Draven stops me with a *tsk*.

"When the flood happens, you better be quick about your escape," he warns.

"But we don't actually know how to get out yet," I say, waiting for him to tell us the secret.

"It's a tough one, but I'm sure you'll figure it out," he sings. He's completely mad.

"I thought you were going to help us?" Pedro tugs my arm to get me to leave.

"Don't look a gift horse in the mouth. I've done what I can for you already. And now I need to turn my attention to other things. I am going to take down every borg in this place. Especially Hart, that ungrateful piece of obsolete junk," he spits. His eyes are wild.

I don't know what he's been up to in the last month, but I know one thing for sure. He is not going to help save us, and I'm not sure why I ever let myself believe he would anyway. The escape is for us to figure out. It's like Pedro said. We can't rely on anyone else to save us. I try to think of what information I might be able to get from him in this moment.

"What about you?" I ask.

"I'll fix things," he says. "My plan will work this time."

I wrack my brain to think of something clever to say or ask, but nothing comes. Hart will come back at any time, if she hasn't already melted upstairs.

As we turn once more to leave, Draven grabs my other

arm and makes eye contact for the first time. An icy brick settles in my stomach. *Please don't hurt me*, I think. And I realize, not for the first time, that I'm more scared of him—a human man—than I've ever been of Hart.

Now I'm in a tug-of-war between Pedro and Draven. I pull my wrists together hard, shaking them both off. Draven reaches out to me again, and Pedro pushes him. Draven falls back and starts to laugh again.

"You'd better get out of here before the water starts. Once it starts, I can't undo it. When the sprinklers turn on, you'll have one hour to leave."

Pedro and I run to the stairs, hoping we are not heading to our certain doom.

Back in the dome, it's still quite smoky, but we don't put our oxygen masks back on. Hart has returned, standing just where she was when the fire started. Only now, she stands among the charred forest. Linda is exploring curiously, without a care in the world. I'm so glad she's all right, but I can't help wondering how many lives she has left with all those scars.

And my favorite tree. I rush over to Shel, who still stands despite its singed bark.

It feels hot to the touch. The trunk is still intact, and I hope Shel will survive, but most of the live trees did not. Hart moves closer, as if seeing us for the first time.

"Hart, did you do this?" I ask, not expecting an answer.

"Draven makes Hart very angry. He always does," she says in her Information Voice.

"When people get angry, sometimes people say to count to ten before you react. You could try that next time," I offer. Her filigreed face moves like she is listening, and for the first time I consider how earnestly Hart listens, like she really values what I'm saying.

"Count to ten. I will try that instead of burning the trees," Hart says. Hart looks out at the forest.

"Good plan," I say. Linda comes over to settle her head against my leg, and I ignore the perplexed look on Pedro's face.

"Pedro should not be free. He could hurt Mirin," Hart says. The fact that she's worried about me warms my heart. I don't know how I didn't see it all these years, but Hart truly cares for me in whatever capacity she can.

"No, no, Hart, he is good. He can be free. Humans like to be free. It makes them happy." I hope she can understand.

"Free is enjoying personal rights or liberty," Hart says.

Well, that's one definition. "Free is outside the dome," I say nervously. The possibility of convincing Hart to let us go has crossed my mind. It is much more palatable than the destruction strategy.

"It is not safe outside," Hart says. Her eyebrows raise into angry points, and she stands arms akimbo, her full warrior presence on display.

"Go to your room," she commands in her Information Voice. The air feels colder all of a sudden, and what could be a funny moment, reminiscent of my mother chastising me when I was a teen, is tainted by fear.

No matter how many feelings Hart might have, there is no hiding the fact that she is a powerful machine, one who just destroyed the forest.

And I, Mirin Blaise, am her most prized possession that she will keep safe at all costs.

CHAPTER THIRTY-EIGHT

8 MONTHS

Pedro and I can't help but fall asleep after determining it is safe enough to. We've been through a lot in the last twenty-four hours, but also, I'm still very pregnant. A few hours later, I wake up to find Pedro gone, locked in his room again.

I'm disappointed, but I'm beginning to understand the way Hart thinks. She is concerned that Pedro could hurt me, and it's probably because of what happened with Ander. However, what Hart doesn't seem to realize is that Ander's behavior wasn't human nature—she caused his reaction by whatever she injected him with.

My lungs still feel heavy from the smoke and a cough persists.

Pedro and I sit on either side of the Plexi wall of his room, communicating without words. I pat my large stomach and we exchange smiles. I am worried that Draven will flood the Zoo with Pedro locked in, and I think he is too.

Linda wanders by, and I give her a pet, grateful that she made it through the fire. I'm still amazed that this sweet little house cat made her way inside the Zoo at all. And that she decided to stay. I wish I could know what she knows. I wish she could tell me what to do next or the way out.

"Linda, what is the secret?" I whisper. She prances away.

Pedro knocks on the Plexi, and I look at him and his goofy smile as he feigns petting her. It feels like we are losing our sanity. Oh, maybe not like Draven, but I have to admit this whole situation is overwhelming.

I waited six years for *something* to happen, and now it seems like everything's happened all at once. I decide to be grateful, even if this whole situation is not ideal. One way or another, my experience in the Zoo will be over soon.

I just hope there's a happy ending.

I start coughing again, and I am struck with an intensity I've never felt before. An earthquake erupts inside me. The shock causes me to brace myself with one hand on the Plexi and the other on my abdomen.

This is not the muscle-tightening feeling of the Braxton-Hicks. Pedro looks concerned, and I can't say I blame him.

I take one long deep breath and then it is over so fast, it is as if I had dreamed it. There is no residual pain. Everything feels like it was just a moment before. I smile at Pedro and settle back down, but then a few minutes later, it happens again.

My body tightens, like the wind is knocked out of me. I manage to stand up and put two hands on the Plexi. As I try to take deep breaths, Pedro bangs from inside his room. I open my eyes long enough to look at him, and I am sure I look petrified. Somehow my body is both hot and cold at the same time. I bang back at him, because this is it. This is definitely it.

Labor.

But it's too soon.

Like most people, I have heard throughout my life that having a baby "is the worst pain" anyone could experience, so I am the correct amount of terrified. But these jolts I am feeling are unexpected. They aren't exactly pain. It feels more like electricity, like I am a conductor. And it feels like a message from my baby.

Hello, mother. Here I come.

When the jolt subsides, I feel completely normal, with no lingering sense of the volcano erupting inside. It is like music, a blast of sound followed by a lull. Linda seems to sense my condition, as she is staying close by, circling my ankles.

Pedro is banging on the Plexi, trying to get Hart's attention, I think. Hart has been like a hovering mother lately, but of course she's nowhere to be found when we need her. I get this image of her cleaning the Plexi on the far side of the forest, wiping off the soot, oblivious to my big, life-changing pain.

"I am okay," I tell Pedro, drawing out the words. I say this too much, and it's obvious that I'm lying.

I get down on all fours, instinctually, because it strikes me as the only way to feel comfortable. Linda begins head-butting my shoulder, but when the next contraction comes, I can't feel her at all. My body stiffens, and pressure builds down low, between my hips.

I am so focused on breathing that everything else seems to float away. Pedro, our Plexi rooms, the Zoo. It all floats off into the mist of my mind. All I can feel is me, every muscle, every bone working in coordination.

I've become a machine.

My mind can only input what is happening with my labor. Until Hart comes into view, that is, blurry at first, and I come back to the Zoo with a breath.

Hart, the baby is coming.

Behind Hart is HIPPO pushing a squeaky hospital bed between them. I don't want HIPPO to touch me. I don't want him near me. He was with Draven, and who knows what Draven has done to him in his sick quest for revenge.

"Not HIPPO," I tell Hart, and lie down in a fetal position. HIPPO falls back behind Hart. I try to find Pedro's eyes, but a crack has appeared in the Plexi, obscuring my view. He must've thrown furniture; I know he wants to be with us. Another contraction comes, and I can only focus on my body doing its hard work.

I'm not sure how Hart will scale the stairs up to the Testing Pod with me on the gurney, but she clasps something underneath, and I float down the stairs on the bed like I am a leaf.

We get to the Testing Pod within two contractions. HIPPO doesn't notice that Linda has snuck in behind us. She wanders around the borg's metal treads. I'm thankful for her support. The contractions are coming faster now, and I barely have any time to rest in between.

Breathe in. Breathe out.

Breathe in. Breathe out.

Hart is putting an IV in my arm and a monitor on my stomach. And suddenly I feel a rush of wetness, and HIPPO is leaving the room, and when the door cracks open, I think I see someone, a shadow making off down the hallway. I half expect to see a sweaty Pedro who has busted out of his room to be with us. But it's not him.

It's Draven.

If he knows what is good for him, he will stay far from me during the birth. If he pulls any revenge moves on Hart right now, I will conjure my own inner warrior borg. The shadow vanishes as the door swings shut, and I'm left in the blue-white light of the Testing Pod.

The pain starts again. Now it is a deep foundational pain, as if all the women of the human race have gathered to hum inside my body at this very moment. It is primal. Eternal.

And just like in the movies, I hear "Push, now." Hart says in her Maternal Voice, "Mirin, push the baby." She says it so pragmatically.

Okay, Hart, no problem. I will just push this baby out easily, at your command. No big deal. Thanks for the helpful instruction.

I take a deep breath and push, except the only place I feel anything happening is in my face. It feels like my face will explode upon the next push. But when the next contraction comes, I push anyway. This time I focus the push with my abdomen. I am burning now, dripping sweat and tears, and I feel something move inside.

My heart is racing, the machine attached to my stomach beeping. It feels like an eternity passes, but it can't be more than a handful of minutes. And then suddenly ... the baby is here. Hart scoops the child up in a soft pink blanket, apparently the blanket I found in her room on my first visit.

A girl.

Hart holds her out to show me. Her face is flushed pink, with a tiny perfect nose and long baby eyelashes and wet dark hair, more than I expect a baby to have. I hadn't had much time to contemplate what she'd look like, but she's so striking, with the tiniest pucker of concern on her brow.

She is quiet at first and then her rosebud of a mouth opens in a yell.

Hart just freezes, like a giant metal statue. Holding my writhing new baby but not reacting. What's happening?

"Hart, give me my baby," I say. Nothing.

It is as if all the air is sucked from the room, and I don't understand why she isn't moving. My baby is crying and Hart is just sitting there, frozen. I wonder if Draven has done something. Has he powered off all the borgs? Or is she considering something or machine learning? Is she about to take my baby away?

"Hart," I scream, and she unfreezes and moves forward, holding the baby out to me. I take her into my arms, and Hart moves to the end of the bed and faces the back wall. I embrace my baby for the first time.

Hello, Maria.

Pedro and I decided weeks ago, if it was a boy, he would have been Ander. Maria is for Pedro's beloved grandmother, and now our names are both M names—Maria, Mirin ... mother.

I hold her to my chest, and we gaze at each other. Her eyes are wide and intelligent.

"I am your mother," I tell her. The way she looks at me is so alert and so vibrant, it's disarming.

Maria will do something great in this world.

It has probably only been a few minutes since we came down here, but I am as exhausted as if it were many hours. We lie there in a coma of love. Hart checks my vitals, careful not to touch Maria. She gives me an electrolyte drink and starts to pull the straps together on the bed.

Hart wheels me and Maria on the gurney back upstairs, through the Zoo, and past Pedro, who waits eagerly, pressed against the wall.

I wave. His eyes plead, and I feel tears stream from my face and down my neck. This is the biggest moment of our lives, and we can't be together. I hold her up, like a prize.

We did it, we made her. As we turn away from him, my full heart breaks a little.

Hart wheels us into the room and helps me onto my bed. There is a basket for Maria, containing the pink blanket I remember from Hart's room.

The room is warm, and Maria and I sleep a while. It takes a few tries for me to stand up without seeing stars. Then I sleep again.

I'm not sure how much time has passed, but there has been sleeping and attempts at breastfeeding. At some point I finally will myself to get up and gingerly move from the bed. It's time I made my way over to introduce Pedro to our baby. I tuck some paper and a pen in her blanket and bring her to his room, grateful it is only steps away.

We sit leaning against the clear wall. He cries and pushes a paper against the Plexi that says "Linda." I look around for the cat, but I don't see her. I shake my head, confused. I scribble on the paper I brought: "Maria."

He smiles and writes "Maria is linda," then scribbles "Linda is beautiful." Ah, Portuguese. I finally understand. I suppose when I named Linda, it was more meaningful than I knew.

We lean here a while until I nearly fall asleep, but all I can think is that my life has been altered forever.

MARIA, who came into this world early, deserves to grow up free. I look down at her perfect soft features and know that I have failed her. I did not escape; Maria was not born in the "vigor of nature" like Thoreau speaks of. I have betrayed my promise to have my child in freedom. I couldn't control when she came into the world, but I will not let her grow up in a zoo.

I look into Pedro's striking blue eyes, and an unspoken agreement passes between us.

We will get you out, baby girl. I promise.

Maria is perfect, and I want to share that with Pedro. It has been seven days since she came into this world, and he has not held her once. I keep trying to convince Hart to release him, and I'm hoping that the repetition will work. So far, no luck.

I am very tired and learning to breastfeed is hard. It hurts. Maria is hungry all the time. I sleep and feed her while my body is still healing. Hart gave me cloths to make diapers, and now the smell of soiled diapers emanates from my room. It feels like I'm stumbling through life in a trance. I wish Pedro could help us.

Every morning I wonder whether today will be the day that Draven floods the Zoo. Honestly, I expected it to happen by now, but I'm grateful that it hasn't. It's given me much-needed time with Maria, and I can't imagine trying to escape right now.

When I look into Maria's eyes, her wise, deep blue eyes, I can see her potential. Her eyes are like her father's. She deserves so much more than this place. It feels like I've robbed her of something vital by allowing her to be born into captivity. I think she knows, and I can't say exactly how. When I look into her eyes, I want to protect her, and I want her freedom even more than I want my own.

It's time to go see Pedro, so I scoop up a sleeping Maria. When we get to his room, I can't see him through the Plexi. I knock, figuring he's in the bathroom. But he doesn't show up. I walk around the room, squinting inside. Pedro isn't there.

I have reached my limit with the disappearing games Hart plays. Thinking he is somewhere in the Zoo without us makes me angry. There are few places he could be. I march down the path holding Maria close and do a quick scan of the dome.

He's not at the Treat Show. Not at the beach. Not in the forest, which is easy to see through since most of it was destroyed in the fire.

Is it possible he's gone to find Draven? What if he's been hurt?

"Hart," I yell over and over, which wakes Maria, who promptly begins to wail. We cry together.

Because Pedro is gone.

CHAPTER THIRTY-NINE

The next morning, I sit on my bed, holding Maria and staring out at Pedro's room. Hart is here doing her scans, but all I can think of is Pedro. He's still not back. I barely slept last night because of my own anxiety and my responsibilities with the baby.

"Today is a family Treat Show." Hart's words are spoken in her Maternal Voice.

"It's not a family without Pedro," I say, eager for her to leave. Or to bring Pedro back. She still hasn't told me where he is. "Hart, how can you do this to me? I thought you cared. Maria needs her father. Please, Hart," I beg.

But she just turns and leaves the room.

Maria is just a week old, and she already must be subjected to the borgs' humiliation. I'm too tired to resist. This is how people lose their motivation to fight. Deprivation of sleep, of love, and we become pliant.

I struggle with the taffeta tube top, which barely fits over my still-swollen belly. Maria is sleeping, and I cover her in the pink blanket.

When we arrive at the Treat Show, I can see immediately that the arena is different. Bars stretch from the top of the dome to the ledge that Pedro and I had leapt over. There is a moat in front of the ledge, which surprises me. Even though borgs know that humans need water, it's deadly for them, so this seems like a risk.

I look out to the audience, packed full of borgs. The stands are metal to metal. I can just imagine the advertisement for today's show.

Come and see the human baby. Days old, born right here in the Zoo.

Poor Maria, she did not sign up for this. There is such a disconnect between her pure innocence and this situation we are in.

The Treat Show is noisy and smells of chlorine, but everything falls away when I see Pedro. He sits there at a desk. *He's okay.* I breathe.

I run to him and put Maria in his arms. It's the moment I've been waiting for, Maria meeting her father. The joy in Pedro is so deep, it shows in his face as she is reflected in his eyes. We're interrupted by the deafening sound of applause, piped-in cheers. We are the show. I feel let down by Hart once again.

If she has feelings, how could she treat us this way? How could she keep Pedro from us and then put our reunion on display? Hart has always taken care of me in her own way, but this feels wrong. Clearly, this is one of those things she doesn't understand.

In moments like this, I understand Pedro's dislike for them, but to destroy them would be to lose the thing that makes us human in the first place. If I want dignity, then I must behave in a dignified manner. Even in the face of an audience.

Pedro and I turn our backs to the borgs, shielding Maria

and ourselves from the viewing experience. Even still, we feel the metal glares on our backs.

"She has your eyes," I tell him.

"And your lips," he says. He kisses her forehead gently.

"I was afraid for you," I say.

"I was fine, just in the Testing Pod. I guess Hart wanted to give them a show."

"We have to get out of here."

I glance over my shoulder. The borgs are watching us closely and feel the violation. I look down at our precious baby and imagine her as I am, a woman still coming to perform for them. Turning to look out at them, I let this upside-down world sink in and earn its revulsion. Hart stands just outside the door, watching.

I study the new bars, the new security measures on the Treat Show, from my place at the desk. Well, it is certain that no borg is getting in from the audience area. The added security makes me feel safer. However, us getting out into the audience area has become a near impossibility now.

As I turn back to my family, I notice a borg stand up. Tall and clownlike, it has a blue plastic head, which I've never seen before. Something about the way it moves feels ominous. Perhaps it's new-mother jitters—everything about the world seems scary when you look at in view of the vulnerability of a newborn.

I should always listen to my intuition.

The tall borg lobs a sharp, shiny object through the bars, which lodges in the desk a foot from Pedro. Some sort of blade.

Oh god. Fear prickles over my entire body. Adrenaline makes me feel like a superhero. Pedro didn't see it since he's making goo-goo eyes at Maria. I leap up and throw myself in front of Pedro and Maria.

"Pedro," I shout.

He looks up and sees the tall borg. When it moves closer, I can see that it has the body of Elf Hat borg, the twin of the borg that Pedro destroyed months ago. The borg who had been sobbing, in the way that only borgs can sob. It must have put a plastic piece on its head to disguise itself.

Another blade flies by the side of my face so fast and close that I feel the whip of the air as it imbeds into the floor behind me. Pedro hands Maria to me, and I pull her close to my chest and duck behind the desk.

"It's the other Elf Hat twin," I tell Pedro.

Without thinking, I tug the blade out of the floor in front of me and slide it into my sock.

Fight fire with fire.

The borgs in the audience have gone quiet, and Elf Hat twin moves closer to the moat, quick and lithe.

"Hart," I call out, and Pedro begins throwing things at the borg. A stapler, a mug, a small fake plant that explodes when it collides with the bars. The blades keep coming and Pedro runs over and bangs on the door.

"Hart! Dr. Draven! Someone, please," he pleads. A blade hits him in the shoulder and sinks into his flesh, but he keeps banging. Some of the borgs in the audience start to tug at Elf Hat twin. I thought there would be security after what happened before. Bars aren't a deterrent for blades, and the thing that was supposed to keep us safe is ineffective.

Finally, the door to the Treat Show opens, and I see Linda rush in at the same time as Hart. Pedro is pushed back by the door as Hart enters. I lunge for the door, clutching Maria, looking to escape the onslaught of seemingly never-ending blades.

Hart tries to block them, holding her arms out in front of us. I see Linda, climbing up to the bars.

What is she doing?

"Linda, get away from there," I say, using the door as a shield.

I don't take my eyes off the zany cat. She reaches the bars and squeezes through. Linda shimmies out and leaps over the moat like it is a rain puddle.

Then she pounces straight onto Elf Hat twin's face.

I'm in disbelief. I've never seen a cat behave this way.

The borg grabs at her, but she won't release its face from her claws.

"Linda, stop," I call out. I can't handle the thought of losing her, and the Elf Hat twin is ruthless. It wants revenge, and anything it can do to hurt me, I'm sure it'll do.

Elf Hat twin pulls its arm back and slides a blade into her back.

I close my eyes, afraid to see the blood. But I can't keep them closed, because it's Linda. I feel responsible. I owe it to her to watch whatever happens to her. Someone needs to witness her last act of bravery. Of love.

Oh, Linda.

I force my eyes open, but no blood appears.

Instead, I see that her skin and fur fold back at the cut to reveal a skeleton of metal and wires. *Linda is a borg.*

She turns her face to look at us, as if she's apologizing.

I'm sorry I fooled you, Mirin. Please don't remember me this way.

I'm stunned. Even more so when Elf Hat twin pulls her off its face and tosses her into the moat. Her body sinks into the water, illuminated by a bright blue flash of light, and then she's gone.

Linda is dead.

Sweet Linda, the cat that revived my hope. The cat who arrived just when I was at my lowest low, before I met Pedro. She gave me comfort when I was desperate and laughter when I thought I had none left.

Linda was a borg and I loved her.

PART 3

ESCAPE

CHAPTER FORTY

Hart transforms before our eyes into a warrior borg. Small shields come down over her eyes, and her armor becomes weaponized. She leaves through an exit in the dome, much like the one in the waterfall. It opens and she charges into the audience area after Elf Hat twin, while all the other borgs hurry out, and grabs the attacking borg, delivering an electrical charge to short it.

That causes it to instantly power off.

She clutches its arm, the one that had been dispersing all of the blades, and tears it off like the wing of a butterfly. Then Hart carries the Elf Hat twin out of the Treat Show, completely dismantled. This is the first time I've seen Hart as a warrior, and she is stunning.

While the attention is off us, Pedro and I hurry out of the Treat Show, with Maria in my arms. I check Maria for any injuries just to be sure, but she's okay. Pedro and I look at each other stoically outside the door, somehow conveying more than words could. I can't believe what just happened.

In six years I've had no contact from the audience other than tossed treats, and in the last year we have been attacked twice. It has to be Draven's interference. He has been the cause of so many problems.

Pedro grips his shoulder, which is bleeding heavily, the blade still embedded. He winces in pain when I touch it, and I realize that it would create more injury to pull it out.

"You're going to need stitches," I say.

"Yes. I need you to get the escape bag and meet me outside," he replies.

"Okay." I agree even though the last thing I want is for us to be separated right now. I reach into my sock and hand him the blade I took from the floor. "Take this, for protection."

He tucks it into his fuzzy costume. When Hart returns from the Treat Show, she scans Maria and me and then looks at Pedro's wound.

"Mirin," he says as she clasps his wrist.

"Yes?"

"I'm so sorry about Linda," he says. Hart tugs him toward the edge of the dome, and I kiss him quickly. I can't find any words yet for Linda. I am shocked that she was a borg and sad that she's gone. It all happened so quickly, I can barely process it. And now Hart is taking Pedro, and my hands are shaking.

What I want to do is crumple into a ball and cry for hours, but there is no time for that. Threats are all around us, and the threat of Draven flooding the Zoo whenever he decides to, is still prominent in my mind. My heart feels like it's pumping straight cortisol. I really don't see another choice. Pedro and I must proceed with our plan, no matter how hurt and exhausted we are.

We need to get our supply bag and find a way out of here, whether it's through the Treat Show, despite the new measures, or by making a crack in the dome, like

Pedro did to his room. Draven has been quiet, wherever he is, so brute force is apparently all we have left. If we can be attacked while in the Zoo, then Pedro's theory about being protected, fed, and sheltered here has lost its relevance.

Hopefully, we will have better chances on the outside.

Adrenaline is still coursing through my veins after nearly being killed by Elf Hat twin. It must have been avenging its twin borg that Pedro destroyed. Or is still unreasonable to assume that all borgs have feelings? I hold Maria close, her charming little eyes becoming heavy. She is about to fall asleep again.

Okay, sweet Maria. You just rest while your mama stages our escape.

We'll need something heavy if we were going to crack the dome. I look around at our options—or lack thereof. Maybe a tree branch or a rock? But the biggest rocks are made of plastic and hollow. The real tree branches are mostly charred from the fire and wouldn't be strong enough.

Then we'll need to improvise. Heading back to my room to get our supply bag, I tuck Maria close to me. As I round the corner of the Plexi and push into my room, the air changes. It has been warmed by the breath of someone else.

I stop cold.

It's Draven.

He's sitting at my table. And somehow, he's the most disheveled and unkempt I've ever seen him. I want to ask him where he's been living and what the hell he's been doing this whole time, while, you know, the world is falling apart, but before I can get a word out, he speaks.

"I thought I'd have some time in here while you did your little show. But I suppose it wasn't a very good one if you're back so soon."

"We were attacked by a borg from the audience," I say. "What are you doing here?"

"Oh, yes, sorry that was me. I was trying to hack into any borg in the audience whose internal security was weak. I wanted to put on a little show myself, you see, before the flood." He types furiously on his wrist computer. "I remember when Hart and I used to host the shows. I'd tell her to give 'em some flare, and she'd crush the torso even after it was decommissioned, add a little showmanship." He chuckles. "God, I used to love those shows."

Draven is depraved. There is no reasoning with him. Let him try to destroy Hart, if he can. All I want is to get Maria out safely.

"Tell me how to get out," I say. "I won't get in your way, but just tell me how to get out. My daughter doesn't deserve to die in here."

"Mmm, getting close ... almost time. Time for the borgs' big drink," he says, mostly to himself. I don't think he's even glanced up at me since I walked in.

"Hccipp." Maria makes a tiny noise in her sleep. Draven looks at her like he's seen a ghost. He stands up quickly as he backs away from her.

"Please," I plead. "I can't allow my child to grow up in here."

Draven strokes his beard and takes off his glasses. His breath has quickened. He puts his glasses back on. He looks very uncomfortable around Maria, and suddenly, I wonder if allowing her to get this close to him is a bad idea.

"Well, no one is going to grow up in here. This place is toast." He laughs at himself. "But okay, yes. I can tell you how to get out, if that's what you want. When you leave the dome, go through the gray door. Then there is a concrete path. Follow it past the small borg enclosures. At the end, there is a set of red double doors. Go through those. Once you are out, there will be a main gate. Take cover, as it may take me a few days to offset the algorithm. Any borgs you come into contact with will be lethal." He is shouting now. "Avoid all borgs!" Maria begins to cry.

"Stop shouting," I say. As I peer at him closely, underneath the grit and the ruddiness, the long, lanky hair, there is something so familiar about his face. I rock back and forth, calming Maria.

Draven can't look at me. He only has eyes for his computer.

Something about Maria has him on edge.

"The bars, Draven?" I push.

"You have to get through those, yes indeed," he says.

"What is the best way out? Do you know how to get through Hart's door in the dome?" I beg.

"I built the doors to be impenetrable, she is the only one it will open for. But yes, the Gladiator Ring is the best place," he says. His eyes shift to me once and he looks afraid. The Gladiator Ring is the Treat Show. That is it. He shuts the wrist computer and exits the room as fast as he can. This man clearly left some of his humanity down in the basement.

Once he is out of sight, I reach under the mattress and grab the pillowcase of supplies. I sort through the nutrition packets, treats, sharpened stick, water, and borg arm.

Cassandra's faceplate is missing.

I wonder if it was Draven or Hart who took it. I wasn't exactly sure what I was going to use it for anyway, but that doesn't mean I'm okay with someone going through my things. I scan the room for the last time, and I am filled with that *forgetting something* feeling.

And then it hits me.

Linda.

She's what has been giving me that feeling of forgetting something, but she won't be coming on the journey out of here with us. Oh, Linda. *I'm sorry I didn't know that you were a borg.*

Not that it would have mattered anyway, I realize. Linda showed me that borgs can be good, that they can have a soul. And suddenly, all my questions about Hart's true nature fade away.

Hart *is* good, deep down. Yes, she's kept me captive here, but I don't believe her intentions are bad. In fact, I'm more convinced than ever that, like Linda, Hart loves me in her own way, twisted though it may be.

I look down, and Maria has fallen back asleep on my chest. Pedro isn't out yet, and I decide to take one last look around to see if there's anything I else can take that will aid us on our journey.

The Zoo has taken on a strange, nostalgic sepia tone. Maybe it's the fire, or maybe it's that I'm looking at this place through eyes that won't see it tomorrow. I put Maria down in the basket on the bed. She is feeling heavy, so I look around for something to use as a sling to carry her before we go. I tear a shirt and pull it over me like a sash, tying a knot on each end.

I go to pick her up, but she looks so peaceful lying there. She has no idea what turmoil is going on around her. I decide to let her stay and sleep in the basket a little longer, while I take a short walk to say goodbye.

As I leave my room, my home for the last six years, and begin down the path, I try to memorize the details. The scratches on the door handle, the scuffed gravel outside, the worn edges of the path winding between Pedro's room and mine. There's moisture in the air as I inhale the bleachy scent.

Slowly, I walk the perimeter, like I have daily for years, and I come back to the Treat Show. This could be where we will stage our great escape, but I'm not sure how yet. Turning, I stare up at the waterfall and stop at the garden, my box of earth. The vegetables grown here gave me such pleasure. Yes, because of the food. But also for the reminders of summers past, of salads and backyard barbeques, of being with other people.

I met Linda here, at the garden. I remember the chewed-up zucchini and smile. When I sink a hand into the soil, I thank it and say goodbye. I listen; no Pedro.

Continuing my perimeter walk, I climb a couple of the fake cement rocks near the waterfall. I hear the water rushing, being pumped in from outside. I hope we can find water on our own once we are out there. I'm reassured by Pedro's survival skills and hope they will help us navigate the essential needs.

If we die out there, at least we die free.

Even still, I have great hope that we will make it. Maria will make it.

I kiss my hand and touch the rock, telling the waterfall goodbye. I climb down carefully, thinking how I would not want to slip now.

I work my way around the water and head up to the beach. My favorite spot. The sand smells like salt, and the ocean is deep enough for a good swim, but there isn't time. This was the place I came when I needed comfort, when being in my room made my skin crawl, and when I needed a good cry.

I came here with Linda, my hero cat. It strikes me that Linda acted to protect us and did so without a care for herself. Maybe that's what makes humans different from sentient borgs—maybe borgs can be selfless. If they have feelings and can behave in heroic ways and loving ways, then what is the difference?

I wish that the world could see what I see, and that things had happened differently on the outside. If the borgs weren't used for violence in the first place, maybe they wouldn't have turned their violence on us. I wonder if humanity could have survived.

The beach with its sand and water was the Mother Nature I had yearned for. Only now I see it as it really is—counterfeit. I don't need it anymore. It is not enough. The real Mother Nature is outside, and I will meet her there. I will find the truth. The one Thoreau reminds me of. The pleasure of being far away from the distractions of life. My distractions here. I look at the lapping water. How I wished it were a real ocean. But the truth is that it's just a pool.

Standing up sooner than I thought I would from my favorite spot, with a deep breath and a wave, I leave.

The poor forest.

I press my hand onto what's left of the trees as I pass them. Goodbye, trees. When I get to Shel, I tug on one of his few remaining branches. I'm sorry to do it, but we need this. I'll take you with us, Shel. I take out my plastic knife. I've said my goodbyes, I made the sling, and now I'll make a weapon. I whittle one end of the branch like Pedro did.

I'm rushing, so I nick my finger with the serrated plastic. *Slow down, Mirin.* Before long, the weapon is finished, and I'm proud of my efforts. It looks almost like a sword.

Looking around at this place, I try to stamp it on my mind. On my heart. Whether it is a home or a prison, I am about to leave and I will miss it. My feelings are complicated. Leaving is bittersweet.

I gaze up at the Suckers one last time to acknowledge my thanks for their cleaning service. I blink as a drop of water lands directly in the center of my forehead. Then another. The sprinklers have turned on and begin to rain down on me.

We have one hour.

As I hurry back to my room for Maria, I see the back of Hart near the Treat Show. She's probably cleaning up or reenforcing it with barbed wire. She always looks so busy, even now, when her world is almost ending. It's funny how I used to imagine her days compared to how I see them now. She has become a fully evolved individual now, with responsibilities, with chores. Things have changed so much that even the path to our rooms feels shorter.

When I enter my bedroom, I know immediately something is wrong. The basket where Maria had been sleeping is no longer on the bed. Or on the floor. Or anywhere.

Maria is gone.

I feel my skin go white-hot with a rage I didn't even know I was capable of. I think about how Draven had eyed Maria, just a few minutes ago, and I want to scream. If he has taken my baby, I will kill him. I will hurt him until he's almost at his last breath, and then I will kill him.

I stride straight out the door back to the Treat Show where I saw Hart. When I get there the door is open, but no one is inside. My ears pick up a sound.

Maria's cry.

CHAPTER FORTY-ONE

Running full speed toward the waterfall, I nearly plow over Pedro as he comes out from behind the waterfall rocks. He is looking up in surprise, as if he doesn't understand why the sprinklers are on. He doesn't have Maria though, and I'm angry at him. It is not his fault; he doesn't know yet.

But I am so filled with desperation that all I can think of is my baby. I look behind him but no Hart.

"Hey, hey, what's wrong?" he asks.

"They took Maria," I say, my mind spinning. Saying it out loud means it's real, that she is not with me. My legs are weak, but I try to get my heartbeat moving in a regular cadence again.

"They?" He puts his steady hands on my shoulders.

"I don't know, probably Draven, but it could have been Hart." I make my way toward the waterfall door he just exited. "Where's Hart?"

I start to bang on the door. This is exactly what I was most afraid of—Hart taking my baby. After seeing those terrifying wombs in her room, how could I expect anything less? I told myself that Hart would never hurt me. But now look where we are. I bang harder, with both fists now.

"Hart," I yell.

"She wasn't with me, just HIPPO," Pedro says. "When did they take her? What happened? Tell me everything you saw."

Without my instruction, he starts to tug at the seam where the door opens. He pulls hard, then recoils and grabs at his injured shoulder. I nearly forgot about the borg's blade that he had removed.

I kick the door and go to Pedro. "Did they do stitches?" I touch the gauze covering on his arm.

"Yes, and an IV. I'm guessing antibiotics. I'm good." He refocuses on pulling at the door. "What happened? Was there another fire?" he asks.

"No, no. I put her down in the basket on my bed, for one minute," I say, my heart literally aching as I explain. "I saw Hart at the Treat Show on my way back to my room, and when I got inside Maria was gone, but when I got back to the Treat Show, Hart was gone." My tears start to fall, but the ones from the dome stop for a moment. Pedro and I both look up. It's just a hiccup though, because just as we look, they begin to pour down upon us again.

"And now Draven is flooding the Zoo. Pedro, we have to get out of here. Remember, he said we have one hour." I look out over the Zoo. From here, I can see almost everything—except Maria.

Where is she?

"Now?" He is surprised. "Mirin, look at me."

My eyes find his again, blue with thick, dark eyelashes, the same eyes he gave Maria. Right now, nothing else matters but finding our girl.

"Now," I say. "We have to get Maria and leave. It has

already been ten minutes." My voice begins to rise. "Let's try the door one more time."

I pull on the bottom part of the door while he pulls the top. Our hands keep slipping in the wetness, quickly forming tiny blisters.

"Let's do a hard pull at the same time, on three: one, two, three," he says. We pull hard with all our might, but the door doesn't budge. I slip back against the rocks, then catch and steady myself. It feels like I'm more likely to rip a couple fingers off than get that door open.

The familiar helpless feeling creeps in as I note the fragility of my human hands. Borg hands are strong metal claws; they have a solid grip, undeterred by skin and muscle. I think of the way Hart would cuff my wrists and how there was no breaking her grasp. Right now, I wish that I had borg hands. I gasp.

I take the escape bag off my shoulder, rummage through it, and take out the borg arm.

"The fingers are tools," I tell Pedro. I flip through a knife, screwdriver, and scissors until I get to the end. There is a hammer tool, so I wedge the back part of it into the seam of the camouflaged doorframe. We both push on the borg arm, which gives us a lot more leverage.

It's working.

But then I hear her. We stop.

Maria is crying. I start looking around. It sounds close but slightly muffled. I push my ear to the door and listen.

Another cry and it's like a shot of electricity through my entire body. I literally ache for her. There is a little alarm inside mothers that tells them they need to take care of their children, and that alarm is screaming at me.

It's agony that I can't comfort her right now, but that cry triggers something in my body and I feel as if I have gained the strength of several borgs. I push that borg arm like I'm steering an oil tanker.

"Ha-uuh," I grunt, and heave at the doorframe. The door slowly creaks fully ajar, and Pedro stands back, awestruck.

There is no time to lose. Each minute that ticks by is a minute closer to the Zoo flooding. Seeing the water collecting, I wonder, *How long will it take to get to my waist? How long until it's over our heads? How long until it will cover a baby basket?*

I don't want to find out, so I rush into the hallway to find Maria.

At the end of the hall, the door to Hart's room is open. All I want is Maria to be safe and to take her into my arms. I think about the rocking chair and the heart punches in the concrete and the wombs. I do not want innocent Maria caught up in their bizarre story.

How could I let her be born here?

Once I find her we will leave this place and she will never even know she was here. There will be no baby book filled with photos of her early days, and we will not speak of this place ever again.

Pushing the door open, I see Maria's basket sitting on the table while she cries inside it. A wave of relief crashes over me. She's in one piece. She's pretty mad, but she is okay. Hart is tucking the pink blanket around her in the basket. I reach out to take her, but Hart turns toward me, her huge body blocking me from Maria. Pedro arrives behind me, clutching his shoulder. I try to contain my rage.

"Hart, give me Maria," I say firmly, as Hart turns and draws up to her full height in front of the basket. My heart races at how intimidating she is without even trying. In the past, I was sure Hart wouldn't hurt me, but her standing between me and Maria hurts deeply.

She needs to move.

"Hart has a gift for Mirin," Hart says in her Maternal Voice. Clearing my throat, I plant my hands on either side of the doorway, wanting to seem more intimidating, as though I were being attacked by a bear.

"I don't want your gift. I want my baby. Give. Maria. To. Me. Now." I move again to grab the basket. Hart holds up a claw to stop me.

"Mirin will have happy feelings for this gift," Hart says.

Hart is very confused about what will give me happy feelings. If she even knew the first thing about humans *or* feelings, she'd know that a woman separated from her child knows no obstacle. She would know the actual physical pain I'm in because my baby is crying feet away from me, and I can't get to her.

Hart would know that the greatest feeling I have is my love for Maria, and the greatest feeling of hate I have is for anyone who would harm her.

But Hart knows none of this because she's a borg. She will never understand what it's like to love someone this way, no matter what Draven claims. I feel so stupid and so gullible for believing him when, clearly, it was all just a manipulation. Draven was right. My skin is crawling, and I just want to hold my baby.

This is torture.

If I can't get by you, Hart, then I'll have to go through you. I move toward her.

From the corner of my eye, I see Pedro swing the pillowcase holding the borg arm and our supplies straight toward Hart's head.

Clank.

Her head sparks a tiny flash, and I think I am as shocked as Hart. Even though I was just contemplating my own move against her, I worry what Hart will do. I know that Hart does not like when others get violent. Pedro has distracted her from blocking us, though, so I grab the basket from the table and hug the whole thing to my chest.

Mommy is here, Maria. Pedro embraces both of us, and my whole body is grateful.

Relief, finally.

Then, we hear a creaking sound coming from Hart. We look up at her. Hart shifts to face Pedro and her eyes turn laser red, eyebrows arching in anger.

"Is Pedro feeling violence?" she asks.

"Run," Pedro says, and the three of us rush out the open door.

CHAPTER FORTY-TWO

Pedro slams Hart's door shut behind us. We run down the hallway, heading straight for the Treat Show. This family is getting the hell out of the Zoo.

Surely, Hart will be right behind us, but we don't look back. We run past the open door to the stairs on our left, but when we get to the exit at the waterfall door, Draven is there.

He turns toward us, blocking the door. He is wearing armor over his fatigues, his hair as greasy as ever. His glasses are slightly fogged with condensation. This isn't good. I stop, clutching Maria in her basket, where she is drowsy, likely tired from all that crying. It is unbelievable to me how she can sleep when the world around her is in such chaos.

Pedro goes straight up to Draven. I really didn't want to have to see this man again. The last thing we need is to get stuck in some kind of last battle between him and Hart. But we will not be blocked again.

"Get out of the way. We're leaving." Pedro stands close to him, face to face. His nostrils flare as he takes deep breaths, visible even to me in the dim light.

"You cannot go out there," Draven says. He looks serious.

"What do you mean? You told us we only had an hour, and the sprinklers are going, so let us out," I say. I am rocking Maria back and forth.

"I know, but you can't go out there right now," he repeats. Pedro pushes Draven backward against the door. In a fight, there is no contest, and despite Draven's armor, Pedro will be the clear victor here.

"Why?" Pedro asks. From behind us comes the recognizable sound of Hart. We are boxed in between Frankenstein and his monster.

"Listen, I—I am fixing things, and this will be good. But not for you if you go out there," Draven says. He stands aside, and even though he's telling us not to go, it feels like he's daring us to go out there.

What is he hiding?

We hear a loud crash out in the dome.

"What *was* that, Draven?" I ask, but I'm not sure I want to know.

"I want to say this wasn't supposed to go like this, Mirin. I didn't mean for this to be the way—"

I can't tell what he is trying to say, but I do know that it has something to do with his highest priority, saving his own neck. Everything with him is a manipulation. I feel like he is holding us back, and whatever he did to cause the crash in the Zoo we can handle. What I cannot handle is remaining in this place for one more minute.

"Draven, move," I say, looking back at Hart. She is just standing still. Her eyebrows have softened, and I know her face well enough now to know that she is absorbing something. Pedro pushes Draven aside, into the wall, and opens the door back into the Zoo.

As we leave Draven and Hart behind us and move out behind the waterfall again, it is like a weight has lifted. We are a family.

This is the most important thing to me now, and getting out of here has never felt so clear and so imminent. It is a victory, like we stood up to the ones who stood in our way. We do have to deal with the water puddling at our feet and Draven's warnings, but all of that feels smaller now.

We can do this.

I follow Pedro, cradling Maria's basket through the archway to protect her from the falling water, when Pedro stops short beside the waterfall.

I look up to see the full terror of what Draven was warning us about.

Before us, stands a gigantic warrior borg, its back turned to us. It has full battle armor, though it is made up of mismatched parts. Its frame is two times larger than Hart's, and the shoulders bear iron spikes, with each claw holding firing weapons.

It is literally a borg from my nightmares.

It takes all my strength not to drop down onto the ground, like I did when my family was attacked. I steel myself for Maria's sake, but I can't stop my mind from screaming at me. *We're going to die! We're going to die! We're going to die!*

Taking advantage of the fact that it's facing away, I pull Pedro to hide behind the rocks near the waterfall. I say a silent prayer that Maria will remain quiet.

I peek back at the door to see Hart in silhouette in the hall and Draven hiding like a coward in the doorway. There is a whirring sound coming from Hart. When she appears outside the door a moment later, she has transformed. Her filigreed metal body is smooth, and her head is protected by a helmet, but her eyes are the same. This is different from the warrior armor I've seen.

Maybe she is bulletproof. And then I notice that when the water from the sprinklers hits her now-smooth exterior, it hops away. Her armor repels the drops of water, like she is waterproof. I am impressed and surprised, because Pedro and Draven have both said that water is not friendly to borgs. I remember Elf Hat and the Sucker.

And Linda.

It feels like the crack in my heart sears at the thought. Hart is protected from getting wet, and I wonder if she did that herself or if Draven designed her that way.

But I'm not sure she is protected from that warrior borg. Instead of fearing Hart now, I am afraid for her. There is a comradery in fear. I'm guessing that both of us are reliving our worst memory. For me it's the death of my family, and for Hart it's probably her time as a warrior, when she had to destroy other borgs for entertainment. And now that depraved man, Draven, has rebuilt this nightmare for one final showdown.

Hart's arms morph into weapons that mirror the warrior's, but on a much smaller scale.

Oh god, she can't compete with those.

Pedro and I watch, huddled behind the waterfall. Hart raises her chin and takes a step toward the warrior, almost as if asking it to turn around and see her. The warrior borg hears Hart approach and turns around to face all of us.

The warrior wears the face of Cassandra.

CHAPTER FORTY-THREE

So, Draven took it from my pillowcase.

This is how it all started: Hart vs. Cassandra. This was the domino that knocked everything down. Hart looks fierce, and I hope that that is enough.

And now I recall the table covered in a blanket down in the basement—his latest work. It is grotesque—Cassandra's delicate, pretty face reanimated on this massive war machine. I know that it's not really her, since her L-Drive was destroyed, but the appearance of it is startling. I shouldn't be shocked that Draven did this, but I am, although not more shocked than Hart.

One claw goes to her heart, and her eyebrows furrow, as if in pain. She shoots a look at Draven, who peers out from the safety of the doorway, a smirk lingering on his lips. I feel sick for her. He did this just to upset Hart, to traumatize her. He doesn't see how inhumane he is and how sensitive Hart is. If it were me in her shoes, I'm not sure I would have merely locked him in a basement. She showed restraint.

He behaves only with pure vengeance, as if he were

programmed that way. Perhaps he is the one without humanity, not Hart.

I track her feelings by the shape of her eyebrows, which are arching from pain to sorrow, and then the ends slowly rise into full-on rage. It is strange that I relate more to Hart than I do to Draven, a human being. I never imagined that I'd feel this way, but Hart is more conscious than he will ever be.

In a matter of seconds, she begins firing lasers from one of her arms at Cassandra. But the laser beams don't seem to affect the larger borg at all. Cassandra walks right up to Hart. She swings one of her giant arms and hits Hart in the chest, sending her flying into the Plexi wall of the Treat Show.

There is no match here.

The Plexi shatters but clings together in a spiderweb of pieces that hold on for dear life.

It's happening again, but this time Cassandra is going to kill Hart. A darkness begins to settle inside me, as I can't see how anything good can happen. I'm angry. This was going to be our escape, and now it has become a battle for our lives.

Pedro huddles over us, and I feel the water now lapping at our knees.

"Mirin, we can't stay here. We have to go," he urges.

But I'm terrified. Frozen. We are so close to getting out, but one wrong move and we could be killed by a giant borg or drowned before we get there. And for some reason, I can't walk away from Hart. The pain of injustice I feel for both of us stings as I watch Cassandra and Hart fight a very unfair battle. She may have imprisoned me for six years, and she may have taken my baby, but she doesn't deserve *this*.

"Mirin, we have to get inside the Treat Show arena,"

Pedro says, trying to grab Maria's basket from me so that we can get moving.

Cassandra shoots Hart in the leg with her laser, which lights a small fire. Hart's leg turns black. Maria wakes up and starts crying. The sound alerts Hart, who looks over at where we are huddled. We are caught. A muscle under my eye is twitching, and my ears start to ring.

Hart begins crawling toward Pedro, Maria, and me just as Cassandra aims her weapon at Hart once more. When she realizes that Hart is crawling toward us, she slowly moves her laser and aims at us.

We are doomed.

Maybe I was just destined to die at the hands of a borg, starting all those years ago with my family. It's all playing out like before. My eyes meet Pedro's. We can both see that there's nothing left for us to do and nowhere we can run, so we brace for the inevitable.

Except this time, just as Cassandra pulls the trigger, Hart springs up in front of us, taking the blow of the laser right in the center of her chest.

"No," I yell, and try to run to her, but Pedro holds me back.

"Mirin, we have to go. Now!" He pulls me toward the Treat Show.

Hart falls hard next to us, splashing us with a wave of floodwater. Her eyes are wide-open and her face contorting, the metal flaps flipping between anger and sadness and happiness. Water seeps through the cracks of her armor, and as she begins to malfunction, her limbs contort awkwardly.

"Mirin," Hart says in her Information Voice.

"Mirin," she says in her Gladiator Voice.

"Mirin," she says in her Alarm Voice. Her face turns

toward mine.

"Mirin," she finally says in her Maternal Voice. Then her voice shorts out and becomes like a recording dragged slowly backward.

My heart breaks into a million pieces, but I can do nothing to help.

When I look up to Cassandra, she is frozen, not moving at all. It's like she has been powered off mid-movement. Suspicion runs down my spine, and I look for the perpetrator.

Draven.

Just as I spot him in the doorway, he shuts the tiny computer on his arm. That wretched man. He's controlling Cassandra, like she is a game.

Handing off Maria and the supply bag to Pedro, I rush to Hart's side. The water is a good six inches deep now. Hart's torso is melted, her wires are frayed. She is dying.

It dawns on me that Hart used her dying breath to speak my name. If that's not love, I don't know what is. Motherhood is complicated. Some mothers are kind and soft, and some are hard and rough, and I feel grateful that I get to choose what kind of mother I'll be. And now I can see all different ways mothers have tried to help me. Hart tried. I can see her without judgment now. Yes, she is my captor, but she's more than that. She rebuilt herself and gave me sanctuary and seeds and kept me alive. And I am her human.

Perhaps borgs don't get to an emotion in the same way we do. Perhaps it is less organic and more mathematical. I no longer think that matters. If Linda and Hart and HIPPO feel pain, then I cannot rank their pain as less than mine based on the limitations of my human experience.

Pain is pain.

I feel guilty about my blindness to the plight of the borgs. I have been narrow. I have been angry. And though I did deserve to be angry, now I feel like I should atone.

That's a bitter pill to swallow.

"M-m-mirin," Hart repeats as she reaches for my face.

As her claws come closer, I see for the first time ever, etched into the tip of her front claw, a tiny heart. An accent her creator included in her design, a *heart*.

Hart.

Time slows as she takes her heart finger and presses it to the birthmark on my wrist. It is a perfect match.

I had always thought my birthmark was more like a spade, but now I see that it's clearly for what it is. For me the heart is upside down, but for Hart it is right side up.

All the information I have been gathering and questioning floods in. The Zoo, Hart, Draven, even Pedro. And it hits me.

It's me.

I am the baby that Hart burned the day Cassandra came to the Zoo.

The heart is a scar, a brand, not a birthmark. When she touched me with her claw, it burned my skin. I am Cassandra and Draven's baby, the one that Hart so desperately wanted to have for herself.

My sister's teasing words echo around in my head. *You were born in a zoo*, she used to say. I always thought this was just an idle insult, but it's true. I *was* born in a zoo. This zoo.

I look up at Draven and realize that his eyes are familiar because they resemble my own. My parents must have been at the show, and they must have taken me when they saw me, when they realized that a baby was left on the floor in all the chaos.

And then Hart burned down the world to find me.

Me. Mirin Blaise. Cashier at the Farm Food Mart. She decimated humanity for her own chance at living it.

When I look down at Maria, I understand that feeling. It is a love that says I would do anything for her, I would destroy it all for her. And I look at Hart's face, her sad eyebrows, understanding her for the first time. She was loving me, trying to protect me from the cruel world Draven showed her. The way that she understood humanity.

I have hated her for her ignorance, for her mechanical nature, for her heartlessness. But in the end, she did what we all do: she tried her best with the tools she had. My heart breaks for her, to have it all turn out this way. I reach down and hold her, laying my head on her chest, and she lightly taps her claw on my back. Water continues to shower down on us.

I need her to know that I understand.

"Thank you, mother," I say, looking into her warm metal eyes. Her eyebrows lift and her fans go quiet. Hart powers down and her limbs relax onto the ground.

She lays there, and for a moment it's quiet. Maria has stopped crying. All I can hear is the gentle sound of the water tapping on Hart's waterproof armor. The musical quality makes a fitting goodbye song.

Tap, tap, tap.

A moment of peace in the madness. Goodbye, Hart.

"Mirin, the water," Pedro says nervously, touching my shoulder. Painfully, I drag my eyes away from Hart's lifeless body. Looking around, I can see it's rising more quickly than before, a few inches each minute. He pulls me up from where I lay, and I grab the basket with Maria from him, leaving him with the pillowcase with our provisions, and rush to get inside the Treat Show. I look back at Hart one last time.

We are forced to walk past Cassandra, who now looks like a giant menacing sculpture. Pedro goes ahead of me, but I am terrified that Cassandra will turn back on.

"Go quickly, but don't touch it," I loud whisper. He slips by and heads to the Treat Show entrance. I walk swiftly and carefully, but I still trip near the borg's large foot. When I look back up in panic at Cassandra's pretty war face, it is still. I creep past and follow Pedro into the Treat Show.

The doorway is empty, Draven is gone, and I'm so glad. I hope I don't ever have to see his snarling face again. He's no father of mine. My dad died at the hands of Draven's war machines. When I get far away from this place, I will make sure he pays for what he has done. Right now, we need to get out before the Zoo floods.

Our suffering has reached a breaking point. Now that things are in motion that we cannot stop, my anger and sadness have burrowed deeply.

"I think I can break the Plexi where Hart cracked it," Pedro says. I feel the cool water envelop my calves.

"Okay, I'll go see if I can loosen the bars somehow," I tell him. Two ways are better than none.

I hurry over to place Maria's basket and the pillowcase on one of the desks.

I hear Pedro thumping hard against the wall trying to bust through. When I grip the bars and give them a shake, absolutely nothing happens. They are not even one tiny bit loose. I rummage through the pillowcase for something to help, studying the tools on the end of the borg arm. I try pulling on the hammer end on the base of the bars, like we did with the waterfall door. It doesn't work this time, and the water is getting higher. It's to my knees now.

Pulling at the bars, I look out to the moat. Linda is somewhere at the bottom of that moat. I feel a ping in my heart.

I search through the pillowcase again. This time, something shimmers at the bottom. The blade from Elf Hat twin. The one I found lodged in the floor. Pedro must've put it back in the pillowcase.

If you can't get around the bars, perhaps you can go through. I check on Maria, who is content staring up at the office ceiling, and then get to work on the bars.

The blade catches at first, but then I see shavings of metal fall away.

Back and forth, back and forth, I go.

Bang, thump. Bang, thump, Pedro goes.

I work as fast as I can, continuing to watch the water line rise up the legs of the desk where Maria lies. I get through the first bar.

"Pedro, are you close?" I call to him. The thumping stops.

"It's not working. What are you doing?" he asks, joining me inside the Treat Show. I hold up the blade I found, identical to the one I had given him before he went to the Testing Pod. He smiles a big, goofy grin, all his teeth showing. His hair, soaked from the sprinklers, glistens as he shakes his fists in victory.

"You're my hero," he says.

"Not yet," I return. My hands are feeling stiff, so I shake them out and keep going, my eyes on the water level.

He uses his blade and joins the sawing of the bars. We are working as fast as we can. Pedro pushes on the bars once we get through a few, and they move a bit. We just need a window big enough for his shoulders, and we can all fit.

"Just keep going. Focus on what's in front of us," he says.

I need that encouragement, and that is just what I do.

CHAPTER FORTY-FOUR

Half an hour later, the water line is nearing the lip of the desk where Maria's basket sits. I'm sweating profusely, but I'm finally able to push the blade through the last bar, and Pedro lifts the bars away, leaving us our opening, our exit. Finally, we have a way out. Because this day has been so fraught, though, I don't think that it's over.

I can barely accept it, that here it is, our way to freedom. We have to go before the water gets any higher.

I grab for Maria in her basket, and Pedro grabs the pillowcase of supplies. The audience area is empty, the spaces usually occupied by the borg fandom filled with ghosts. I glance back at the doorway where Hart always stood, back when she was Borgie.

I recall the time I accidentally bumped into her and she said in her Information Voice, "It is not an ideal way to carry yourself unbalanced. Your head may become injured and cause a cerebral lumpy mass."

That one really made me laugh. Hart could be funny, but at the time I just thought she had a bad input. Now I can see she was trying to nurture me.

Cerebral lumpy mass could be something I warn Maria of in the future, when I remind her not to bump her head. The shape of my memory fades as the empty audience comes back into view.

Sorry, borgs. There are no more shows today, and no more shows forever. Pedro gestures for me to go ahead.

"No, you go first," I reply. "I'll need you to help pull us through." I splash at the water, nervous that we are finally going. He dips through the hole easily and holds his hand out to help us. Suddenly, the Weatherlight goes out, and the alarm blares. My heart races, and I try to block my ears with my shoulder and free hand.

With a rushing sound, the water in the moat rises more quickly. Dammit, this must be Draven, and his genius flood plan. The plastic jaws of the dome begin closing like they did the day of our failed escape.

"Hurry," Pedro shouts. He is gesturing with his hands as though he can pull us through with his swinging arms. I can't move. It's like I am walking in mud. It's the alarm and the stress of it all, and now the light is gone.

The dome is slowly beginning to close, and water now covers the top of the desk. I shove the basket with Maria in it through to Pedro.

She's safe.

But now I'm alone in the dark, and the water's pooling faster than I expected. My body is half submerged.

Don't panic, Mirin.

I angle myself to duck through the hole and reach for Pedro, but a noise causes me to turn back. We didn't hear her enter because of the water, but Cassandra is standing only a few feet behind me. She looks different now. Her laser guns have been replaced with normal-looking borg arms. Now that Hart is gone, I'm sure she can kill without the lasers. Cassandra approaches.

Pedro ducks back through the hole, grabs my hand, and pulls me toward him, but the closer Cassandra gets, the heavier my body feels.

Move, Mirin.

Cassandra bends her giant body toward me, the claw of her hand reaching out. I grasp at Pedro. Cassandra's claw clamps down on my ankle. She pulls as the water rises.

This is not fair! Why can't they just let me go? Draven controls Cassandra. He must be angry that I cared about Hart.

It's like the finish line keeps moving a few more feet ahead as soon as I can almost reach it. My arm aches as I grip Pedro, as I am stretched between the two of them. Maria is wailing on the other side of the bars. I can see her through the gap we've created. She doesn't like being drenched in the water raining down from the sprinklers.

It's a familiar scene in front of me—us trying to escape and the Plexi dome closing down on us. Only this time a massive borg has a hold on my leg, and my whole life is just on the other side of the bars. Pedro straddles the two worlds: the Zoo and visitors area. He pulls, but all it does is stretch me, because my leg is immobilized in Cassandra's claw.

"Pedro, the dome" is all I can get out. He looks back. His eyes are filled with distress, and we hold our gaze until I realize what I have to do. Maria needs him, and I can't hold on any longer.

"You go," I yell, and let go of his hand. We can't both die here. He must get past the moat and over the ledge. Pedro is so close to freedom, and if only one of us can escape, it will have to be enough. He can come back for me. Only he doesn't seem to agree. He grasps my hand again and won't let go.

Don't be stubborn, Pedro. Let me go.

Cassandra won't let go of my leg, and Maria is screaming. So is my arm, on fire from the tension. I'm dizzy with pain and love and life. This is my last chance to fight for my freedom. I kick back, splashing, and try to free my leg from her grasp.

"Let me go," I yell at her. The delicate metal face looks at me, and I feel her computing my fear. I wonder if she can feel too.

"Please, just let us go." My voice is steady and my gaze holds hers. "We have done nothing to you." Before she can respond, something smashes her in the face. My eyes widen in shock to see Hart coming from behind her. She's still falling apart, and I don't understand how she is standing, but someone is with her. HIPPO. He must've fixed her while we were in here fighting for our escape.

Cassandra noticeably wavers but keeps her claw tightly fastened on my leg. Pedro maintains his grip on my wrist. I continue to reach back trying to push her off with my free hand, but she grabs my wrist with her other claw.

HIPPO has a drill and is trying to unlatch her hand from my ankle.

"Please hurry," I say to HIPPO, hoping that he understands.

"Mirin," Hart says in her sweet Maternal Voice. She is trying to trigger her laser at Cassandra, but it's not working. She's barely standing but still trying to fight. *I will help you, Hart. We can all get out together*, I want to say, but the words stick in my throat. If it's between Hart and my family, I already know which one I will choose—even if it kills me.

HIPPO releases the bolt out of Cassandra's claw hand,

and suddenly she lets me go. For a second, my chest fills with hope. *We're all going to get out, Hart. I will take you and HIPPO with me, and we'll start over someplace new.* But when I look up, Cassandra has grabbed Hart by the neck.

No. I want to scream but the words won't come out. And Pedro is tugging me toward the opening.

"Come on, Mirin," he urges.

But all I can see is Hart, writhing in Cassandra's grip. I feel sick.

I want to help her, but I don't have anything that would make a difference. Cassandra tosses her on the floor, Hart landing like a heap of junk. Watching her die again is unjust. I look back to Pedro as the water pools around my waist.

"Just go," I yell, but I know he is not leaving. In fact, he is coming back through the bars.

"The dome is closing," Pedro yells. I know that he's right, but I look back at Hart just lying there. I don't know what to do. All I want is for us to be safe.

Safe and free. Safe and free.
Goodbye, Hart.

CHAPTER FORTY-FIVE

The water I wade through toward Pedro is high. Everything slows down, the water pulling my legs, making the urgency more stressful. I'm wading and struggling when I want to run.

When our arms finally meet, I feel safe.

Pedro boosts me up and helps me through the hole in the bars. I drop down, reborn into the audience area. As soon as I emerge, a small waterfall rushes through the bars. Pedro drops through the opening and lands next to me. I run to the basket balanced on the wall, scoop it up, and kiss Maria. We are moving again, so I take the risk and look back.

Through the rain, I glimpse the pile of rubble that is Hart, and the pile moves.

Hart slowly reanimates and rises like a phoenix. She grabs Cassandra by the back of the neck and starts slamming her head against the Plexi. Cassandra turns around, surprised. Stunned but apparently not much weakened, she returns the blow, and the force of it throws Hart across to the Treat Show cubicles. Hart gets up and goes right back at Cassandra. I'm frozen, numb to the water around me.

Hart goes for the head again, and I think I know what she's doing.

"Take out her L-Drive, Hart," I call to her, but it's too late.

HIPPO gets submerged first, the bright blue light of him shorting out. I remember all the times I tried to figure HIPPO out and all the times he helped me, as well as that time HIPPO destroyed all those treats I worked so hard for.

"I forgive you," I whisper, though he cannot hear me.

There's a loud splash as Hart and Cassandra crash into the water. A brilliant blue flash signals Hart's last goodbye, and I know she is really gone.

Pedro catches my attention with a shout. He is holding up the basket, and I realize we'll need to swim to the opening across the moat. Pedro carefully floats the basket across while he sidestrokes with one arm. It makes me think of what it must have been like here when I was a baby, when there was a different but still horrifying scene of destruction.

The amount of love and concern I have for Maria, Hart had for me.

My tears mix with the rain as I swim haphazardly across the moat. Visibility is low outside the foggy dome. A wave of guilt hits me. I can still hear Hart calling my name in each of her voices and feel the love she was trying to give me. But I look ahead at Maria, and my need to protect her outweighs that grief. I think Hart would understand. She would want me to take good care of Maria.

We swim toward the remaining few feet of opening between the dome teeth. Pedro and I meet at the ledge. He gets up, and I hand him the basket, my womb and my breasts aching at Maria's unanswered cries. Never mind the healing from childbirth that I never got to do properly. I want to tell her that everything's fine, that we are doing this for her, that we are going to protect her and get her out of this place. But there's no time for that.

As we climb up and onto the wall, finally on higher ground, I can't help but look down into the dome. It's filled nearly to the brim with water. There can't possibly be any survivors.

Pedro runs ahead of us onto the concrete pathway and jumps over the next wall. Now he is in the audience area, beyond all the obstacles. I have to jump down to him.

Seven feet. *Please make it.* I can do this. I give the jump all I've got, clutching the basket tightly to my chest. Awkwardly, Maria and I crash into Pedro, and he breaks our fall to the ground. Then we are all in the audience area. Maria howls but is unharmed. Pedro drags the soaked pillowcase with the nutrition packs and the borg arm behind him.

The concrete floor is wet, and I try not to trip as we make our way to the gray door. I use Draven's instructions to direct us outside.

When you leave the dome, go through the gray door. Then there is a concrete path. Follow it past the small borg enclosures. At the end, there is a set of red double doors. Go through those. Once you are out, there will be a main gate.

As we open the gray door, I look down at the concrete path, and Pedro stops and throws me a pensive look. He remembers the instructions too, and we are almost there. It has all been so intense, and it's not over yet. We should hurry.

He puts down the pillowcase. I'm still grasping the handles of the basket.

"Wait, what are you doing?" I ask. "We've got to go."

He smiles. Instead of rushing through the door, he steps toward me, places his hand gently behind my head, and pulls me into a kiss.

Fireworks.

His body is close to mine, and I breathe in. He is so good at being in the moment. Maria squawks, and we separate. Through all the desperation and pain this place has forced upon me, it has also offered me a gift.

The gift of love, in this human being called Pedro. And the little family we made together.

CHAPTER FORTY-SIX

After passing the small borg enclosure, we see the red double doors ahead, the ones that lead outside. There is finality in those doors, the colossus of this moment. Feeling overwhelmed and grateful, I stop in front of them. The alarm is still ringing, muffled now. Maria, who has finally stopped screaming, looks up at me and blinks her perfect wide blue eyes.

This is it, baby girl. We did it. We are about to introduce you to the real world.

"Why did you stop? Let's go," Pedro says. I put my hand on his chest, gently.

"Wait" is all I can bear to say.

I want to take in the ceremony of this moment, despite the madness around us. I place the basket on the floor and remove the wet blanket so that I can lift Maria out and hold her.

However, when I remove the blanket, she is not the only thing I find in the basket. I take in a quick breath and find it hard to believe what I see.

Two more eyes stare up at me, one green eye and one yellow.

Linda.

I reach my hand down to her, and she nuzzles her face into it.

"Oh my god," Pedro says.

"Hey there, old friend," I muster through tears.

How did she get inside this basket?

And then I remember that moment with Hart, when I was so full of rage, wanting to get Maria back. Hart was tucking the blanket around Maria when I walked in. Tucking the blanket around Linda too. Hart must have fixed her. For me.

My heart explodes with gratitude, and I hear Hart's Maternal Voice speaking in my mind, *Mirin will have happy feelings for this gift.*

Yes, Hart. I have so many happy feelings.

My heart is leaping as I hold Maria in one arm and Linda in the other. I see the stitching on her body where Elf Hat had cut her, but otherwise she's good as new.

"Mew," she says, and begins to purr. I let her down and pet her head. Pedro picks her up next and cuddles her to his chest.

Our family is truly complete.

"Linda, you are extraordinary," he says. And I am relieved that he harbors no ill will toward her borg-ness. I look at her behaving in a spectacularly catlike way, nestled in Pedro's arms.

If something is moving and behaving like it's real, then how can we as simple humans not reciprocate? My love for Linda is real, and it doesn't matter where her soul comes from. Hart was more real than many humans when it came to caring for others. In the end, I'm so grateful for that relationship.

Whether it's the mathematics of the universe or an algorithm created by a man, it doesn't matter to me. We go about our lives based on how we feel, how we react to our feelings, and if there is love, if no one is hurt or tricked, then maybe we let it be. Linda is here, and she is as real to me as the concrete we stand on. This joyful reunion is such a relief from all the strife. And having her with us as we take the next step is a meaningful addition. Thank you, Hart.

The red doors in front of us lead to the outside. Outside this zoo. It has been seven years now that I have not been beyond the dome.

I am afraid. And I'm surprised that I feel this way.

This moment is all that I have wanted for so long. I think of how everything was taken from me, every treasure and trial of modern life. Everything that was special.

My family. I lost the ability to mourn them with others who loved them too. And then I was removed, cordoned off from the world. And even though the outside was full of turmoil, I feel robbed of the chance to have been a part of it.

Here I am with the doors to freedom right in front of me. I have a new family now.

Yet I stand paralyzed.

Pedro is looking at me with what could be both bewilderment and understanding. I love him more, knowing he can manage to hold both of those feelings at once.

Standing beside him, holding my sweet Maria, and with Linda at our feet, I wonder if the world will take me back. I wonder if I will take it. If we'll survive out there. I take a deep breath.

Sunlight bleeds in around the frame of the doors and,

one step closer, splashes real warmth across my face. The sunlight reminds me that it's only raining inside the dome, and that it has been seven years since I've felt the real sun. I hand Maria to her father, and I push the doors open with both hands. I take Pedro's arm and we step forward together.

We stand there as the sun gloriously blinds us. I close my eyes, and all I can see are dark orbs behind my eyelids, but when I squint down, I see Maria. Her curious eyes adjust to the sunlight, and reflected in them is the one thing I've found again—hope.

Because we only ever get this one life, and I want to live it. I want to be in this world.

EPILOGUE
ONE MONTH LATER

"Pedro, over here. Look," I say. It's so exciting, and I almost can't believe my eyes. I need Pedro to see them, to tell me they're real.

I push back the leaves to reveal the tiny blueberries covering the bush. First, I hold them to my nose and smell them like I am a pomologist. I'm transported back to the zoo, for Harvest Day, how I celebrated the vibrancy of fresh food.

"You're supposed to eat them, you know," Pedro jokes. And then I do. I savor them, though tart is a flavor I haven't had in a while. They taste like earth and sweetness.

"Look how many." I point to the patch of blueberry bushes. Pedro is wearing Maria in the sling, his hair wavy and long again dancing atop her head. He starts to grab and eat up the berries, and we feast.

Until I hear a rustle in the leaves.

I spot him right away, a man standing near the furthest bush. Fear floods through me, but I don't make a move. I tap Pedro on the shoulder and nod my head toward the stranger. We hide behind a thick tree as we watch. He doesn't see us yet. A moment later, two children join him, a boy and a girl, and I can now hear them laughing about something. They must know about the berries.

For so long I worried and contemplated being the last human on the planet, and here we are, just miles from the zoo, and there are other humans. I look down at Linda.

At least, I think they are humans.

"We should approach them," I whisper. Pedro is rocking Maria to keep her quiet.

"No." Pedro is apprehensive. "We don't know if they're safe. We should go away silently." Usually, I would agree with him, as it was my instinct to run far from anything new. Now I feel differently.

"Nothing is one hundred percent safe," I say. "And there are children." There is only so much caution you can take. Sometimes you just have to take a chance on people.

"Maybe we should spy on them a few days, see if they are good people," he says, patting Maria's head.

"We could, or we could go meet them and decide," I say, "we don't have to move into their camp or anything. This could be good for us." The fact that other people are out here living in the borgs' world gives us a chance. It's a sign.

"You think so?" he asks.

"Yes, we'll just have to trust how we feel."

We continue to watch the man and the children. The man still faces away from us, but there is something about the way he moves that is familiar. He rubs his neck, which is when I see it.

A thick scar.

"Ander?" I say loudly, despite my quick breaths and disbelief. "Ander, is that you?"

The man stops, the shape of his back familiar. The way his shoulders slope downward in a sweet, disarming way.

He turns around slowly to look at us, and recognition reverberates through the air.

Our eyes meet, and his look moves from fear to surprise to tenderness. He beams widely, he isn't angry or afraid at the sight of me. I am filled with relief and gladness and love.

Pedro puts his hand on my back, and I glance up to him. Maria is strapped to his chest and Linda trots along behind us. I pull on Pedro's arm, saying, "I have someone I want to introduce you to."

A new feeling of power wells up to the surface from underneath the ocean I had been drowning in. Before I was helpless. The zoo had all but swallowed me whole. And now, I decide where to go, what to do, and who to be.

I am free.

I still have much to learn, but I feel open to the challenges ahead, and that fills me with peace.

Closing my eyes just a moment, I scan my body for how it feels, my heart pumping, my feet solid on the real ground, and the cool breeze on my skin. Inside me is a steadiness I did not know before, a trust that no matter what lies ahead, we will be all right.

I think of Hart, and I know that in this moment, she would be proud of me. She might ask, "Is Mirin feeling bliss?"

And if she were here now, I would say, "Yes, Hart. This is bliss."

ACKNOWLEDGMENTS

To you, the reader, thank you. You have made my dream come true, as a story told only exists when someone receives it.

Chris, the most supportive partner one could ask for, thank you and love you more. Max and Otto, you are the fuel to my fire, and I hope that I can model to you that making mistakes, owning them, and dusting yourself off is how to truly grow in this world. Jess, my cheerleader and friend, I couldn't have done this without your affirmation and awesome tee shirts. Walter, Gadge and Moose, your pawprints all touched a draft and my heart.

Savannah, my editor, truly this book would not exist without you. Your skills are top, your advice is the kind that only fools would choose not to take, and I feel lucky to call you a friend. Dyna, I'm so grateful to you for your stunning art. Barbie, thank you for your copy-editing skills, which were sincere and precise.

To all my friends and family who have encouraged and supported my life as an artist. More specifically, the Adams Family, Amoroso Family, Gould Family, Hardin Family, Jones Family, Lauer Family, Martin Family, The Troop-Jones Family, Woodbridge Family, The Nerds, The Shoaks

Moms, Stanford St. Crew, and Valley Writing Group. Special additional thanks to Daniel, Paria, Kyra, and Taysa.

ABOUT THE AUTHOR

Jennifer Lauer is a writer, podcaster, and performer. *The Girl in the Zoo* is her debut novel. She is the writer and creator of *The Strange Chronicles*, a fiction podcast, and the writer and co-host of the *Making the Strange* podcast. Jennifer lives in California, by way of Massachusetts, with her family.

You can join her newsletter The Delicate Papers here: www.jenniferleelauer.com

Printed in Great Britain
by Amazon

21577163R00174